FAMILY
TIES

Also by Ernest Hill

A Person of Interest

Cry Me a River

It's All About the Moon When the Sun Ain't Shining

Published by Kensington Publishing Corp.

FAMILY TIES

ERNEST HILL

KENSINGTON PUBLISHING CORP.
www.kensingtonbooks.com

DAFINA BOOKS are published by

Kensington Publishing Corp.
119 West 40th Street
New York, NY 10018

All Kensington titles, imprints, and distributed lines are available at special quantity discounts for bulk purchases for sales promotion, premiums, fund-raising, educational, or institutional use.

Special book excerpts or customized printings can also be created to fit specific needs. For details, write or phone the office of the Kensington Special Sales Manager: Kensington Publishing Corp., 119 West 40th Street, New York, NY 10018, Attn. Special Sales Department. Phone: 1-800-221-2647.

Dafina and the Dafina logo Reg. U.S. Pat. & TM Off.

ISBN-13: 978-0-7582-1314-3
ISBN-10: 0-7582-1314-X

First Printing: September 2010
10 9 8 7 6 5 4 3 2 1

Printed in the United States of America

For my three little Angels,
Priya, Jioni, and Amiya.
I am proud of the spirited girls that you are,
and I look forward to the dynamic women
that you will become.
You are my heart.

Acknowledgments

Thanks to my agent, Frank Weimann, for his excellent representation; my editor, Selena James, for her insightful questions and comments; my family and friends, for their unwavering support; my readers, for their continued interest in these characters; and all the dedicated souls who make up the Kensington family.

FAMILY TIES

1

I stood before the window watching large torrents of rain fall from the eave of the roof. But my mind formed no lasting image of the rain; instead, the sound of the rain cast a strange spell upon me, a spell that cautioned me to fully contemplate what had just happened. And as I did, fresh tears formed in the corners of my eyes, and I mourned from a place deep within my soul, and as I mourned, I felt rise in me a rage that echoed the voice that told me to leave this place and to forget these people and to begin life anew in a town where I was not known. A town hundreds of miles from Lake Providence, Louisiana.

I turned from the window and removed the tiny suitcase from the closet. I pulled open the dresser drawer, and I was about to remove my clothes when footsteps in the corridor made me turn and look. Behind me, in the shadows of the hallway, I saw the dim form of a heavyset woman. It was Mr. Henry's sister, the one we called Miss Big Siss. She eased forward, and I could see that she was still wearing the long black dress and wide brim hat she had worn at the funeral. She made it to the doorway, then stopped. She looked at me. Our eyes met.

"Are you alright?" she asked.

Her question caused me to pause. I looked at her, then sank onto the bed, fighting against raw emotions tugging at my already moist eyes. I opened my mouth to answer her, but no words came. I turned my head back toward the window again. Outside, the rain had ceased, and in its place hung a dreary, ominous-looking haze. But I was neither seeing the haze, nor the trees, nor the tiny vegetable garden nestled just beyond the hurricane fence; instead, I was seeing the undertaker as he slowly lowered the steel blue coffin into the recently excavated earth. Suddenly my emotions broke and I began to sob again.

"Hush, now," she said. "Henry wouldn't want that."

I felt the bed give, and then I felt her arm about my shoulders, hugging me tight, gently rocking me from side to side.

A moment passed and then she spoke again. "Henry lived a good life," she said, then paused. I closed my eyes. I felt my body begin to tremble. "But he had gotten old and tired, and it was just his time to go." She paused again, waiting for me to say something, but I remained quiet. "He was proud of you," she said. "I hope you know that."

I didn't answer.

"You were like a son to him."

I still didn't answer.

"And I thank you for what you did for him."

Suddenly a lump filled my throat; I opened my eyes and looked at her. "I didn't do anything," I said.

"Yes, you did."

"No, ma'am . . . I didn't."

"You did," she said. "Before he closed his eyes, you allowed him to see his dream. And I thank you for that."

I didn't answer. I couldn't.

"But now there's something I want you to do for me," she said.

Suddenly, I pulled away and looked at her with eager eyes.

"Anything," I said. "Anything at all."

"I want you to go home," she said. "I want you to talk to your mother. I want you to work things out."

Stunned, I rose and moved next to the window. It had been ten years since I had seen my mother, and at that time she had made it perfectly clear—she never wanted to see me again. I turned and looked at Miss Big Siss. I opened my mouth to speak, but sorrow choked back my words. I raised my fist to my mouth and cleared my throat. My eyes blurred, and I shook my head.

"I can't."

"Why not?"

"She doesn't want to see me," I said.

My voice broke again, and I lowered my head, feeling warm tears collecting underneath my chin.

"Nonsense," she said. "What mother doesn't want to see her child?"

"Mine."

"You don't believe that."

"She told me not to come back."

"When?"

"Just before the judge sentenced me."

"She didn't mean it."

"I was fifteen years old, and she told me I was dead."

"People say a lot of things, especially when they're angry."

"I wrote her when I was locked up. I tried to apologize. I tried to explain. But she would never write back. So, I kept writing and I kept telling her that I had changed. And she finally sent me a note." My voice trembled and I broke down again. "You know what it said?"

"No, child," she said. "I don't."

I opened my mouth to answer but I could not. Suddenly

my mind began to whirl. I turned from the window and made my way to the far wall, feeling the tightness in my legs, hearing the mounting tide of blood pulsating through my veins. I leaned into the wall, balancing myself with sweaty palms. Anger seized me. I bowed my head and lowered my eyes, seeing the letter again. I bit my lip and pushed hard against the wall. I stared at the floor a moment, then spoke again.

" 'Time will tell.' "

"Excuse me?"

"That's all she said."

I paused. But Miss Big Siss remained quiet.

"She never came to visit," I said, sobbing. "And she never wrote me again. She doesn't want to see me. She's made that perfectly clear. And if she doesn't want to see me, I don't want to see her."

"Life is short," Miss Big Siss said, "even when it's long."

"I can't go back there," I said. "I can't go back there and take a chance on her rejecting me again."

"I have never asked you for anything," Miss Big Siss said. "Not as long as you've been living in Henry's house—but I'm asking you now . . . No, I'm begging you. . . . Please go see your mother while you still have a mother to see."

"I can't," I said.

"Why not?"

"I just can't."

"How do you think you would feel if something happened to her before you had a chance to make things right?"

I didn't answer. I wanted to, but I did not know what to say.

"You would feel terrible," Miss Big Siss said. "That's how."

"I don't know," I said.

"Well, I do," she said.

In the hallway, I heard footsteps moving toward us. I looked at the door. Miss Ida entered the room, and like Miss Big Siss, she was still wearing the clothes she had worn to the funeral.

Miss Ida looked at me and then at her sister. "You tell him yet?" she asked.

"No," Miss Big Siss said. "Not yet."

"Tell me what?" I asked.

"Sis and I talked it over," Ida said. "And we want you to know that you can stay in Henry's house as long as you want to, and we want you to have his truck."

I shook my head. "No," I said. "I can't accept that."

"It's what Henry would want," Miss Big Siss said.

"No," I said again. "You all divide his things among yourselves. You're his family. Not me. I can't take his things."

"When I first saw you, I hated you," Ida said.

"Ida!" Miss Big Siss said, shocked.

"All I could think about is what you took from us."

"Ida!" Miss Big Siss said again.

"But then, over the years, I got to know you," she said. "And I watched how hard you worked to make things right with Henry. And gradually I saw some of the pain leave his eyes. And I saw him get up and live again. You did that. You took his life from him; then you gave it back. And as the years passed, it was like he wasn't mad at you anymore. At first, I couldn't understand it. Oh, I knew Henry was a true believer. And I knew his faith was strong and that he believed in love and forgiveness, but not me. I just wanted him to keep on hating you just like I was hating you. But he didn't. And over time, I guess I figured if Henry could forgive you, I could forgive you too. Son, take his truck, and live in his house. It's what he would want."

"His family should have his things," I said.

Miss Big Siss rose and moved next to me.

"In Henry's eyes, you are his family," she said.

"That's right," Ida said. "As far as Henry was concerned,

you're just as much his family as anyone else. Child, Henry loved you. Don't you know that?"

I nodded.

"Then it's settled," she said.

"No, ma'am," I said, shaking my head again. "I can't."

"You can and you will," Ida said. "It's what he would have wanted."

"But I'm leaving."

"Leaving!" Miss Big Siss shouted, stunned.

"Yes, ma'am," I said. "Leaving."

She looked at me and then at the suitcase.

"Where are you going?"

"Texas."

"Where in Texas?"

"Dallas."

"Didn't know you knew anyone in Dallas."

"I don't," I said. "I was offered a job. A good job with an engineering firm."

"And you decided to take it."

"Yes, ma'am," I said.

"Why?" Ida asked. "Why so far away?"

"Just figure it might be a good time to start over somewhere."

"Well, ain't nothing wrong with starting over," Miss Big Siss said, "as long as you running to something and not from something."

I didn't answer.

"When you planning on leaving?" Ida asked.

"In an hour or two," I said.

"That soon!"

"Yes, ma'am."

"Well, at least take his truck," Ida said. "The house will be here if you ever decide to come back."

I nodded. Then I saw her turn and look toward the front door.

"We got a house full of folks across the street," she said. "I guess I better go back over there and check on Mama. She's been real quiet since the funeral."

"I'll be on directly," Miss Big Siss said.

Ida looked at me again. "Plenty food over there," she said. "You better come on and get something to eat."

"I'm not hungry," I said.

"Well, I'll fix you a plate," she said. "It'll be over there when you want it."

"Yes, ma'am."

Then she turned and disappeared into the living room. I heard the screen door open and close as she made her way out of the house and back across the street. I was sitting there thinking about what she had said, when I heard the sound of Miss Big Siss's voice again.

"Family is everything," she said. "But family ain't much good when the circle has been broken."

I remained quiet.

"I'm not worried about Henry," she said. "He's with his wife and child, and all three of them with Jesus. But I am worried about you. Your papa is in jail. Henry is dead. And you and your mama ain't talking. Before you leave here, I want you to go home," she said. "I want you to go home while there is still a home to go to."

"I'm alright," I said.

"You're not alright," she said. "And you won't be alright until you make things right with your mother. . . . Go home. Go home and talk to your mother. Sometimes, time changes things."

"I can't."

"You think your mother hates you," she said, "but you're wrong."

I didn't answer. Instead, I looked around the old house. I could feel Mr. Henry's presence lingering in the space that he had once occupied. I shook my head again. I wanted to hate my mother, and I wanted to hate my father, and I wanted that hatred to give me the strength to leave this place.

"Son, your mama loves you," she said. "And I suspect deep down you know that." She paused. I remained quiet. "When your mother said those things to you, you were a troubled little boy caught up in a bad situation. But you're not that boy anymore. Now you're a man—a twenty-five-year-old man with a college education. Go home and let your mama see what kind of man her child has become."

There was silence. I looked at her, but I did not speak.

"Will you go?" she asked.

I hesitated again. Maybe she was right. Maybe it was time that I went back to Brownsville. After all, I *wasn't* a child anymore; I *was* a grown man with a college degree. And perhaps my mother would be proud of what I had become. Perhaps she would see that I was not like my "no-good daddy." No, her child, the one they had called outlaw, the one who had done six years in juvenile hall for first-degree murder, the one for whom she had cried a river of tears, her son, D'Ray Reid, had made something of himself. Yes, I would go, and like the prodigal son, my return would be cause for celebration.

"Will you?" I heard Miss Big Siss ask again.

"Will you go with me?" I asked her.

"Of course I will," she said.

Then there was silence.

"Does that mean you're going?" she asked.

I looked up. Our eyes met. I nodded.

2

Mr. Henry's old green pickup truck was parked next to the house beneath the carport. Miss Big Siss followed me out to the truck, and once I had helped her climb inside, I went around to the driver's side, got in, and slowly pulled out of the driveway, heading north toward the still blue waters of Lake Providence.

As I drove, I formulated a plan. When I reached Brownsville, I would park in front of my mother's house, then cross the yard and take the stairs like one who belonged. And when she opened the door, her eyes would fall upon me, and she would cry, and then she would stretch forth her arms and pull me into her bosom, and all that had been wrong between us would be made right, and she would apologize for the ugly words she had directed at me all those years ago, and I would accept her apology, and the nightmare that had been our relationship would be never more. Involuntarily, I let out a deep sigh. Oh, if only this vision, which danced so vividly in my head, could somehow morph into the reality that I was so desperate to claim.

I turned left at the caution light and headed west toward Brownsville. The truck rumbled over the tracks, and I heard Miss Big Siss grunt. I looked at her; she was bracing herself

against the door. I had been driving too fast. I gently pressed
the brake and the truck slowed. Through the windshield, I
spied a sign neatly nestled on the far shoulder: BROWNSVILLE
8 MILES. I swallowed hard, feeling my tepid skin flash hot. It
just did not seem fair that I should have to deal with so
much. Suddenly, I frowned. I could not picture my mother's
face. It had been so long since I had been in her presence that
I simply could not picture her. How strange this was to me;
she was my mother, and I could not picture her face.

In Brownsville, I spied a flower shop on the corner just
off Main Street. Suddenly, a thought occurred to me. I should
bring her something—a peace offering of sorts. I pulled into
the parking lot and stopped, my eager eyes fastened on the
sign hanging high above the tiny flower shop. I looked at the
sign and then at Miss Big Siss.

"Maybe I ought to buy Mama some flowers?"

"That would be nice."

"What kind?"

"Roses," she said. "A lady is always partial to roses."

"Roses it is," I said. "A dozen red roses."

I hurried from the truck and bound toward the door. Inside, I paused and looked around. An arrangement in the far
corner caught my eye. I was starting toward it when a woman
called to me. I snapped around, startled. Our eyes met. I
paused and looked at her. She was a beautiful lady. I guessed
she was in her midtwenties. She was wearing an elegant gray
skirt with matching high heels. Her shoulder-length hair was
down, and she was carrying a rather expensive-looking purse.
Then, suddenly, I recognized her.

"Peaches," I exclaimed. "Is it really you?"

Involuntarily, I felt the corners of my mouth form a smile.
And in that instant, I was in Jackson again, looking through
the peephole, staring at a young, beautiful woman standing
before the door, seeking entrance into the seedy hotel room
that served as my temporary hideout.

"It's me," she said.

I took her into my arms and held her for a long time. "What in the world are you doing here?" I asked, finally releasing her.

"I live here," she said.

"In Brownsville?"

"Yes."

"You're lying."

"No," she said. "It's true."

"But how can that be?"

"It's a long story," she said.

Through the large bay window, I could see Miss Big Siss. She was still sitting in the truck, only now her head was bowed and I figured she was looking through her purse for something. I looked at her for a moment, then at Peaches. No, I couldn't keep her waiting. That would be rude.

"Right now I'm pushed for time," I said.

"How about the abridged version?" she asked me.

"Sure," I said.

"In short," she said, smiling, "I came looking for you."

"For me!" I said, frowning.

"Yes," she said. "For you."

"But how did you know where to find me? I mean, I never told you where I lived."

"Your cousin told me."

"What cousin?"

"Glenda."

I hesitated. "How do you know Glenda?"

"I met her at a church retreat."

"Really."

"Yes. The two of us shared a room. As a matter of fact, that's how your name came up. One night, I saw a picture of you in her photo album. When I saw the picture, I asked her how she knew you, and she said that you were her cousin. Then I asked where you were, and she told me that you had been sent away to Louisiana Youth Authority and that after you were released, the family lost contact with you. So then I asked her where she thought I ought to look for you, and she said Brownsville, because sooner or later, you were bound to come back."

"So you moved to Brownsville."

"That's right," she said. "Three years ago."

"And you waited all this time?"

"Yes," she said.

"Why?"

"First of all, you saved my life—"

"No," I interrupted her. "That's not true."

"It is true," she said. "Because of you, I got off the streets and I went to college—I'm a teacher now."

"A teacher!" I shouted.

My reaction amused her and she smiled again before offering an explanation. "After I was arrested, I went to college. And I earned a degree in elementary education from UL Monroe."

"UL Monroe!"

"Yes."

"That's unbelievable." I shook my head from side to side. "I just graduated from ULM a few days ago."

"Get out of here!"

"I'm serious," I said.

"Boy, this is a small world."

"Tell me about it."

I stared at her for a moment. "And you're really a teacher?"

"I am a teacher."

"And you teach here."

"Yes," she said. "I teach at Brownsville Elementary."

"Do you like it?"

"I love it," she said.

"Really!"

"Yes . . . this little town is the best thing that ever happened to me."

"What!"

"I mean it. I was able to reinvent myself here. Now I'm Miss Lewis—Peaches does not exist."

"No Peaches," I mumbled. "That just doesn't seem right."

"Aw, she wasn't real anyway. She was just a frightened little girl who found herself on the streets of Jackson. And if she had not been fortunate enough to stumble upon a wonderful soul who took her under his wing and guided her through that terrible nightmare, I shudder to think what would have become of her." She hesitated and looked at me again. "You saved me. And I came here to say thank you and to let you know that I owe you big-time."

"You don't owe me anything," I said.

"I owe you my life."

She paused and I remained silent. Then she looked at me with quizzical eyes. "What finally brought you back here anyway?" she asked.

"The same thing that took me away," I said.

"And what's that?"

"Death."

She paused again. My answer baffled her.

"I don't understand."

"I'll tell you about it sometime," I said. "But right now I have to go. Someone's waiting for me."

"I understand," she said. "Maybe you can give me a call when you have a moment."

I looked at my watch. "I'll do that," I said. "But right now, I really have to go. Are you in the book?"

"Yes," she said. "I'm in the book."

"Good." I turned to leave.

She stopped me. "Don't keep me waiting."

"I won't," I said.

"You promise?"

"I promise," I said. "I'll call right after I see Mama."

Suddenly, her expression changed. "Are you going to see her now?"

"Yes," I said. "Why?"

"I got so caught up in seeing you again that I didn't ask if you had heard."

"Heard what?"

"About Curtis."

"What about Curtis?"

"He escaped last night."

"Escaped!"

"Yes," she said.

"From where?"

"The parish jail," she said, then paused again. "I guess you didn't know he was locked up."

"No," I said. "I didn't know. I didn't know anything."

"Well, the cops are looking for him. They say he's armed and dangerous. They even closed the schools early. They said they didn't want anyone on the streets until he's caught."

"My God!" I said. "What did he do?"

"He was convicted for burglary and assault."

"What!" Suddenly, my head began to whirl. "I've got to go talk to Mama," I said. "Maybe she can tell me what's going on."

3

I raced out of the shop and climbed into the truck. As I settled on the seat, fumbling for my keys, I could feel Miss Big Siss's eyes on the side of my face.

"Lawd, child, what's wrong?" she asked.

I turned and looked at her. Her mouth was agape, and her jittery eyes danced with concern. "It's my brother," I said, pulling the key from my pocket and inserting it into the ignition. "He's in trouble."

"Trouble!"

"Yes, ma'am."

Out of the corner of my eye, I saw her turn on her seat and face me. "What kind of trouble?" she asked me.

"He broke out of jail last night."

"Jail!"

"Yes, ma'am. And now they're after him."

"Who's after him?"

"The police!"

"My God!" she said, then paused. "Maybe you oughtn't go over there right now. Maybe you ought to wait."

"No, ma'am," I said. "I need to find out what's going on."

I pulled the truck into gear and stepped on the accelerator. The tires screeched, the truck lurched forward, and Miss Big Siss fell back against the seat. After a moment or two, she raised herself upright, and I knew she was trying to think of something to make me turn back. But I did not; instead, I concentrated on the highway, seeing before me an image of Little Man held up somewhere, hiding from a police force that was closing in on him. I closed my eyes and opened them again. Yes, I had to hurry. I pressed the accelerator and raced toward the old neighborhood. At the railroad tracks, I slowed, then rounded the corner and turned down the street to my mother's house. When I arrived, I parked the truck on the shoulder and jumped out.

"I'm coming in with you," Miss Big Siss said.

"No, ma'am," I said. "Under the circumstances, it would probably be better if you waited in the truck."

I turned toward the house again. There were two cars and a truck parked in Mama's yard, and though I did not recognize either of them, I assumed they had something to do with Little Man's escape. I studied them for a moment, and then I looked at the house. The front door was closed and the curtains were drawn. Yes, they were home, but they were hiding behind locked doors and closed windows. I crossed the yard and climbed up on the porch. Then I raised my fist and pounded on the door. I waited. No one answered. I raised my fist to knock again, but before I could, I heard a woman's voice calling to me from the other side of the door.

"Who is it?" she whispered.

"It's me!" I shouted. "D'Ray!"

Suddenly, I heard chains rattling. A moment later, the door swung open; it was Aunt Peggy. She looked at me and her eyes grew wide.

"Sweet Jesus!" she exclaimed, raising her trembling hands to her mouth. "Sweet Jesus in heaven. What are you doing here?"

"I just heard," I said. My comment seemed to alarm her. I saw her look past me with jittery eyes.

"May I come in?" I asked.

"Yes," she said. "Hurry."

She stepped aside and I walked in. Behind me I heard her fumbling with the lock. I turned and looked. She had chained the door shut again. I looked about nervously. The lights were out, and the tiny living room was vacant.

"Where's Mama?"

"In there," she whispered, pointing toward the kitchen.

"Is she alone?" I asked.

"No," she said, shaking her head, "Papa and Miss Irene in there too. They're talking about Curtis."

"What are they saying?"

"They're just trying to figure out where he is."

"Do they have any ideas?"

"No," she said, shaking her head again. "I'm afraid not." She paused, and I looked at her and then toward the kitchen.

"Well, I need to talk to them."

"Come on," she said. "Follow me."

We moved deeper into the house, walking down a short hallway before turning into the kitchen. I paused in the door-way and looked. Mama was sitting at the table. Miss Irene was sitting next to her. Grandpa Boot was leaning against the stove. I looked at Mama. I could tell she had been crying.

"Look who's here," Aunt Peggy said, announcing my presence. Instantly, all heads turned toward me. Grandpa frowned, then leaped to his feet.

"Well, I'll just be," he exclaimed. He hurried across the room and gave me a big hug. "If you ain't a sight for sore eyes."

When he released me, I looked at Mama. Her mouth hung open, and she stared at me but did not speak.

"Mama," I said softly.

She didn't answer.

"Mama," I called to her a second time, and when I did, I saw a tear roll down her face. Then I saw Miss Irene put her arms around her. And I saw Grandpa look at her for a moment and then back at me.

"Where have you been all this time?" he asked me.

"College," I mumbled.

"College!"

"Yes, sir," I said.

"You mean to tell me you went to college."

"Yes, sir," I said, looking past him. "I graduated a few days ago."

"Graduated!"

"Yes, sir."

"You fooling!"

"No, sir," I said.

He grabbed me again, lifting me from the floor.

"You hear that, Mira?" he said, smiling. "This child done made something of hisself. Did you hear that?"

Mama didn't answer.

"You're a college man?" Grandpa said.

"Yes, sir."

"Boy, I'm so proud of you that I don't know what to do," he said.

"Me too," Aunt Peggy said.

"That's what you come to tell us?" Mama said, speaking for the first time. Her voice was dry—no, cold.

"No, ma'am," I said.

"Then what is it?"

"Mira!" Aunt Peggy said.

"I just heard about Curtis," I said, offering an explanation. "I was hoping you could tell me what's going on."

"Why?" Mama asked. "What can you do about it?"

"Mira, please," Aunt Peggy pleaded.

"He was in the parish jail," Grandpa said. "And he broke out sometime last night. That's all we know."

"You have any idea where he might be headed?" I asked.

"We don't have a clue," Grandpa said. "Just know that he run off."

"And I'm glad he did," Mama said defiantly.

Grandpa whirled and looked at her.

"Well, I am," she said.

"He's just making matters worse," Grandpa said. "That's all he doing—just making matters worse."

"He didn't do what they said," Mama said. "They lied on him."

"It doesn't matter."

"It matters to me."

"Well, it doesn't matter to the law," Grandpa said.

"I don't care about the law," she said. "Just care about my child."

"You better care," Grandpa said.

"They ain't had no business locking him up in the first place," Mama said. "He ain't did nothing."

"How do you know that?" Grandpa asked her.

" 'Cause he wouldn't do nothing like that."

"Was he still doing drugs?"

"Nah," Mama said. "And anybody who say he was is lying."

"Then what was he doing in that white gal's house?"

"He wasn't."

"She say he was."

"She lying."

"She said he hit her upside her head. And she said if the other one hadn't stopped him, she was sure he would have raped her."

"She lying."

"Was the nigger who pulled the job lying too?" Grandpa asked. "When they caught him, he said that Little Man was with him too. He even testified against Little Man. Said that Little Man was the one who hit the girl. Didn't he?"

"I don't care what he said," Mama said. "I know my child."

"Well, somebody hit her," Grandpa said. "She had a big ole gash on the side of her head."

"I don't care," Mama said for the third time.

"You better care," Grandpa said again.

"Lord, I wonder where he is right now?" Aunt Peggy asked. She had turned her back toward Mama and was looking at the window.

"Only God knows," Grandpa said.

"I just hope he's safe," she said. And then I saw her look toward the window again. "Maybe he got away."

"On foot?" Grandpa exclaimed.

"Maybe he wasn't on foot," Aunt Peggy said. "Maybe somebody helped him."

"Somebody like who?" Grandpa asked.

"I don't know," she said.

Suddenly, everyone turned and looked at me.

"Was it you?" Mama asked me. "Did you help him?"

"Me!"

"Yes," she shouted. "You!"

"No, ma'am!" I said, stunned.

"Mighty strange you showing up here now," she said, staring at me with suspicious eyes.

"I haven't seen anybody," I said. "I swear."

"If you know something," Grandpa said, "you need to tell us."

"I don't know a thing," I said. "I just got here."

"What are we going to do, Papa?" Aunt Peggy asked.

"I don't know," he said.

"Pray," Mama said. "Pray that he gets away."

"You think you can find him?" Grandpa asked me.

"Stay out of it," Mama said to me.

"Mira!" Grandpa yelled.

"I mean it," she said, looking at me. "Stay out of it."

"Maybe I can help," I said.

"You just stay out of it."

"But, Mama."

"But, Mama, nothing," she said. "This is all your fault."

"Mira!" Grandpa shouted again.

"Well, it is," Mama said.

"No," Aunt Peggy said, shaking her head. "You can't blame him for this."

"I can," she said. "And I do."

"You don't mean that."

"I do mean it," she said.

"I didn't have anything to do with this," I said. "I haven't been here in years."

"You had everything to do with it."

"No, I didn't," I said.

"Mira, why are you saying this?" Aunt Peggy asked her. But Mama didn't answer her. Instead, she spoke to me.

"You couldn't rest," she said. "You couldn't rest until you got him in the streets. Well, now the streets got him and ain't nothing you or nobody can do about it."

"This ain't his fault," Aunt Peggy said again.

"Then whose fault is it?" Mama asked.

"It's nobody's fault."

"You took him to that place," she said to me. "Didn't you?"

"What place?" I asked, confused.

"That juke joint."

"What juke joint?"

"Kojak's Place."

"That doesn't have anything to do with this," Aunt Peggy said.

"It has everything to do with it," Mama said.

"No," Aunt Peggy said. "It doesn't."

"You exposed him to all those hoodlums," she said. "Didn't you?"

"Mira!" Grandpa said. "Now, that's enough."

"And you got him hooked on that old dope," she said. "Didn't you?"

"That's not true," I said.

"Don't lie to me," Mama snapped.

"Mira!" Grandpa shouted. "This is not helping anything."

"You and World didn't care about nobody but yourself," she said. "But Little Man was different. He could have been somebody. If you would have just left him alone, he could have been somebody. But, no, you wouldn't let him. You had to turn him into another you."

"Back then I was just trying to help him," I said, feeling the need to defend myself. "But that don't have anything to do with this."

"Help him!" she shouted.

"Yes, ma'am," I said. "Help him be a man."

"He didn't need your kind of help."

"I did what I knew to do," I said.

"This is not helping anything," Grandpa said again.

"Why did you come back here?" Mama snapped.

"Mira," Grandpa said. "Now, that's enough."

"That's alright, Grandpa," I said, staring at her. "She's right. This was a mistake. I shouldn't have come back here." I turned to leave.

Grandpa stopped me. "Hold on," he said.

"No," I said. "I'm leaving."

"Let him go," Mama said.

"No," Grandpa said. "Ain't nobody going nowhere."

"I know where I'm not wanted," I said sullenly.

"Please!" Aunt Peggy said.

"Let him stay," Mama said. "I'll leave." She rose from the table and hurried out into the hallway. Miss Irene dashed after her.

"Mira!" Miss Irene called after her. "Mira!"

"Leave me be," I heard Mama say.

"Mira, you need to calm down before you make yourself sick."

"I'm already sick," Mama said. "My child is out there somewhere, and I don't know if he's dead or alive."

"Come on," Miss Irene said. "Sit down on the sofa and rest."

I heard them walking across the floor, and then I heard the springs on the old sofa creak, and I knew they had gone into the living room.

"Don't pay her no mind," Grandpa said to me. "She's just worried about that child, that's all." He paused and looked at me. I remained quiet.

"What time is it anyway?" Aunt Peggy asked.

"Almost five," Grandpa said, looking at his watch. "Why?"

"It'll be dark in a few hours," she said.

"Yeah," he said. "I know."

"I have a feeling it's going to be a long night."

"Tell me about it," Grandpa said.

Outside, I heard the sound of a car door opening and closing. Then I heard footsteps hurrying across the porch. A moment later, someone knocked on the door. We went into the living room. Mama was sitting on the sofa, crying. Miss Irene was sitting next to her, trying to console her.

Aunt Peggy paused, then cautiously made her way to the door.

"Who is it?" she whispered.

"The police!"

Aunt Peggy slowly pulled the door open. I saw two police officers standing in the doorway, staring at me.

4

I stood gaping at the two officers as they entered the house. Yes, I had seen them before. The black one was Sonny, my mother's old boyfriend. And the white one was Harland Jefferies, the chief of police. I saw the chief look at me and then back at Sonny.

"That's not him," he asked Sonny. "Is it?"

"No, Chief," Sonny said, staring at me. "It's not."

"What's the meaning of this?" Grandpa asked.

The chief did not answer, instead he kept his eyes on me. "Do I know you?" he asked me.

"What's this all about?" Grandpa asked again.

The chief stared at me, and though he did not answer Grandpa, I understood. They had seen me arrive, and they had assumed I was Little Man. I saw Sonny look at me, then back at the chief.

"I know him, Chief," Sonny said. "That's Reid's older brother. The one they call D'Ray."

And at that moment, I felt rise in me an anger I thought I had long ago subdued. I had never liked Sonny. He was a mark. I was convinced of that. I heard the chief sigh; then his lips parted and he spoke to me again.

"What are you doing here?"

"He came to visit his mother," a voice called from behind him.

The chief whirled and looked. It was Miss Big Siss. She had gotten out of the truck and made her way onto the porch.

"And who are you?" he asked, looking her over.

"Sissy," she said. "Sissy Earl."

The chief frowned. He did not recognize the name.

"You aren't from around here," he said, "are you?"

"No, sir," she said. "I'm from Lake Providence."

The chief looked at her and then at me. "You and him related?"

"No, sir," she said.

"Then how do you know him?"

"My brother took him in a few years ago."

"Your brother?"

"Yes, sir," she said.

"And who is your brother?"

"Henry," she said. "Henry Earl."

Suddenly, the two men gasped.

"Henry Earl was your brother!" Sonny said.

"Yes, sir," Miss Big Siss said. "We just buried him not more than an hour ago. Then we came here so this boy could see his mother. He hasn't seen her in years."

"My condolences," Sonny said, fumbling with his hat.

"So this boy was with you last night?" the chief pressed.

"Yes, sir," she said. "This young *man* was with me."

The chief frowned. "All night?" he asked through clenched teeth.

"Sir?" Miss Big Siss responded, confused by the question.

"Did he stay in the house with you all night?"

"No, sir," she said. "He stayed in Henry's house."

"Alone?" the chief asked her.

"As far as I know," she said.

"Then you don't know who he saw," the chief said. "Do you?"

"I know he was with us," Miss Big Siss said.

"Us?" the chief asked.

"Yes, sir," she said, "the family." She paused again, then explained further. "Henry's wake was last night, and several of us, including him, sat up the better part of the night talking."

The chief was done with her. He focused again on me.

"How long have you been in town?" he asked me.

I didn't answer.

"He just got here," Miss Big Siss answered for me.

"I wasn't talking to you," the chief said. "I was talking to him." He continued to stare at me; I stared back. When I didn't say anything, he spoke again. "You sure you didn't get here last night?"

I remained quiet.

"We got here a few minutes ago," Miss Big Siss said. "We just left the funeral. We didn't even take time to change clothes."

Sonny looked at me, then squinted.

"Where's Curtis?" he snapped.

"You tell me," I said, "you the law."

The chief's face flushed red. He raised an angry finger and pointed it at me. "Did Curtis come to you for help?"

I remained quiet.

The chief turned his attention to Mama. "Mira," he said. "Enough is enough. Now, I want you to tell me where that boy is. And I want you to tell me right now. You hear?"

"I don't know where he is," Mama said.

"Didn't you see him last night?" the chief asked.

"I saw him," Mama said.

"And he didn't tell you anything?"

"No, sir," she said. "He didn't."

"That boy wouldn't leave here without saying something to you," the chief said.

"Well, he did," Mama said.

"I was good to him," the chief mumbled. "I let him have the run of the place. And this is how he repays me." He paused. Everyone remained quiet. "He's trying to embarrass me," the chief said. "And I'm not going to stand for that, you hear?"

He looked at Mama. She remained quiet.

"Mira," Sonny said pleadingly. "You're not helping him."

"I told you all I know," she snapped.

"You know where he is," the chief said. "I know you do."

"No, sir," she said. "I don't."

"What happened last night?" Sonny asked.

"I cooked him some food and brought it to him in the jail. Just like I always do," she said. "That's all."

"Just like I always let you," the chief said.

"How was he acting?" Sonny asked her.

"Like he always acted," she told him.

The chief didn't like her answer; he frowned again, displaying angry eyes. "And how was that?" he asked.

"Like he didn't have a care in the world," she said.

"Are you sure he didn't say anything?" Sonny said.

"He didn't say a word. He just ate his food."

"What time did you leave?" the chief asked.

"About twelve-thirty," she said. "Just like always."

The chief grabbed her shoulders with both hands. "Did you help that boy escape?" he snapped.

"No," she shouted, pulling away. "But I'm glad he's gone."

"Mira!" Sonny said.

"Well, I am," she said. "He ain't done nothing. He ain't done nothing at all. And you know it."

The chief paused, fuming. "Alright," he said. "Be glad. But when you see that boy, you tell him something for me. You tell him to run. And you tell him to run hard—and you tell him I said he better not slip up, because when he do, I'm gonna be there, and when I catch up to him, I'm gonna blow a hole in him big as Texas." He whirled and looked at Sonny. "Let's go," he said.

He stormed out of the house and Sonny followed him. When Mama was sure they were gone, she fell on the sofa and sobbed. I closed the door, then eased next to her. Inside my head, I heard Miss Big Siss's words again: *family is everything, and right now she and Little Man are the only family you got.*

"Mama," I said. "I know you don't want to talk to me, but we need to put our differences aside for now because this is trouble. This is big trouble."

She didn't answer.

"Mama," I said. "You need to talk to me."

She still didn't answer.

"I can't help Little Man if I don't know what's going on." I paused. Again, still no answer.

"Mama," I said pleadingly. "You need to tell me what you know."

A moment passed and she began to speak. "He told me to cook him a big meal." She paused and shook her head. "He said he needed some food that would stick to his ribs. He said he was going to run."

"He told you that?" Grandpa said.

"I told him not to," she said. "I told him that he was going to make matters worse. But he wouldn't listen. He said he didn't have any choice. He said he had been cleaning the chief's office, and while he was in there, he saw some papers on the chief's desk. He said they were getting ready to send him to Angola and that he wasn't going to go to no Angola."

She paused and began sobbing again.

"What else did he say?" I asked her.

"That's all."

"Did he tell you where he was going?"

"No," she said. "He didn't tell me where he was going, and he didn't tell me how he was going to get there. Just ate his food like he didn't have a worry in the world."

"None of this makes sense," I said, looking around. "Why would the chief leave papers on his desk when he knew that Little Man cleaned his office? And why would he give Little Man so much freedom?"

I turned toward Mama again. She was sitting with her hands folded across her lap. Her body was taut, and she was gently rocking back and forth.

"Why would the police allow you to visit like that?" I asked her.

"Sonny fixed it that way."

"Why?"

"Because I asked him to."

"No," I said. "There's more to it than that."

"Little Man gave Sonny his word," she explained. "He told Sonny that he would behave. And Sonny believed him."

I paused again, thinking. "When did they allow you to see him?"

"Whenever I wanted," she said.

"They gave you access to the jail whenever you wanted it?"

"Sometimes I would go to the jail," she said. "And sometimes Sonny would bring him here."

"What!" I said. "Are you telling me that the chief allowed Sonny to bring Little Man home?"

"Yes," she said.

"When?" I asked, still not believing what I was hearing.

"They would usually get here around midnight, and the three of us would watch TV and talk."

"How long would he stay?"

"An hour or two, then Sonny would take him back."

"That doesn't make any sense," I said.

"He did it for me," she said.

"Why would the chief agree to that?"

"This is a small town," she said. "And them white folks can do whatever they want. I didn't ask why. I just accepted it."

"Something about this ain't right," I said.

"Right and wrong ain't got nothing to do with this," she said.

"I don't trust the chief," I said. "And I sure don't trust that Sonny. I never did, and I never will."

"Sonny's a good man," Mama said, becoming defensive.

"I don't trust him," I said again.

"He's been good to me," she said. "And he's been good to Little Man. Through it all, he's been good to us."

I shifted my feet and listened to the faint sound of cars passing on the street. My nerves were taut. Why was I having this conversation? None of this mattered now. I was beyond the world of Sonny, and I was beyond the world of men like the chief. My eyes fell again upon my mother; I could see her broad shoulders shuddering as she sobbed heavily. I moved next to her and eased onto the sofa.

I collected myself, then spoke again. "Little Man is on drugs," I said. "Ain't he?"

"No," she said between sobs. "He was at one time, before he went into rehab and before he joined the church."

"You think he had a relapse?"

"No," she said. "He's been clean for years."

"Are you sure?"

"I'm positive," she said. "When all of this happened, he was a drug counselor at the church. He had come to hate drugs."

"If that's the case," I said, "why would he break into someone's house?"

"He didn't," she snapped.

"Wasn't he convicted for breaking and entering?" I asked.

"And for burglary," Grandpa said.

"And assault," Aunt Peggy added.

"But he didn't do it," Mama insisted.

I paused and looked at her. Her eyes were wide and her mouth was open. "How much time did they give him?" I asked.

"Twenty-five to life," she said.

"What!" I shouted.

Suddenly, she fell facedown on the sofa, sobbing.

"It's gonna be alright, Sister Reid," Miss Irene said. "It's gonna be alright."

I wanted to console her, too, but at that moment, there was something in me that resented her. She had not grieved for me when I was sent away. She had simply turned her back and declared me dead. I turned toward the window, seeing heavy, gray clouds gathering from the west. It would rain again, but neither the wind, nor the strong currents of water could wash away that which was before me. I cautioned myself to be calm and not give in to the wave of hot rage rapidly rising within me. Suddenly, things were as they had always been. Inside of me I felt an overbearing need to protect the naive little brother who did not have the ability to protect himself. And then I heard the voice again telling me to forget about Mama and concentrate on him, for you are your brother's keeper.

"Where do you think he might have gone?"

"I don't know," she said.

"He must've told you something."

"No," she said. "He didn't."

"Did he have any money?"

"Not that I know of."

"Did he have anybody who might have helped him get out of town?"

"Nobody that I can think of."

"Who did he hang out with before he went to jail?"

"Nobody," she said. "He mainly kept to himself."

"Does he have a girlfriend?"

"No," she said, "at least not to my knowledge."

There was silence.

"Think you can find him?" Grandpa asked me.

"I'll find him," I said.

"No!" Mama protested. "I don't want him found."

"You heard the chief," I said. "If they catch him, they'll kill him."

"And if he goes to prison, he'll die."

"Doing time won't kill him," I said. "But the chief will."

She stopped sobbing and her eyes became stern. "He ain't like his daddy," she said. "And he ain't like you. He can't do time."

"He can if he has to."

She started to say something else and I interrupted her. "Did you say he was active in the church?"

"Yes," she said. "Why?"

I paused. Peaches had spoken about the church. Perhaps she knew him, or perhaps she knew someone who knew him. And if she did, maybe they knew where he was. Yes, I had to speak to her, and I had to speak to her right now.

"I got to go," I said.

"Go where?" Mama wanted to know.

"To see somebody," I told her.

"Stay out of it," she yelled. "You hear me? Stay out of it."

I didn't answer.

"I mean it," she yelled again. "Stay out of it."

I went through the door. Miss Big Siss followed me. I drove her home and then I called Peaches. She agreed to meet me in Lake Providence, at the little sandwich shop on the lake. I changed clothes, then headed to the sandwich shop.

5

When I arrived at the sandwich shop, I selected a table outside on the deck. While I waited, I ordered a glass of soda. After I drank it dry, I placed the glass back on the table and looked about, seeing the murky waters of Lake Providence part as a lone boat whizzed by with a young female skier in tow. I watched her for only a moment. Anxiousness made me think of Little Man again. "Oh, God," I mumbled to myself. "Please keep him safe." Suddenly, I heard the sound of footsteps on the wooden deck. I turned toward the door. I saw Peaches walking toward me. I rose to my feet, and when she made it to me, I embraced her.

"I got here as quick as I could," she said.

I released her; then she pulled out a chair and sat down across from me. I looked at her. She seemed worried.

"Is anything wrong?" I asked her.

"I'm afraid so," she said, her voice barely audible.

"What is it?"

"They just profiled Little Man on the five o'clock news."

"My God!" I said. I started to say more, but before I could, the waitress returned to the table. She removed a pencil and pad from her apron and looked at me.

"Ready to order?" she asked.

I shook my head.

She looked at Peaches. "Would you like something to drink while you decide?"

"Iced tea," Peaches said, "if you have it."

"We have it," the waitress said.

She left. A few minutes later, she returned and placed a glass of iced tea on the table.

"Let me know when you're ready to order," she said.

I nodded and she left again. When she did, Peaches raised her glass and sipped her tea. Then she sat the glass back on the table. I looked at her and shook my head.

"They're boxing him in," I said. "Aren't they?"

"I don't know," she said. "But it certainly appears that way."

I looked away for a moment. I had just lost Mr. Henry. I could not lose my brother too. I just couldn't. Suddenly, my anxious mind began to whirl. Little Man and I had been close before I was sent to youth authority. But now I did not know him. I focused my eyes and stared at Peaches.

"Tell me about him," I said.

She frowned. "Excuse me?"

"Tell me about Little Man," I said. "If I can figure out how his mind works, I can find him."

"You know how his mind works," she said. "He's your brother."

"No, I don't," I said. "He was a ten-year-old kid when I left here. He's a man now, a twenty-year-old man." I paused and looked at her. "Do you know him?"

"Not very well," she said.

I hesitated, then really stared at her. "How well is not well?"

"Well, before he got in trouble, we used to attend the same church. I ran their literacy program, and he ran their substance-abuse program. We would bump into each other from time to time. But I can't tell you much about him except that he was extremely quiet and usually kept to himself."

"Did you ever see him talking to anyone?"

"Just the boys he counseled."

"Is that it?"

"That's it," she said.

"Are you sure?" I asked.

"I'm positive," she said.

"There has to be someone else," I said. "Someone he leaned on."

"Not that I know of," she said. "I never saw him with anyone except the boys he counseled and Reverend Jacobs."

"Reverend Jacobs."

"Yes."

I paused again. "Are they close?"

"Yeah," she said, "now that you mention it, they are."

"Maybe he contacted the reverend."

"I don't know," she said, "maybe."

"I need to talk to him," I said. "Can you arrange that?"

"Sure."

"When?" I asked impatiently.

"Whenever you like."

"Do you think he would talk to me this evening?"

"I don't see why not."

"Would you ask him?"

"Sure," she said, pushing from the table. "I left my cell phone in the car. I'll go call him now."

When she left, I leaned back and buried my face in my hands—first Mr. Henry and now this. Why was this happening? Why now? Why to me? Why? I was mulling it over in my head, trying to make sense of things when I heard someone call to me.

"Didn't know you knew Miss Lewis," he said.

I looked up. It was Sonny. I had to be careful. It appeared that he was following me. I looked directly at him, agitated.

"What do you want?" I asked.

"We need to talk."

"Nothing to talk about," I snapped.

"I beg to differ," he said.

"I don't have anything to say to you."

"Well, I have something to say to you."

"Not interested," I said.

"I'm not here to fight with you—"

"Then why are you here?" I interrupted him.

"I'm here to help you."

"I don't want your help."

"Just hear me out."

"Not interested," I said again.

"Look," he said. "This thing has gotten serious. The chief has issued an all points bulletin. Do you know what that means?"

"I don't want to talk to you," I said again.

"It means every cop in the state of Louisiana is looking for Curtis," he said. "That's what it means."

"Why don't you leave me alone?" I said.

"And by tomorrow morning, Curtis will have been profiled in every newspaper in the ArkLaMiss. Do you hear me?"

I didn't respond.

"What's wrong with you?" he asked. "Don't you understand what I'm trying to tell you? The chief has put a freaking net over this entire state. And sooner or later, he's going to catch Curtis. And when he does, I'm afraid something bad is going to happen. Now, maybe I can prevent that if you just tell me where he is."

"I don't know where he is," I said. "And if I did, I sure as hell wouldn't tell you. Not in a million years."

"If we work together—"

"Not interested," I said.

"Son—"

"Don't call me that."

"Look," he said.

"No," I said. "You look. You're a cop. And I don't trust cops. You understand?"

"I'm not speaking to you as a cop," he said. "I'm speaking to you as a friend."

"A friend!"

"Yes," he said. "A friend."

"I ain't your friend," I said. "Believe that."

"Well, you believe this," he said. "Curtis is in a lot of trouble. And if I don't get to him before they do, he's going to get himself hurt. Now, he picked the wrong time to pull this stunt. This is an election year, and the chief sure as hell ain't going to let this become a campaign issue. Now, if we work together—"

"Get out of my face," I said.

He paused. I could see that he was getting angry.

"Why don't you think of somebody besides yourself for once in your life? This ain't about you. And it ain't about me. This is about your brother."

I didn't answer.

"Alright," he said. "Suit yourself. But if something goes wrong, it's on your head, not mine."

I remained quiet.

"Look . . . You don't have to tell me where he is—just tell me if he has contacted you."

I still remained quiet.

"Has anyone told you anything?"

I turned my head and looked away.

"Son—"

"Leave me alone!" I shouted.

"Alright," he said with a sigh. "I'll leave you alone."

"Thank you!" I said.

He turned to leave, then stopped.

"If I get to Curtis before they do, I'll do what I can for him. When you talk to him, let him know I said that."

He paused again and waited, but when I didn't answer, he shook his head and left. A few minutes later, Peaches returned to the table.

"Was that Sonny?" she asked.

"Yeah," I said. "That was him." I paused. "Do you know him too?"

"Not really," she said, shaking her head. "I see him around town, and he goes to our church, but I wouldn't say that I know him." She looked at me, puzzled. "What did he want?"

"He was just sweating me," I said. "That's all." I paused and looked at her. She was carrying her cell phone. "Did you get him?"

"I got him," she said.

"What did he say?"

"He can see you."

"When?"

"Right now."

"Great!" I said. I pushed away from the table, then rose to leave. "Are you coming with me?" I asked her.

"If you want me to."

"I do," I said. "But one thing."

"What's that?"

"Let's take your car," I said. "I think they're following me."

"I think you're right," she said.

I looked at her and then at the rear door.

"I'll leave my truck here and meet you behind Pizza Hut."

"Okay."

I turned to leave.

"D'Ray," she called to me. I turned back and looked at her. She was fiddling with her hands.

"I hope this doesn't sound out of place. But I'm glad you're back. I missed you so much. I hope you don't mind me telling you that."

"I don't," I said.

She smiled. "Good . . . because I really missed you."

"I missed you too."

"If you missed me," she said, "why didn't you look for me?"

"You mean after I got out?"

"Yes."

"I guess I was afraid."

"Afraid of what?"

"Of what I might find."

"You shouldn't have been," she said. "I know we were young. But we were in love. You should have trusted that. D'Ray, my feelings for you were real. They still are."

"I didn't know."

"Now you do." She smiled and kissed me on the cheek. "Let's go see Reverend Jacobs, and after this is all over, maybe we can sit down and talk about us."

"Alright," I said. "I would like that."

After she left, I exited through the rear door and walked along the lake for a few blocks before crossing the street and making my way back to Pizza Hut. And as promised, she was waiting for me in the rear parking lot. I climbed inside her car, and we headed back to Brownsville. And every now and then, as the car gobbled up the highway, I secretly stole a glance at her. And though I did not say it, my feelings for her had not changed either. I had never stopped loving her.

6

At the church, we found Reverend Jacobs sitting behind his desk, reading over some papers. When he saw us, he rose to his feet.

"You made it," he said.

"Yes, sir," Peaches said. Then she paused and looked at me. "This is the young man I spoke to you about."

I stepped forward and extended my hand. "I'm D'Ray," I said. "D'Ray Reid."

"Pleased to meet you, Mr. Reid," Reverend Jacobs said; then he shook my hand and motioned to two chairs that had been positioned before his desk. "Please, have a seat."

We sat, and as we did, I studied the man. He was a little younger than I had anticipated. I guessed he was in his late thirties or early forties. He was a well-groomed man with a cleanly shaven head. He was wearing a nylon jogging suit, and from his build, it appeared that at one time or another, he could have been a serious athlete. Once we were settled, Reverend Jacobs sat in his chair again, leaned back, and looked directly at me.

"Miss Lewis tells me you want to talk about Curtis."

"Yes, sir," I said. "I don't know if you know it, but he escaped last night."

"Actually, it was early this morning," the reverend corrected me.

"So you heard?"

"The police called me around three a.m. They wanted to know if I had talked to him or if I had any idea where he might be."

"Do you?"

"No, I don't."

"That's too bad," I said, sighing deeply. "I was hoping you did."

"I'm sorry," he said. "But I don't have a clue."

"Do you think he's still in town?" Peaches asked softly.

"I don't know," Reverend Jacobs said. "But if he hasn't made it out of the city by now, chances are he won't."

"Why do you say that?" she asked.

"From my understanding, most of the roads are blocked and the chief has called in the state police."

"The state police!" she exclaimed.

"That's what I heard."

"My God!" she said.

"I also received a phone call from the mayor about an hour or so ago. According to him, the town has been cordoned off, and the police have been ordered to search every dwelling in Brownsville."

"Do you think someone is hiding him?" she asked.

"I don't know," Reverend Jacobs said. "It's possible."

"Maybe he's held up in the woods?" Peaches said.

"I doubt it," Reverend Jacobs said. "This is May. The mosquitoes would eat him alive."

"Do you think someone is helping him?" I asked.

"Maybe," Reverend Jacobs said.

"Who?" Peaches asked.

"I don't know," he said, and then he was quiet.

"The chief has a vendetta against him," I said. "It's imperative that I find him before they do."

Reverend Jacobs had been looking off, but now he turned directly to me. "If you find him," he said, "what do you plan to do?"

"Help him," I said.

"Help him how?"

"Any way I can," I said.

Reverend Jacobs hesitated, then began again. "I spoke to Sister Reid earlier this morning," he said. "She seems to believe that Curtis did the right thing. She seems to believe that his only chance is to get away from here and never come back. I don't agree with that," Reverend Jacobs said. "Do you?"

"No, sir," I said. "I don't."

Reverend Jacobs let out a deep sigh, then leaned back in his chair. "I know he's frightened, but running is not the answer. If I could talk to him, I would tell him that."

"What is the answer, Reverend?" I asked.

"Jesus," he said.

His answer caught me off guard. I frowned but remained silent. I saw the reverend studying my face.

"You believe that, don't you, son?"

I hesitated. Yes, I knew what was going on. He was seeking to know me. He was trying to determine whether he could trust me or not.

"Well, Reverend," I said. "Right now it doesn't really matter what I believe. It only matters what Little Man believes. And when it comes to faith, I have to defer to you."

"His faith is strong," Peaches said. "I can vouch for that."

"Yes," Reverend Jacobs said, nodding as he spoke. "The Curtis I know is a good and faithful servant."

"I just want to find him," I said, attempting to drive home my concern. "I just want to find him before they do."

"You will," the reverend said. "God willing."

I decided to change the subject. I did not want to talk about God, nor did I want to talk about myself. I wanted to talk about Little Man. I looked at the reverend. He was still looking at me.

"Did you visit him much while he was incarcerated?" I asked, hoping that Little Man might have said something to him that might give me some indication where he might be.

"At least once a week," he said, "sometimes more. Why?"

"How was he handling jail?"

"Not very well," Reverend Jacobs said. "He was having trouble sleeping, and he had all but stopped eating."

"Did he ever talk to you about prison?"

"He talked about it constantly."

"What did he say?"

"He said he would rather die than be locked up for the rest of his life for a crime he didn't commit."

"He said that?"

"On more than one occasion."

"And what did you tell him?"

"I told him he couldn't think like that. And I promised him that I would do everything I could to help him get to the truth. I would always end our conversation by giving him some Scriptures to read, Scriptures that I thought would keep him encouraged."

"So, you believe he's innocent?"

"With all of my heart," the reverend said.

"So do I," Peaches said.

"Really?" I said, looking at her.

"Really," she said

I looked at the reverend. He leaned back in his chair and stared into the distance.

"I've stood by him," he said. "I've stood by him every step of the way. And I will continue to stand by him."

"If he comes back, does he have a chance to beat this thing?" I asked.

"Yes," Reverend Jacobs said. "He does."

"You really believe that."

"Son, I've hired one of the best appeals attorneys in the state. And he's been working on Curtis's case for the last five months. And he assures me that in time, he believes Curtis's conviction will be overturned."

"Does Curtis know that?" Peaches asked. "I mean, have you told him?"

"He knows," the reverend said. "But for some reason or another, I guess he panicked." The reverend shook his head. "I never figured he would run."

"Why not?" I asked him.

"I just didn't," the reverend said.

"Reverend, when a man's facing twenty-five years to life, he might do anything—especially if he's doing somebody else's time."

"He should have been patient," Reverend Jacobs said.

"You ever been locked up, Reverend?"

"D'Ray!" Peaches said in a tone indicating she felt the question to be inappropriate.

"It's okay," Reverend Jacobs said. "I'll answer the question." He looked up at me again. "No, I haven't."

"Then you don't know what it's like," I said. "Do you?"

"No," he said. "I don't."

I saw Peaches open her mouth as if she was going to say something else, but before she could, I interrupted her.

"Well, Reverend," I said. "Let me tell you what it's like. You sit in a tiny cell day after day, night after night, watching those cement walls close in on you while hoping against hope that time will hurry up and pass. But time don't hurry up and pass. So you just sit there trying to talk your mind into maintaining its sanity. And you keep telling yourself that you're a man. And as a man, you'll do the time because you did the crime. But what if you didn't do the crime, Reverend? What do you tell yourself then? Do you know what that must be like, Reverend—facing twenty-five years to life for a crime you didn't commit?"

"No," he said. "I don't. But I do know Curtis. Something spooked him. I don't know what. But I do know it's not in his character to run."

"I don't know his character," I said. "I've been away too long."

"Well I do," Reverend Jacobs said. "It's impeccable."

"He's a good person," Peaches said. "Everybody says so."

"Is he violent?" I asked, looking at her.

"No," Reverend Jacobs said, answering for her, "absolutely not." I looked at the reverend.

"Do you think he's still using drugs?"

"No," he said. "I'm certain he's not."

"Did he hang out with people who were doing drugs?"

"He didn't hang out," the reverend said. "He went to work during the week, and he ran his substance-abuse program on the weekend."

"Where did he work?"

"He worked for the utility company."

"Doing what?"

"He drove one of the utility trucks. I believe he repaired power lines, but I'm not sure. But whatever he did, he was usually alone. I believe he liked it that way."

"Reverend, I know you don't know where he is, but if you had to guess based on what you know about him, where would you think he might go?"

The reverend paused. "I just don't know," he said.

"But if you had to guess," Peaches said, pressing him.

He paused again. "Well." He sighed, then looked at me. "If I just had to guess, I would guess that he would probably try to find you."

"Me!" I said, shocked.

"It's just a hunch," the reverend said.

"But that doesn't make sense."

"Perhaps it doesn't, but that's what I believe."

"Why?"

"He idolizes you," the reverend said.

"He told you that."

"He didn't have to."

"I don't understand."

"I'm his spiritual advisor."

"And?" I said.

"And over the years, whenever he was in the midst of a problem, he would often tell me he wished he could talk to you."

"Really?"

"Yes," he said, "really."

There was silence for a moment.

"You seem surprised," the reverend said.

"I am."

"Why?"

"I didn't know he still felt that way."

"You're his brother and he loves you," Reverend Jacobs said. "Time and distance haven't changed that."

I was quiet.

"Put yourself in his shoes," Reverend Jacobs said, offering his advice. "Where would you go if you were him?"

"As far away from here as I could get," I said.

The reverend looked far into the distance. Suddenly, he thought of something. He leaned forward and gazed at me. "What about your mother's sister?" he said. "The one they call Peggy. Where does she live?"

"Chicago," I said.

"Perhaps he would go to her."

I hesitated before answering. That was a possibility, but would it be wise to admit that to the reverend? After all, the police had come to him once, and who was to say they would not come again? And if they did, would he share with them that which I had shared with him? No, I did not know him and because I did not, it would be crazy to trust him.

"No," I said. "Not in a million years."

"Why not?" he asked.

"Aunt Peggy is a straight arrow," I said, making up the story as I went along. "She would turn him in, in a heartbeat. Curtis knows that. He would never go to her. Besides, she's here—I just spoke to her a few minutes ago."

"Would he go to your father's people?"

"I doubt it."

"Why not?"

"He never met Daddy," I said. "And Mama kept him away from Daddy's people. So he doesn't know them and they don't know him."

Reverend Jacobs leaned back in his chair and rubbed his chin with his fingers. "Then it's a crapshoot," he said. "And your guess is just as good as mine—he could be anywhere."

I looked at my watch, then at Peaches. "Well, we better go," I said.

We rose to our feet. So did Reverend Jacobs.

"Sorry I couldn't be of more help."

"Yes, sir," I said.

We all walked to the door.

"What are you going to do now?" Reverend Jacobs asked me.

"Keep looking," I said.

"Where?"

"Any place I think he might be."

Reverend took a deep breath. "I wish I could have been of more assistance," he said again. "But this thing has me baffled."

"Well, if you think of anything, please let me know."

"I'll do that," he said.

I turned to leave, but he stopped me.

"Wait a minute!" he said.

I turned back to face him.

"What is it?"

"There is somebody he may have turned to."

"Who?" I asked.

"Reggie Wayne."

"Excuse me?"

"If he didn't come to me, and he didn't go to your mother, he probably went to Reggie."

"Who is he?" I asked, confused.

"One of the kids he counseled," Peaches said.

"Where can I find him?"

"In the Quarters," Reverend Jacobs said. "He lives with Junior Miller in a house near the cemetery."

"Which house?"

"I know where it is," Peaches said.

"Good," I said. "Let's go."

Outside, I paused and looked toward the dense forest just behind the church, and then I turned and looked down the long, narrow road winding its way deep into the countryside. Little Man was out there somewhere. If only I knew where. In the distance, I heard the sound of a siren blaring. My frazzled nerves flared. Yes, this was a manhunt, a full-fledged manhunt. One in which the chief did not want to take Little Man alive. No, he wanted him dead. Oh, but that would not happen. I would get a gun and kill him dead before I allowed him to kill the little brother I long ago vowed to protect.

7

We crossed the church grounds and made our way to Peaches's car. I heard the menacing sound of the sirens again. Convinced they had something to do with Little Man, I quickly climbed in and clicked on the radio. If he had been captured, surely the station manager would interrupt the broadcast to inform us of the news. I listened for a moment. The voice emanating from the radio spoke calmly of local happenings and of weather forecasts, but nothing about Little Man. I concentrated on the radio until instinct made me turn and look back toward the church. Reverend Jacobs had exited his office and was now standing near the window watching us. Our eyes met, and in that instant, I wondered if he had told the police what he had just told me. Suddenly, I felt my level of anxiety rise. What if he had told them? What if the police got to Reggie before me? No, I did not trust the good reverend, and I knew exactly why I did not trust him. I had done time, and the time I had done had taught me to trust no one.

I watched him for a moment and then turned back in my seat as Peaches guided the car off the church grounds and onto the narrow streets leading back to town. Inside, I was overcome by a strong sense of urgency. I was convinced that I could not trust Reverend Jacobs. But could I trust Reggie? Who was he? And why would Little Man turn to him? None of this made sense to me. I looked at Peaches, but she was not looking at me. She was staring straight ahead, and I could tell from the expression on her face that she was also thinking about the conversation we had just had.

"So, do you know this guy?" I asked her.

"Yeah," she said. "I know him."

"What can you tell me about him?"

"Not much to tell," she said. "He's just another black kid from Brownsville with another sad story."

"Well, if he's from Brownsville, I should know him," I said. "Who are his people?"

"I don't know," she said. "The Millers raised him, but no one knows where he came from."

"Why not?"

"He's a throwaway baby."

"What are you talking about?"

"He was abandoned at birth."

"Abandoned!"

"Yes. Someone left him near the door of one of the hotel rooms at the Brownsville Inn."

"Are you serious?"

"That's what I heard."

"Wow," I said. "That's unreal."

"They say the manager found him and turned him over to the police. Then the police gave him to a foster family to keep while they searched for the birth mother."

"But they never found her."

"No . . . they never did. At first, they thought she was a local girl. You know, some frightened teenager who gave birth to a child and was afraid to tell her parents. And then they thought she was a streetwalker. But after they couldn't find her, they figured she was just some stranger who gave birth somewhere near Brownsville that night and took the child to the hotel for someone to find."

"Was the baby found inside the hotel?"

"No, they found him on the stoop in front of the manager's office. And when they found him, he wasn't even wearing any cloths. He was just wrapped up in a sheet."

"Really?"

"That's what I heard."

"Man, that's crazy."

"Who're you telling?"

"And no one ever came forward?"

"No. And after they didn't, Junior Miller and his wife adopted him. And folks say over the years, that boy gave them pure hell. I mean, he stayed in trouble, especially after Junior's wife died."

"What kind of trouble?"

"Drugs mostly."

"He's an addict?"

"He was a crackhead," she said. "But he's not anymore. Curtis helped him get off drugs and back on the right track. He's been clean for years."

"Curtis helped him?"

"Yeah," she said. "And the two of them have been close ever since."

"Really?"

"Really," she said. "That's why it doesn't surprise me that Reverend Jacobs thinks Curtis may have turned to him. It doesn't surprise me at all."

"Yeah," I said. "That makes sense. It makes a lot of sense."

Satisfied, I leaned back against the seat, watching quietly as she guided the car south along Highway 17, slowing a few minutes later to turn off the main highway onto a side street, which she followed through a steep curve. She stopped at a little white house just across from the cemetery. It was strange but even though we had been separated for nearly a decade, nothing seemed to have changed. She was still the same sweet, caring person who I had fallen in love with. I stared at her, thinking that when this was over, I would take up with her where we had left off before I had gotten into trouble and jail separated us.

"That's it," she said, pointing out the house.

"Come on," I said. "Let's see if he's home."

We got out and made our way to the porch. At the front door, I raised my hand and knocked. A moment later, I heard the dead bolt click. Then, the door creaked open, revealing a middle-aged black man standing on unsteady legs. He had been drinking. I could smell the liquor on his breath.

"Mr. Miller," I said.

He leaned back and looked at me. "What's left of him," he said, swaying from side to side.

"Is Reggie home?"

"Reggie," he stammered. "What you want with Reggie?"

"I need to talk to him," I said.

He furrowed his brow, then leaned slightly forward, gawking at me with narrow, bloodshot eyes. I was still wearing my funeral suit, and I saw him look at my tie and then at my shoes.

"You a cop?"

"No, sir."

"Then who are you?" he asked, slurring his words.

"My name is Reid," I said. "D'Ray Reid."

"Reid!" he said, lifting his unsteady head. "You some kin to that convict they looking for?"

"Yes, sir," I said. "He's my brother."

"Your brother!"

"Yes, sir."

Suddenly, he furrowed his brow again and backed against the door frame for support. He looked at me with furious eyes.

"Reggie ain't got nothing to say to you," he said. "You hear?"

"I understand they were friends," I said.

"Yeah," he said. "But that ain't got nothing to do with nothing."

"Well, I was hoping he—"

"Look! I done told you he ain't got nothing to say to you."

"But—"

"But nothing," he said. "Now, I'm gonna have to ask you to leave."

"Mr. Miller—"

"Alright," he slurred. "I see you hard of understanding. Be here when I get back if you want to."

"Mr. Miller," I called to him. But he didn't answer.

He staggered inside the house, and when he returned, he was holding a shotgun. He raised the gun and pointed it at me.

"Now, I said leave."

"Mr. Miller!" Peaches said, stepping forward. "Don't you remember me? I'm Miss Lewis . . . you know . . . from the church."

He staggered back and looked at her through squinted eyes. Suddenly he recognized her.

"Miss Lewis!" He repeated her name in a tone indicating his surprise at seeing her.

"Yes," she said, smiling. "It's me."

"He's drunk," I mumbled.

Peaches raised her finger to her lips and shushed me. Then she turned back to him again. "I haven't seen you at church lately," she said.

"No, ma'am," he mumbled, lowering the gun and averting his eyes. "It's been real busy at work lately."

"I understand," she said.

"Yes, ma'am," he said.

He had been wearing a dirty baseball cap. He removed it from his head and clumsily clutched it in his hands. He looked about nervously for a moment or two, and I sensed that he was ashamed of having her see him in his state of drunkenness.

"Would you like to come in?" he asked, stepping aside. His eyes were still averted.

"No," she said. "We don't have much time. We're trying to find Curtis."

"Yes, ma'am," he said.

"We sure could use your help," she said.

"Yes, ma'am," he said again.

"Is Reggie home?"

"Yes, ma'am," he said. "He in there."

"Could we talk to him for a minute?"

"Yes, ma'am," he said. He turned his back and yelled into the house. "Reggie! Uh, Reggie! Get your tail out here, boy."

A moment later, Reggie emerged from the shadows. It appeared he had been sleeping.

"These folks want to talk to you."

"What folks?"

"Miss Lewis," he said. "And Mr. Reid."

"Talk to me about what?"

"Have you seen Curtis?" I asked, interrupting them.

"Curtis!" he said, seemingly stunned.

"Yeah," I said. "I'm his brother."

He hesitated. I saw him looking me over with narrow, shifty eyes. "No, sir," he blurted after a moment or two. "I haven't seen him."

He was lying. I could tell.

"Are you sure?" I asked.

Suddenly, Junior Miller stepped forward. "He told you he ain't seen him. Now leave him alone."

"When was the last time you saw him?" I asked Reggie, ignoring Junior.

"It's been a while."

"How long is a while?"

"I don't know," he said. "Just know it's been a while."

"Have you seen him since he escaped?"

"No, sir," he said. "I haven't."

"Well, I need to find him," I said. "And I need to find him quick." I waited. He didn't say anything. "Like to help him," I said, "if I can."

"To get away?" he asked me.

"No," I said.

"You mean you want him to turn himself in."

"Yeah," I said. "I do."

"Why?"

"Because they'll kill him if he don't."

"And he'll go to prison if he do."

"I can get him out of prison," I said. "But I can't get him out of the cemetery."

"I can't help you," he said.

"Did he talk to you before he left?" Peaches asked.

"No, ma'am, he didn't."

"I told you he didn't know nothing," Mr. Miller said. "Now you done talked to him. Leave him alone."

"He told me what you did for him," Reggie said in a faraway tone.

"Excuse me?" I said.

"He told me you saved his life. He told me you went to prison for him. Is that true?"

"It's true," I said. "But that was a long time ago."

"You know he's been looking for you," he said. "Don't you?"

"No," I said. "I didn't know that."

"Well, he has," Reggie said. "He's been looking for years."

"Well, I guess that makes us even," I said, "because now I'm looking for him. Will you help me find him?"

"I don't know where he is," Reggie said.

"I think you do."

"I don't care what you think," Reggie said.

"Take me to him," I said.

"He told you he don't know where he is," Mr. Miller said. "Now, leave him alone. And I ain't gonna ask you no mo'."

"They'll kill him if they catch him," I said. "Is that what you want?"

"Don't put that on him," Mr. Miller said.

"Then help me find him," I said.

"I don't know where he is," Reggie said. "But I'll ask around and see what I can find out. That's all I can do."

"When?" I pressed him.

"Right now," he told me.

"I'll go with you," I said.

"No," he said. "Be better if I go by myself."

"How long will you be?" I asked.

"An hour or two," he said.

"Then what?" I asked him.

"Meet me at your mama's house," he said. "And I'll tell you what I find out."

8

I walked out onto the porch and leaned against one of the small wooden posts. Two hours. What in the world was I supposed to do for two hours? Behind me, I heard the screen door open and close. Peaches emerged from the house and walked next to me. She had hung back to speak to Reggie in private, about what I did not know.

"Do you want to go to my place?" she asked me. "We can wait there."

"No," I said. "I need to sit outside where I can breathe."

"How about the park?"

I shook my head. "Too many people."

"Then where?"

I was quiet a moment. "The old baseball field," I said. "It's not too far from Mama's house, and there shouldn't be anyone out there this time of day."

"Alright," she said. "The old baseball field it is."

We went to the car and drove back to the projects. At the community center, she parked before the gymnasium. We made our way across the campus and sat beneath the large oak tree on a bench overlooking the diamond. It had been years since I had been here, and to my surprise, the field was overrun with weeds, the wooden bleachers had rotted, and the tall wire screen behind home plate was filled with gaping holes. In the distance, two young boys were walking across the campus toward the community center. They were brothers—I could tell by the striking resemblance they bore to each other. I watched them for a moment; then my mind fell upon Little Man again. Suddenly, I thought about Reggie.

"I should have followed him," I said.

"No," Peaches said, shaking her head. "You did the right thing."

"But what if he doesn't come back?"

"He'll be back," she said.

"How do you know?"

"I just know," she said.

I rose and paced back and forth before the old dugout. I looked at my watch again. Reggie had been gone a little less than an hour, and my nerves were already shot. I checked my watch again. Behind us, there was a slight crack in the woods.

"What was that?" Peaches asked. I looked at her. She had snapped around on the bench and was staring nervously at the woods.

"I don't know," I said. "I better go see."

I walked to the edge of the woods. Dusk had settled, and in the shadows I could see the faint outline of a large deer, forging about, looking for something to eat. "It's just a deer," I mumbled. I watched him for a minute or two, then returned to the bench and sat next to Peaches. She placed her hand on top of mine and began to massage it. I looked at my watch again.

"Don't worry," she whispered. "It's going to be alright."

"I wish I could believe that."

"You can," she said.

I looked across the field again. Time seemed to be standing still. Oh, what if Mama was right? What if this was my fault? The thought made me move about uneasily in my seat.

Frustration made me take a deep breath and then exhale hard. Suddenly, my mind began to drift again.

"I had the fellows take him over there that day," I finally said.

"Take him where?"

"To Kojak's Place."

"So?" she said.

"I knew from the start that he was too young to go there. But I let them take him anyway. And while he was there, one of the ladies gave him some crack. He was only ten. If I—"

"This is not your fault," she said sternly.

"Mama thinks it is."

"Well, she's wrong."

"I don't know."

"Well, I do."

"She loves him," I said. "She loves him more than life itself. And when that happened—"

"She loves both of you," she interrupted me again.

"Oh, no," I said. "She loves him. She just tolerated me. Two of us don't get along. We never did and I don't expect we ever will."

"Why not?"

"It's a long story."

"Tell it to me."

"I don't know where to begin."

"Begin at the beginning."

I paused. A long moment passed.

"She stopped loving me when Daddy went away," I finally said.

"I don't believe that," Peaches said, vehemently denying my assertion.

"It's true," I said.

"That doesn't make any sense," she said, turning in her seat and facing me. "That doesn't make sense at all."

"After Daddy went away, she wanted me to be something I couldn't be, and when I refused, she gave up on me."

"What did she want you to be?"

"Normal," I said. "In spite of where we lived and all the problems we had, she wanted me to be normal."

"What's wrong with that?"

"It wasn't possible."

"Why not?"

I turned from her, and I sensed that she was trying to comprehend what I was trying to tell her. But how could she? How could she understand that which I had not understood myself?

"To me, the world Mama believed in was a fairy tale. She actually believed we could pull ourselves up by our bootstraps."

"And you didn't?"

"No," I said. "I didn't."

"Why not?"

"Because we were so poor that we didn't have any bootstraps to pull."

"A lot of people are poor."

"Not like us," I said. "We were poorer than poor. Do you understand what I'm telling you?"

"Make me understand."

"I don't know if I can."

"I wish you would try," she said.

"Alright," I said. "I'll try." I got up from the bench and began pacing again. "After Daddy went to prison, we fell on real hard times. And nobody would hire Mama, because they didn't like my daddy. So, she used to sit around reading books. I mean, she read all the time. And I guess the stories she read led her to believe that we could rise above Chatman Avenue. She used to say, 'Boys, you don't have to be like everybody else. You can go to school and get an education, and be whatever you want to be.' "

"What's wrong with that?"

"I didn't believe it."

"Did Curtis?"

"Curtis was young and didn't know what to believe. So he believed whatever I believed."

"And your mother knew that."

"Knew it and hated it."

"What did she do about it?"

"She just kept reading those books and saying we could be somebody. We could go to college and be anything we wanted."

"She's a dreamer?"

"Yeah, and I wanted to believe in her dreams, but our circumstances just wouldn't let me. So, whenever she started talking like that, I just let her know that I wasn't trying to hear it and that I wasn't going to let Little Man hear it either."

"You told her that?"

"No, I didn't tell her. I showed her."

"Showed her how?"

"I started running the streets and hustling."

"What about Curtis?"

"I took him under my wing and started working on his head. You know, I told him to forget all of that talk about school and college. I told him he had to learn how to fight because that was the only way he was going to make them Negroes in the streets respect him. And then I reminded him that we were living in the projects and that nobody in the whole world gave a flying flip about us, so we had to learn how to hustle if we were going to survive. And that's what I tried to teach him—how to survive."

"What about school?"

"I thought it was a waste of time because we were living on death row."

"What!"

"Death row," I said. "That's what folks called Chatman Avenue."

"Why?"

"Because didn't nothing happen on Chatman Avenue except strong Negroes killing weak Negroes. And by the time I was thirteen, I had figured it out. There wasn't any way off of death row except in a casket or in handcuffs. So I made up my mind that they could take me to prison, but come hell or high water, I wasn't going to let any of them crazy niggers send me to the cemetery."

"That's sad."

"Yeah," I said. "But at the time it was how I felt. I mean, by the time I was thirteen years old, the ways of the world were crystal clear to me. We were black, and we were poor, and there was a fence around us, separating us from everything that would make our lives better. And I hated that fence, and I hated the life that those of us behind the fence were forced to live. So, I decided to do the only thing I thought I could do—I became a hustler, a hustler named Outlaw. And Mama hated me for that. And she hated herself because she had to depend on me to make ends meet. So, she took the money that I brought home, and she never asked where it came from. But she swore that my life wouldn't be Little Man's life. She gave up on me and focused all of her attention on Little Man. And when she did, I wasn't even mad at her, because I knew she couldn't see that fence. And as long as she couldn't see it, I knew she couldn't see me. She could only hate me. But at the time, that didn't matter to me. Daddy was in prison, and it was my responsibility to make sure that my family was fed and that Little Man was safe. And that's what I did, the only way I knew how."

"How old were you when your daddy was sent to prison?"

"I was five."

"Which prison?"

"Angola."

"What did he do?"

"He killed a white man. Everybody saw it was an accident. But that didn't matter. They still gave him life."

We were silent for a moment, then she spoke again. "How old were you when you quit school?"

"I quit when I was fourteen, and a year later, I was living in a facility for boys serving juvenile life."

"Wow!"

I paused again. I felt myself becoming emotional.

"The night I met you at the hotel in Jackson, I was running from the police. I had just killed a boy." I hesitated again, feeling the magnitude of what I had just said. I opened my mouth to speak again, but my voice broke, and my hands began to shake. "I didn't mean to kill him," I said. "But just like now, Little Man was in trouble. He had taken some drugs from a drug dealer, and he couldn't pay for them. And that dealer was going to kill him if I didn't pay him a hundred dollars to spare Little Man's life. So I robbed a store to get money to pay the dealer. The boy I killed was tending the store. I didn't want to kill him . . . but he pulled a gun . . . and I shot him to keep him from shooting me. At the time, I was just a boy myself, living in this crazy place, trying to keep my brother alive. I didn't know what to do. Just like now, I didn't know what to do, so, I decided to do whatever it took to save my brother's life. And that's what I did—I took another boy's life to save his. After the police found out I was the killer, I thought I could run from them, but I couldn't. . . . No matter how far I ran, it wasn't far enough, so they caught me, and I went to jail. It ended up being the best thing that ever happened to me, because I got to know the boy's father—in spite of all I had done to him, he spent time with me at the prison, and over time, as hard as it is to believe, he forgave me, and after he forgave me, he taught me how to be a man. That's what I'm trying to do for my brother. I don't want him to destroy his life before he has had a chance to live it. I want him to face this thing like a man, and when it's all over, I want him to live his life like a man and not like some sad, trifling nigger walking around here blaming white folk for all of his troubles."

"So you feel like Curtis is your responsibility."

"He's my baby brother. If I don't look out for him, who will? Besides, if it ends like this, it will all have been for nothing."

"I understand," she said; then she looked out across the field, and I could tell she wanted to cry.

"Mama thinks I want him to go to jail, but I don't. I wouldn't wish jail on anybody. But if he doesn't come back and face this thing, he'll never live again, because as long as this thing is hanging over his head, he'll always be looking over his shoulder. And at some point, when it all closes in on him, desperation will set in, and then he will do whatever he has to do to survive. He'll rob; he'll steal—he'll even kill."

"Just like you?"

"Just like me," I said.

There was silence. I waited for her to speak, but she said nothing. I looked at her and then continued. "I don't want that for him," I said. "I graduated from college, and I want him to do the same thing."

I looked at her. She was crying.

"I hope Reggie finds him," she said.

"Yeah," I said, "me too."

"It's been a long time since you've seen him," she said. "If you get a chance to speak to him, do you think he will listen to you?"

"He'll listen," I said. "If I can talk to him like I'm talking to you, he'll listen."

"Well, Curtis is a good man," she said. "Everybody who knows him knows that."

"Not the chief."

"I wasn't talking about the chief," she said. "I was talking about folks in the community."

"Right now, the chief is all that matters."

"I suppose you're right."

"I am right," I said. "The chief will kill him if he catches him. Ain't no doubt about that. He'll kill him dead."

"My God," she said. "I'll be so glad when this is over."

"Yeah," I said. "So will I."

"D'Ray," she said softly.

"Yeah," I said.

"Does your mother know that you've turned your life around?"

"No," I said. "She doesn't."

"Don't you think you should tell her?"

"No."

"Why not?"

"She knows, but it doesn't matter to her now."

"Why not?"

"Because in her mind, Little Man's life has been destroyed and I'm the one who destroyed it."

"When all of this is over, the two of you should talk."

"Maybe we will," I said.

After that, it was quiet again. I looked at her and she was looking far across the field.

"Do you really think your mother stopped loving you?" she asked me.

"I don't know," I said. "I just know that I never stopped loving her."

"That's the thing that made me fall in love with you," she said. "You were so compassionate. And it doesn't seem that has changed."

"I don't know if that has changed or not. But seeing you again has made me realize one thing."

"What's that?"

"The way I feel about you has not changed. I know it sounds crazy, but it's like we've never been apart."

"I know," she said. "I feel the same way."

It was quiet a moment; then I looked at her.

"I am glad you're back," she said.

"So am I," I said.

9

When it was time to go, I said good-bye to Peaches, then walked across the campus and out into the streets. I had been away from Brownsville for nearly a decade, and the world that I now gazed upon seemed as foreign to me as if I were a complete stranger. To my amazement, most of the houses were gone and the old trailer homes that now lined both sides of the street were in such disrepair that they seemed uninhabitable. Vacant lots were overgrown with weeds, and the pothole-riddled streets were void of any activity save for an occasional bicyclist pedaling past or a pedestrian aimlessly wandering about.

I followed School Street to Chatman Avenue, turned left, and walked to the end of the block. At Mama's house, I made my way across the yard to the front porch and mounted the steps. I raised my hand to knock, but before I could, the door opened and Mama poked her head out. Her eyes were wide, and I could tell that something was wrong.

"Come in," she said frantically.

I entered and she hastily closed the door. I looked past her. Reggie was sitting on the sofa. Our eyes met.

"Did you find out anything?" I asked him.

"I saw him," he said.

"What!" I exclaimed.

I waited for him to say more, but he remained quiet. I stared at him for a moment, then looked at Mama. The two of them had already talked. I could tell by the awkward way in which they both attempted to avoid looking into my eyes. I frowned. I was becoming agitated again.

"Well, how is he?"

"He's alright," Reggie said, and then he looked at Mama again.

"Is he hurt?" I asked.

"No." Reggie shook his head. "He's fine."

"Where is he?" I asked.

"I can't tell you," he said. "At least not until we talk."

"Talk about what?"

Reggie didn't answer. Instead, he turned and looked at Mama again.

"Go ahead," she said. "Tell him."

"Tell me what?" I asked, frowning.

"He wants to know if you will help him."

"Help him," I said. "Help him how?"

"Help him get away."

"No," I said. "I won't."

"He needs money and he needs transportation."

"No," I said again.

"And he's running out of food," Reggie added.

"No," I said for the third time.

"I'm begging you," Mama said.

"I can't," I said.

"Please," she whispered. "He needs your help."

"He needs to turn himself in," I said. "That's what he needs to do."

"He's not asking for your opinion," she said. "He done already made up his mind to run. He's asking you to help him get away."

"I can't."

"He's your brother," Mama said. "If you don't help him, who will?"

"He'll help himself," Reggie said.

"And what's that supposed to mean?" I asked.

"He has a gun," Reggie said. "That's what."

"A gun!"

"That's right."

"He's going to get himself killed," I said.

"Not if you help him," Reggie said.

"Look," I said forcefully. "Go tell him I said to turn himself in, you hear?"

"No!" Mama shouted. "That's not what he wants."

"I don't care what he wants."

"You should care," she said. "He's your flesh and blood. Don't that mean anything to you? Don't this family mean anything to you?"

I felt the anger rise within me. I whirled and looked at her, then opened my mouth to speak, but before I could, Reggie interrupted me.

"What you gonna do?" he asked. "We ain't got all day."

"I already told you."

"Then it's settled."

"No," I said. "Take me to him."

"I can't do that."

"Please," Mama said. "I'm begging you."

"Don't beg him," Reggie said. "We don't need him."

"You're right," Mama said; then she looked at me and shook her head. "I should have known we couldn't depend on you."

"What?" I said.

"You heard me," she said.

"You got your nerve," I said.

"Me?" she said. "When you were in prison, I prayed that one day you would see fit to change. And I had hoped that one day you would be able to think of someone other than yourself. But I see my prayers went unanswered. You haven't changed. And you never will."

"Take me to him," I said, ignoring her.

"No!" Mama said. "Not until we have an understanding."

"This is crazy," I said.

"I don't want him going to prison," she said. "I want him to be free. Even if it means I'll never see him again."

I rose to leave, but Mama stopped me.

"If you leave, don't come back. You hear?"

I turned and faced her. "Where will he go?" I asked. "How will he live?"

"He'll go wherever you take him," she said. "And he'll live by the grace of God."

"Me," I said. "Why me?"

"Because there ain't nobody else."

I didn't say anything.

"Today, before you came, I was on my knees," she said. "I was on my knees asking God to make a way. Two hours later, he sent you."

"God didn't send me," I said. "Miss Big Siss did."

"What you gonna do?" Reggie asked. "We're running out of time."

"I'm going outside," I said.

"For what?"

"To think."

"Ain't nothing to think about," Mama said. "He's your brother, and you're going to help him." She paused and her face became stern. "Now, I'm not asking anymore—I'm telling."

"I could get in big trouble," I said. "We all could. He's a fugitive."

"You been in trouble before," she said.

"Excuse me?" I said, shocked.

"I didn't stutter," she said.

"I'm leaving," I said.

"If you do," she said, "don't come back."

"I won't," I said.

I stormed out. Behind me I heard the door slam. I descended the steps, feeling hot tears rolling down my face. Suddenly, the door opened again and I heard Mama's voice.

"Don't come back," she yelled. "I mean it—don't ever come back."

10

I stood for a moment trying to digest what she had just said. I had either to join them or leave them alone. Well, I would not join them. The whole thing was crazy. Curtis was not going to get away. He was going to get himself killed. Well, if that was his choice, who was I to try and convince him otherwise? Suddenly, my head began to ache, and I had an overwhelming desire to put distance between me and this place. I made my way back to the campus. Peaches had parked the car in the front lot next to the gym. When I arrived, she was sitting behind the wheel, waiting. I pulled the door open and climbed in on the passenger's side. Then I grabbed the seat belt, pulled it across my shoulder, and buckled it. Out of the corner of my eye, I could see that she was staring at me.

"What happened?" she asked.

"Nothing," I told her.

"Something happened," she said. "I can tell by the look on your face. What is it? Is Curtis alright?"

"I'm done," I said.

"Done!" she said. "What do you mean, you're done?"

"Just what I said."

She paused for a moment, and I could tell she was trying to figure out what was going on.

"Did you talk to Reggie?" she asked.

"I talked to him."

"What did he say?"

"They want me to help Curtis get away."

"They actually told you that?"

"Yes," I said. "They did."

"And what did you tell 'em?"

"I told them no."

"They had no right to ask that of you," she said. "No right at all."

"Well, they did," I said. "And now they're angry."

"That's not your problem."

"He's armed," I said. "Is that my problem?"

"My God!" she exclaimed. "You have to do something."

"Like what?" I snapped.

"I don't know."

"Let's just go," I said.

"Where?"

"As far away from Brownsville as we can get."

"What about Curtis?"

"I can't help him," I said. "Don't you understand that? I can't help him."

"But—"

"But nothing," I said. "He's made up his mind. He's going to run. And when he does, they're going to catch him. And they're going to kill him. Then Mama will cry. And life will go on."

"And you can live with that?"

"I guess I'll have to."

"This is crazy," she said.

"Tell me something I don't know," I said sarcastically.

She looked at me but did not speak.

"Go away with me," I said.

"What?"

"Let's just gas up and go."

"No," she said. "You can't just leave and pretend that this isn't happening."

"Why not?" I asked.

"It's irresponsible."

"Irresponsible!"

"Yes," she said. "And selfish."

"I don't care about this anymore," I said. "Can't you understand that? I just don't care."

"I don't believe you."

"Let's go," I said. "Let's go home and pack our clothes and leave."

"No!"

"Please."

"No," she said again. "I can't."

"Why can't you?"

"I'm a teacher," she said. "Or did you forget?"

"School is out," I said. "Isn't it?"

"Not for three days."

"Three days."

"Yes," she said. "Three days."

"So in three days you will be free."

She nodded.

"Then will you go away with me?"

"No," she said. "Not until all of this is over."

"Then I'll go by myself."

"You can't leave him," she said. "I don't care how angry you are—you can't leave him."

"I can and I will."

"No," she said. "I won't let you."

"I need to get away," I said. "Don't you understand that?"

"Then let's get away," she said. "Let's go to dinner and take in a movie. Maybe see something light, something to take your mind off Brownsville . . . but afterward, we're coming back."

"No," I said. "I'm not coming back here."

"You have to."

"No, I don't."

"He needs your help."

"He doesn't want it."

"I won't let you abandon him just because you're angry at them."

"I can't handle this," I said. "Not right now. Not after all I've been through today."

"You have to," she said. "He's your brother." She paused but I didn't respond. "If you leave, and something happens to him, you will never be able to forgive yourself."

"Why is this happening to me?" I shouted. "Why?"

"Let's go to Monroe and get something to eat," she said. "Things will look different when we get back."

"Okay, but I need to go home first. I need to get out of this suit."

"Alright," she said, starting the engine. "We'll stop by your house first."

She drove me back to the sandwich shop to retrieve my truck; then I made the short trek home. When I arrived, I parked my truck next to the house and got out. I looked around. Everything was as I had left it. The doors to the house were closed, the lights were off, and the only noticeable sound was the soft, steady hum of the tiny air conditioner sitting in the window just off the porch. Peaches had pulled her car behind my truck and stopped. I walked back to her and leaned against the window.

"Would you like to come in?"

Peaches looked around as if she was trying to see if anyone else was there. There were a few cars parked across the street at Mr. Henry's mother's house. One belonged to Miss Big Siss and one belonged to Ida. But I had no idea who the remaining three or four vehicles belonged to.

"Do you think it will be alright?" she asked, staring at the cars parked along the street. "I mean, I don't want to be disrespectful."

I looked at the cars and then back at her. "It's alright," I said. Then I helped her out and she followed me inside. I flicked on the lights.

"I'm going to get out of this suit," I said.

She nodded. I turned to leave, then stopped.

"If you would like something to drink, the kitchen is over there," I said, pointing to the door just off the living room. "Make yourself at home."

I left the room and heard her moving about the house. In all the madness, I had not had time to think about Mr. Henry. But now that I was home, I was overcome by the heaviness of it all. I had lost him, and now it appeared that I might also lose Little Man. Suddenly, my head began to swirl. No, I could not stay here. In a few days, I would leave this place and start all over again, just me and Peaches and the promise of a better day.

I changed and returned to the living room. When I got there, Peaches was sitting on the sofa staring into space.

"Ready?" I asked.

"If you are," she said.

She rose, then stopped.

"There's something I didn't tell you," she said. "Something I heard on the radio while I was waiting for you to return from your mother's house." She paused to collect herself. I remained quiet. "The chief has issued a reward," she said after a moment or two.

"A reward!"

"Yes," she said. "Ten thousand dollars."

"Ten thousand dollars!" I said, shaking my head. "That's not good. . . . That's not good at all."

"It's going to be alright," she said.

I didn't answer. She looked at me for a moment, then handed me the keys to her car.

"Let's go," she said.

A few minutes later, I found myself leaning back, clutching the steering wheel, feeling the power of the vehicle as the car sailed along the asphalt highway. I looked at her. After a moment or two, she slid next to me, and when she did, I placed my arm around her shoulder, and she leaned her head against me. At that moment, I was not concerned with Little Man or my mother; I was concerned only with her and the moment and all of the moments that were to come. Oh, why did we have to wait? Why couldn't we keep going, just her and me?

"I don't want to go back," I blurted.

"You have to."

"I can't do what they're asking."

"I know," she said. "I don't expect you to."

"And I may not be able to do anything for him either."

"I know that too," she said.

"Then what is this all about?" I asked her.

"Just don't leave him," she said. "Don't leave him like you left me."

Suddenly, I snapped my head around and looked at her. "I didn't leave you," I said defensively.

"It doesn't matter," she said.

"It does matter," I said. "It was never my intent to leave you."

She frowned, and I knew she did not believe me. I took a deep breath and tried to explain it to her.

"When I came back to the hotel that day, I had come back to get you. I just had located a car and I was going to purchase it that evening. Then I was going to take you to Detroit with me. But when I got back to the hotel parking lot, I saw you standing there with that policeman, and I saw that he had cuffed you. It was never my intent to leave you. It was my intent to lay low for a day or two and then bail you out. But a few days later, the police caught me too. They brought me back to Louisiana, and I spent the next six years in juvenile prison. I didn't leave you. They took me away. I would have never left you. I was in love with you. Don't you know that?"

She remained quiet.

"I would have written you to explain everything, but I didn't know where you were or what had become of you."

"I was in jail," she said. Then she was silent, and I could tell she was reliving the moment. "They did arrest me that day. . . . I ended up doing thirty days in county jail for solicitation."

"I didn't know," I said.

I looked at her, but she was not looking at me. She was staring straight ahead, looking far up the road.

Suddenly, her voice broke. "I was so scared."

"I didn't know," I said again. I glanced at her. I saw her shake her head, and her eyes began to water.

"I had never been to jail before, and I didn't know what to expect, so I just freaked out. I started shouting and screaming and pulling on those bars. I guess I was having some kind of panic attack. After a while, a guard came to my cell. I thought she was going to torment me, but she didn't. Instead, she asked me what I was in for, and when I told her, she just shook her head and said that I didn't belong in jail and that I didn't belong on the streets either. She said that when I got out, I needed to find myself a good church and enroll in a good school, and then get about the business of living the life that God had put me on this earth to live."

"She told you that?"

"Yeah . . . and that's just what I did. I got myself together and I became a teacher."

"A teacher," I repeated, still in disbelief.

"Yes," she said, "a teacher." She paused and smiled. "It's

funny, but when I was first locked up, all I could think about was you. But as time went on, all I could think about was my father."

"Were the two of you close?"

"No," she said, and her voice began to quiver again. "He left us when I was a child."

"Really," I said.

"Yes." She paused. "I never told you that?"

"No," I said. "You didn't."

"I used to tell everybody that he was dead. But he wasn't dead. He left us. He just got in his car one morning, started the engine, and drove away."

"Why?"

"I don't know."

"Your mother never told you?"

"No."

"And you never asked her?"

"No, I didn't."

"Why not?"

"My mother is not a very nice person. In fact, the night I met you, she had just put me out."

"I remember you telling me that."

"Did I ever tell you why?"

"No, I don't think so."

"She threw me out because of a man. Can you believe that? I was seventeen years old, and she threw me out in the streets over a man."

"Who was he?"

"He was her boyfriend."

"What happened?"

"He tried to rape me."

"Oh, my God," I said, and then I looked at her, but she didn't answer me. She raised her hands to her face. They were shaking.

"Did you tell your mother?"

"Yes."

"What did she do?"

"She threw me out. She threw me out like an old shoe—just opened the door and said *leave*."

"Just like that?"

"Just like that."

She paused again and I saw the tears streaming down her face.

"You don't have to talk about it," I said.

"I don't mind," she whispered. "I want you to know." Then suddenly her eyes narrowed and I could see the pain on her face. "It was a Friday night and Mama was at work. I guess the two of them had argued about sex before she left, because a few minutes after she had gone, he stormed into my room and said, 'You gonna do what your mama won't.' Then he grabbed me and threw me on the bed and started trying to pull down my panties. But I fought him off. And when Mama came home, I told her what happened and she slapped me in the face and said I was lying. I told her that I was telling the truth and that he wasn't no good and that I was scared of him. Then she got mad at me and told me to get out and don't ever come back. I begged her not to put me out. I kept telling her that I didn't have anywhere to go, but she didn't listen. She just kept saying that Harold was a good man, and she wasn't about to lose another good man over a pack of lies. So I left, and I was walking down the street trying to figure out where to go when a car pulled up next to me, and a white man asked me how much. At first, I didn't know what he was talking about. Then it dawned on me—he was trying to buy sex. Then I thought about my mother and her boyfriend and my situation, and I said to myself, *Why not?* And I told him one hundred dollars. I got in the car with him, and he took me to his hotel room. As it turned out, it was the same hotel that you were staying in. His room was next to yours."

Suddenly, I remembered. The man refused to pay her. "He tried to stiff you," I said. "Didn't he?"

"Yes," she said. "And I was feeling real low. But I still needed money, so I knocked on your door, thinking I could sell you some sex. But when I told you my story and you helped me get my money from him and said that I could stay with you, I knew that you were the answer to my prayers— that God had sent you to protect me. And that night while you were sleeping, I thanked Him for sending you. And I told myself right then and there that I would be yours as long as you wanted me. Then after a while, that vow became easier and easier to keep, because I fell in love with you." She looked at me with warm, compassionate eyes. "I know we said we would talk about it later. But after all of this time, I still want you and you still want me." She paused. "You do still want me, don't you?"

"Of course I do."

"Do you think it can be like it was before?"

"I don't see why not."

She smiled and laid her head on my shoulder again, and as I drove, I thought about the story she had just told me, and I thought about how good it felt having her next to me. I had lost Mr. Henry and my brother was missing, but I had my girl back. Maybe this was *divine* intervention. I looked at her.

"So you think God sent me, huh?"

"I know he did."

"This is so strange," I said. "But my mother said something like that to me a few minutes ago."

"Really?"

"Yeah . . . she said that God had sent me to save Little Man."

"Maybe He did."

"And maybe she's just trying to manipulate me."

"Do you think she would do that?"

"I know she would," I said. "My mother and your mother

seem to be cut from the same cloth. They seem to think only about themselves, and they don't mind hurting the ones they love."

"That's true," she said. "But in spite of all my mother has put me through . . . I still love her to death. . . . And deep down I know you love your mother too. You might not like her, but I know you love her. Am I right?"

I didn't say anything. Yes, I loved her. But what good had it done?

"When was the last time you told her how you felt?"

"I don't remember."

"That's not good," she said.

"Oh, I know what would happen," I said.

"What?"

"She wouldn't hear me. She would just twist what I said and keep blaming me for everything bad that has happened to this family."

"You don't know that."

"She's blaming me for this," I said. "And I wasn't even here. She hates me. She always has and she always will."

Suddenly, all was quiet. My mind began to drift. I thought about Mr. Henry again, and I thought about Little Man. It all seemed so overwhelming. Involuntarily, I sighed, and my lips parted.

"What a day," I heard myself say. Then I felt Peaches's hand on my knee. I tilted my head and looked at her.

"Oh, it hasn't been all bad," she said.

"Hasn't it?" I asked.

"No," she said. "It hasn't."

"Well, I sure wish you would tell me what's been good about it."

"I found you," she said. "Didn't I?"

"Yeah," I said teasingly. "But now that you've found me, what are you going to do with me?"

"I don't know." She smirked. "But I'm sure I'll think of something."

"Is that a promise?" I goaded her.

"It's a promise," she whispered.

Then she leaned over and kissed me on the cheek. I looked up. We were in Monroe. And, yes, I had my girl back.

11

My anger subsided, and as planned, we went to dinner and took in a movie, then drove to ULM's campus. Near ten-thirty, we parked and mounted the footbridge, holding hands while walking slowly and gazing at the flickering light from the full moon cascading off the murky waters of Bayou Desiard. Halfway across the bridge, we paused and leaned against the metal rail.

"This is so beautiful," she said. "Isn't it?"

I smiled and nodded.

"I just love this campus. Don't you?"

"Yes," I said. "It's a nice place."

There was a cool breeze blowing off the water. I stood for a moment, enjoying the serenity of the moment and feeling glad that we were together in a place that seemed thousands of miles from Brownsville. I looked at her, and I could not help but think how beautiful she appeared, standing in the moonlight with the soft, gentle breeze blowing through her hair.

"I can't believe you were actually on this campus," she said. "I just can't believe it."

"Well, it's true," I said.

I lifted my hand and placed it on her shoulder, then gently pulled her to me. Her body relaxed and she leaned against my chest.

"Oh, it's such a shame we never bumped into each other," she said. "It would have been so nice to sit out here on the water with you on a beautiful night like this."

"Let's sit now," I said.

I took her hand and we made our way across the bridge, then found a bench just off the water beneath a large oak tree. As we sat, looking at the moon, the stars, the sky, and the water, I could not help but think if only the world was as peaceful as this. Who knows, perhaps it was, somewhere far, far away from Brownsville.

To the left of us, I heard the sound of people talking. I turned and looked. A man was standing on the balcony of one of the dormitories. Next to him was a much younger man, a boy, really. As I watched them, I figured they were father and son, and the father had come to take the son home for summer break. Then I thought about Peaches and the story she had told me earlier. Then I thought about Little Man and me, and I wondered how we had gotten to this god-awful place. I exhaled hard, then turned and looked at Peaches, whose head was tilted back. She was still looking toward the sky.

"Curtis never knew his father," I blurted. I hadn't meant to say it. It just came out. When it did, she looked at me awkwardly.

A pensive moment passed. Out of the corner of my eye, I saw the man put his arm around his son and I saw the two of them disappear inside the room, as if to say, *It has been a good year, but now it's time to go home.* I thought about my father again.

"Sometimes it seems cruel," I said. "Them taking our father away from us like that. And other times it just seems like one of those things you have to deal with."

"Did you deal with it?"

"As best I could."

"You ever hear from him?"

"No, I thought about writing him once but I didn't. So, he's never written me and I've never written him."

"Not even once?"

"Not even once."

"Wow."

"When I was younger, I tried to talk to Curtis about him. But he always pretended it didn't matter to him. But I knew it did. I could tell by the way he acted whenever somebody mentioned Daddy's name."

"And how was that?"

"Oh, he would act like he was going to cry or something."

"He was probably hurting."

"Ain't no probably to it," I said. "He was hurting, and I'm sure he's still hurting. Can you imagine what it's like to have never seen your daddy?" I paused and looked across the water. "As long as he has been in this world, Curtis has never treated me like a big brother. He always acted like I was his daddy. He used to cling to me—Mama hated that. She hated it with all of her heart. But in spite of how she felt, I promised him that if he ever needed me, I would be there for him."

"Why did she hate it?"

"In her mind, Curtis was going to be somebody, but I wasn't. My fate was sealed. I was going to end up like my no-good daddy. That's all she used to say to me: 'Boy, you gonna end up like your no-good daddy.' "

"She actually said that?"

"Constantly."

"She probably didn't mean it. She was just hurting too."

"I don't know if she meant it or not. But after a while, I started believing it. I mean, I just felt like I was nothing and I wasn't ever going to be anything. So, one day, I declared myself a man. And I took to the streets and I started hustling, and

I didn't care what happened, because in my mind, the world had taken my daddy and didn't a single soul on God's green planet give a flip about me, so I didn't give a flip about no-body—except Little Man. I had made up my mind that I was going to be the daddy he never had. So that's what I did. And like I said before, that's how I got in trouble. I killed a boy so that Little Man could live."

"Mr. Henry's son?"

"Yeah," I said, then paused. "His name was Stanley, and from what I hear, he was a really good kid." I paused again, remembering the day, the hour, the second that I had killed Stanley. After a moment, I continued. "After I killed him, I made myself hard and I acted like it didn't bother me. But it did. And it still does."

I stopped talking and looked at her. But she wasn't look-ing at me. She was looking out across the water again. Her eyes were moist.

"When I met you, I didn't want to care about you." I saw a tear roll down her cheek. "I was a young, frightened fugitive looking for a quick way to make some money so that I could get out of Jackson. But you kept being good to me. I didn't want you to. But you kept on doing it anyway. And I started hating myself for liking you. And I kept trying to resist, but I couldn't. And during the few weeks that we were hiding out in that dingy hotel room, I fell in love with you. I didn't want to, it just happened."

I looked at her. She was crying.

"I'm sorry," I said. "I didn't mean to make you cry."

"It's not you," she said. "It's the situation." She hesitated and I could see that she was searching for the right words to express what she was feeling. "Sometimes it seems like it's all for naught—my life, your life, your brother's life, Reggie's life, the lives of the kids I teach. It all seems for naught. It seems like so many of us were born for nothing."

"The old folks used to say we're cursed."

"We're not cursed," she said. "We just keep living the same life over and over again—never learning and never adjusting."

I was silent, considering her thought carefully.

"Somebody has to stand up," she said. "Somebody has to stand up and set a different course." She looked at me. "That's why I want you to go back. I want you to go back and find Curtis. I want you to convince him to turn himself in—just like you had planned."

"What if he doesn't want to go back?"

"Then you make him go."

"What if they send him to prison?"

"Maybe that's what he has to do to become a man."

"Going to jail won't make him a man," I said forcefully.

"Maybe not," she said. "But facing his problems will."

"He'll hate me."

"At first," she said. "But after it's all said and done, he'll thank you. So will your mother." She paused. I remained quiet. "Please," she said. "Will you do it?"

"I'll try."

"That's all I'm asking," she said.

I nodded. She eased closer and I took her in my arms, feeling her breath on the side of my face. A slow moment passed. Then we kissed each other, slowly, softly, gently, on the edge of the bayou, beneath the moon and the stars. I released her and looked deeply into her eyes. She smiled at me. Then I raised my hand and gently caressed her face, secretly wishing that this moment would never end. But it did end, and when it did, I made my wishes known.

"Let's stay here tonight," I said.

"In Monroe?"

"Yes," I said. "Let's get a hotel and spend the night."

I waited, but she didn't answer.

"I'm sorry," I said. "I've offended you, haven't I?"

"No," she said. "You could never offend me by asking me to be with you. I love you."

"Then let's do it," I said. "Nobody knows us here. Here, we can be free. Let's be free tonight. Let's be free tonight and worry about the world tomorrow."

"Okay," she said.

"Do you mean it?"

"I mean it."

I took her in my arms and kissed her softly.

12

At the hotel, I entered the room first and flicked on the switch. There was a small radio on the nightstand next to the bed. I crossed the room and switched it on. A soft tune was playing. The soothing music calmed me.

"Dance, madam?" I said, extending my hand.

"I would be honored," Peaches said, playing along.

I took her hand and led her to the center of the floor. "I'm so glad we decided to stay," I said.

"So am I," she said softly.

I drew her close, and as we danced, I looked deeply into her eyes. In them I saw something that reminded me of the good times. And in recalling those times, I realized why I had loved her and why I still loved her. Suddenly, I wanted her. No, I needed her, for I longed to be reminded of what it felt like to love someone and to have that someone love you back. I drew her closer, and as we continued to dance, moving slowly, keeping perfect time to the soft, melodic tune emanating from the radio, I kissed her, and she kissed me back. I felt desire rise in me, and in that instant, I wanted to possess her again as I had possessed her long ago. And that desire filled me with an urge to speak.

"I want you," I whispered.

She melted into my arms, then I drew her to the bed and I kissed her greedily. Suddenly, the fear and anxiety I had felt only minutes ago dissipated, and in its place was a peaceful excitement fueled by the swirling passion her response caused to rise in me. I undressed her and kissed her breast. I felt her body shudder. And though we were lying naked on the bed in the semidarkness, I sensed that her eyes were closed and her mouth was open, for I could hear her panting, softly and seductively through lips positioned only inches from my ear.

I closed my eyes and gave in to the moment, feeling our bodies press together, hearing the bed creak, sensing the sensual movement of our hips rising and falling together in love. I attempted to slow the moment and control my breathing, but the hypnotic rhythm of her swaying body excited me. I felt my body respond. Suddenly, I was caught in a whirlwind of emotions. I bit down on my lip and held on to her until the titillating roll of her hips overwhelmed me. My emotions erupted. I moaned and fell forward, feeling the urgency of her embrace.

"I love you," she whispered.

"I love you back," I said.

Then I closed my eyes, vowing that I would never let her get away again. No, as soon as this was over, I would make her my wife, and we would begin life anew in a place of our own choosing, a place where our past and our present were not acquainted.

"You're smiling," she said.

"Thinking about you always did make me smile," I said.

"I don't ever want to lose you again."

"You won't," I said.

"You promise?"

"I promise," I said.

Then I heard her chuckle.

"What?" I said.

"I still can't believe you were here all of this time."

"I know," I said.

Peaches rose to her elbows and stared at me. "You never thought about coming home?"

"I thought about it. But I knew that I couldn't."

"Why not?"

"I just couldn't," I said.

"Has to be more to it than that," she said. "Didn't you miss your mother? Didn't you miss your brother?"

"I missed them."

"Then I don't understand."

"Don't know if I can explain it."

"I wish you would try."

"I already did."

"When?" she asked.

"Back on the bayou," I said. "I tried to tell you then."

"Well, I wish you would try again."

I put on my pants, then rose from the bed and walked to the window. I pulled the curtains back and looked out. We were on the second floor overlooking the pool. From where I stood, I could see Highway 165 stretching back toward the city. I could feel my heart pounding. My lips parted and I spoke without facing her.

"Stanley couldn't ever go home," I said. "So I didn't think I should ever go home either."

"So you were punishing yourself," she said. "Is that it?"

"No," I said. "I was just trying to deal with what I did. That's all."

"But that was a long time ago."

"I know," I said. "But I just can't get it out of my head."

"You're going to have to find a way to move on."

"How can I?" I asked. "I mean, for ten years, I've been going to bed at night hoping that things will be better when I wake up in the morning. But they aren't. When I get up, he's still dead. And he's gonna always be dead."

"You can't grieve for the rest of your life."

"At least I have a life."

"Then live it."

"I don't know how—I mean, how am I supposed to live? What am I supposed to do? Every morning, I get up and act like I'm okay. But I'm not. I'm just going through the motions. And I'm hurting inside. But I don't feel I have the right to talk about it. And up until this moment with you, I never have."

"Why not?"

"Because as bad as I feel, I know the people I hurt feel even worse. I deserve what I'm feeling, but they don't. When I think of them, feeling bad just doesn't seem like it's enough. I don't know if you understand what I'm trying to say."

"I think I do."

"When we buried Mr. Henry today, I was sitting there looking at his coffin. He was a great man, a born-again Christian, and I know he went to heaven. But as I watched them lower him into the ground, all I could think about was what I took from him. Over the years, he was good to me. He taught me a lot about life. But today, when I was trying to say good-bye to him, all I could remember was something he said to me the first time I met him."

"What was that?"

"He said that when I killed Stanley, I killed everything that he was and everything that he was going to be. That made everything real. I mean, I had been in fights before, and I had hurt people before. But I had never done anything like this. I tried to deal with it. I kept telling myself that it didn't matter. But it did matter. Because all I could think about was what Mr. Henry said; 'You killed everything he was going to be.' "

I paused and looked at her, but she did not speak.

"He was right," I said. "Wasn't he?"

I paused again. She still remained silent.

"How can I ever atone for that?" I asked. "How?"

"By living a good life," she said.

"And what will that prove?"

"That you're a good man."

"So was Stanley."

"Didn't his father forgive you?" she asked.

"He said he did."

"Do you believe him?"

"In my heart I do," I said. "But in my head, I don't understand how it's possible. I mean, I killed his only child. I know we were both kids. Stanley and I were the same age. And I know that he knew I had not intended to kill him. But I did kill him. How could he forgive me for that?"

"Paul killed," she said. "And God forgave him."

"That's religion," I said. "I'm talking about life."

"Religion is life," she said. "Mr. Henry understood that. That's why he could forgive you. That's the only thing that could have enabled him to forgive you."

"Maybe forgiveness is not enough," I said. "Somewhere deep inside of me, I feel the need to make it right. But I just don't know how. Do you understand what I'm telling you?"

"I understand that you're a good person," she said. "And I'm sure that after Mr. Henry got to know you, he understood that too."

I shook my head.

"You are," she said. "You're a good person who was caught up in a bad situation. You made a choice. The only choice you thought you had at the time. And because of that choice, a boy died. But that's not all that happened that day, is it?"

I didn't answer.

"No," she said. "It's not. You know what else happened that day? Another boy lived."

She paused. I averted my eyes.

"Now maybe you can't do anything about the boy who died," she said, "but you can do something about the one who lived."

"What?" I said, looking up again. "Please tell me. What can I do?"

"I don't know," she said. "But Little Man's life has to mean something. You have to make him understand that."

"So we're back to that," I said.

"That's all there is," she said.

I became quiet again.

"He has a gun," she said. "Right?"

"Yes," I said. "He has a gun."

"Then you have to make sure he doesn't use it."

"I'm not sure that I can," I said.

"You can," she said. "Because if he uses it, the cycle continues."

"What cycle?"

"The vicious cycle your family seems to be caught up in," she said. "Your father killed, you killed, and now the pendulum has swung to Curtis. The only question is, what is he going to do?"

She paused. I didn't answer.

"I have so much respect for Curtis," she said. "I truly admire what he had done with those boys. But if he uses that gun, it's all for naught. He will just be another black man who has taken a life. And the cycle will continue. He'll go to jail, and another generation of black folk will suffer. Is that what you want?"

I shook my head.

"Then let's go home," she said. "Let's go home and find Curtis before it's too late."

I looked at the clock.

"But it's almost eleven-thirty," I said. "It'll be well after midnight by the time we make it back to Brownsville."

"Let's just go," she said. "Let's just leave the key on the nightstand and go."

"Are you sure?"

"I'm positive."

"Alright," I said. "Let's go home."

13

Through the darkness of night, I guided the car along the desolate highway back to Brownsville. And, yes, I was thinking about what I had to do. Like it or not, Peaches was right. I had to go to Reggie's house, and I had to say whatever I needed to say to convince him to take me to Little Man. And once he did, I had to try to convince Little Man to turn himself in, and if he refused, I had to make him go. I did not know how, but I had to make him get in my truck, drive back to the police station, and turn himself in. Oh, but what about Mama? How would she feel about this? She would hate me. That's how she would feel. And she would hate Peaches, and she would hate anyone who had anything to do with this. But none of that mattered now. If she never spoke to me again, so be it. I had made up my mind. The family curse would be broken. It would stop with Little Man, and it would stop with me.

In Brownsville, I parked the car on the street before Reggie's house and killed the engine. Then I looked over at Peaches. Somewhere along the highway, she had fallen asleep. I reached over and tapped her on the knee. She did not move. I tapped her again. Her eyes opened and she looked about wildly. And as I watched her reorient herself, I knew that I loved her and that she loved me, and I prayed that when this was all over, she and I would be able to find the happiness that had eluded us our entire lives.

"Where are we?" she mumbled.

"Brownsville," I told her.

She tilted her head back and yawned. "What time is it?"

I raised my arm and looked at my watch. "A quarter to one," I told her.

"You think they're still up?"

I look toward the house. The living room light was on. I could see the dim yellow glow through the thin white curtains.

"Looks like it," I said. "I guess we ought to go see."

She yawned again, then turned in her seat to open the door. She stopped suddenly. "Don't look now," she said, "but we've got trouble."

"What kind of trouble?" I asked.

She pointed to the rearview mirror. I looked up to see bright flashing lights. A police car had pulled behind us. I stared at the flashing lights, then turned back to Peaches.

"I'm getting tired of this." I sighed.

"Just be calm," she said.

In the rearview mirror, I watched the officer exit his car and walk toward us. I took a deep breath and waited. When he reached the car, he shined a light on me, then on Peaches. I saw Peaches raise her hands and shield her eyes.

"You two live around here?"

"No, sir," I said.

"Then what are you two doing out here this time of night?"

"We came to visit a friend," Peaches said.

"A friend."

"Yes, sir."

"At one o'clock in the morning?"

"Yes, sir."

He looked at me and frowned. "Let me see your license."

"Why?" I asked him.

"Because I said so," he snapped. "That's why."

"But we weren't doing anything."

"Just give him your license," Peaches said, her voice trembling.

"But we weren't doing anything," I said again.

The officer squinted. His face became one huge, angry frown. "Step out of the car," he ordered.

"Excuse me?"

"You heard me," he said. "Step out of the car!"

I opened the door and stepped out.

"Place your hands on the car!"

"What?!"

"Place your hands on the car!" he shouted a second time.

"But I haven't done anything."

I heard the car door open. Peaches jumped out.

"D'Ray!" she shouted. "Please!"

"Not until he tells me what's going on."

I saw the officer place his hand on the nightstick. I looked at the stick, then back at him. Inside my chest, I felt my heart racing. I took a slow step back, and when I did, he advanced toward me.

"I mean it," he said. "Put your hands on the car."

"D'Ray! Please!" Peaches said. "Just do what he asked."

An urgent anxiety gripped me. I doubled my fist, then averted my eyes, searching for a weapon. Suddenly, I felt the stick crash against the side of my head. I wobbled, stunned.

"No!" Peaches yelled.

"On the ground," the officer shouted.

I looked at him but did not move. My head felt light, giddy. Warm red blood trickled down my face. I heard Peaches scream; then I felt the sting of the stick again, crashing hard against the side of my face. Darkness flashed and I raised my hands to protect myself. Through fuzzy eyes, I saw

the huge black man raise the stick above his head again. I
ducked, struggling to maintain my balance; then I rushed
him. He stepped to the side and brought the stick down hard
across my back. My knees buckled. Hot pain raced down my
spine. I looked up; he was standing over me.

"Stop it," Peaches yelled. "Please, stop it."

I looked about feverishly for something to fight with. I
saw an empty whisky bottle lying in a tuft of grass. I reached
for it. Instantly, I felt the stick again, this time across the wrist
of my outstretched hand. I snapped my hand back, feeling an
enormous tide of pain roll up my arm and explode near my
elbow. My lips parted to scream but no sound came. Suddenly, terror seized me, and I was no longer myself. Instead, I
was in juvenile prison again, lying naked upon the floor as a
rogue cop stood over me, beating me with a stick. And I was
asking God to help me, while promising myself that no cop
would ever beat me again. In the moment of my recollection,
anger overtook me and I willed myself upright. And as I did,
I grew conscious of the swirling stream of blood collecting
just beneath the swell of my pulsating tongue. I was weak and
my arms were trembling, and through the haze of my blurred
vision, I saw the stick again. Though my mind told me what
to do, my battered body could not respond. Instead, it went
limp and fell facedown upon the highway. Involuntarily, I
looked up. The officer dropped the stick and drew his
weapon. His gun was aimed at my head.

"Don't shoot him!" Peaches yelled.

The office looked at her. "Get back against the car," he
yelled at her. She complied and looked at me again.

"Spread your arms."

I spread my arms, and instantly I felt the full force of his
knee pressing hard against my back. Then I felt him twisting
my arm. I moaned in agony, feeling the coldness of the steel
cuffs binding one of my wrists to the other.

"You think you bad," he said. "Don't you?"

He flipped the gun in his hand, clutching it by the barrel. Then he raised it above his head and brought it down hard against the side of my face. My head snapped down. I felt warm blood trickling.

"Why don't you leave him alone?" Peaches yelled.

"What's wrong, tough guy?" He smirked. "Cat got your tongue?"

"I'm not scared of you," I mumbled.

"You don't have to be scared to die," he said, placing the barrel of the gun against my temple. I heard Peaches scream again. Behind me, I heard a door open and shut. I turned my head and looked. Junior Miller emerged from the shadows of his house. He was wearing pants but no shirt and no shoes.

"Pete!" I heard him shout.

The officer hesitated, then looked up.

"Junior!" he said. "Is that you?"

"It's me."

I felt the officer relax. Then I saw him lower the gun.

"Do you know this fool?"

"I know him," Junior said. "He's a friend of mine."

"A friend!"

"That's right."

"What's the problem?"

"I pulled him over because his taillight is out. Then he attacked me." He paused. "You better tell him who I am before he gets himself killed."

"I'll tell him."

The officer removed the cuffs, then rose and slowly made his way to Peaches's car. He paused, then raised the stick and smashed the rear light. I heard the loud sound of glass breaking. "You better tell him," he said. Then I saw him climb into his car and drive off. I looked at Peaches. She was crying. Junior Miller helped me to my feet.

"Can you walk?" he asked me.

I nodded.

"Come on," he said to Peaches. "Let's get him inside."

The two of them lifted me from the ground. He held one arm while Peaches held the other.

"Easy," he said. "Easy now."

They helped me into the house and laid me on the sofa. He left and when he returned, he was carrying a small basin filled with water and a washcloth. He dipped the cloth into the basin and dabbed at the bruises on my face. When he finished, I raised my hand and felt my face. It was swollen. And there was a large lump on the side of my head where the officer had hit me with the stick.

"You alright?" he asked.

I nodded again.

And when I did, Junior lit a cigarette and raised it to his mouth. He took a long drag, then exhaled, releasing a thin cloud of white smoke.

"You need a doctor," Peaches said.

"No," I said. "I'm alright."

"You should have given him your license."

"Why?" I said. "We weren't doing anything."

"Aw, don't worry about that fool," Junior said. "His day is coming."

"Who is he?" I asked.

"His name is Pete," he said, taking another drag on his cigarette. "But everybody around here calls him Bulldog."

"Bulldog," I mumbled. "I don't remember him."

"He ain't from around here," Junior said. "He's from New Orleans. The mayor brought him in to head his drug task force. Ever since he got here, he's been trying to prove to white folks that he hates black folks as much as they do. He's been kicking in doors and beating the hell out of Negroes for over a year now—all with the blessings of the chief."

"Is that right?" I said.

"You better believe it," he said. He took another drag on

the cigarette and exhaled. "Nah, you ain't the first somebody he hit with that stick, and you won't be the last."

"Well, somebody ought to do something," Peaches said. "My taillight's not out. At least it wasn't out before he smashed it."

"I know it wasn't," Junior said.

"Somebody ought to do something," she said again.

"He gonna git his," Junior said, and then I saw him dip the rag in the pan of water and felt him place the cold, wet rag on the side of my face. "As a matter of fact, he almost got his due a few months back. He acted a fool and jumped Dirty Red back there on Skinner Lane. And before he knew what hit him, Red had damn near beat him to death. Only reason Red didn't kill him was because he said the nigguh begged and cried like a little sissy. Didn't change nothing, though. Soon as that nigguh healed, he was back in the bottoms swinging that stick. He just don't give a flying flip—none of them cops do—and everybody around here know it, including your brother. That's why he ran."

Junior lifted the cigarette to his mouth again.

"Need to talk to your son," I said.

Junior turned toward the hallway.

"Reggie!" he yelled at the top of his lungs. A moment later, Reggie entered the room. He looked at his father and then at me.

"What happened?" he asked.

"Pete," his father told him.

"Oh."

I looked up at him. "Take me to him," I said.

"To who?"

"Curtis," I said.

"Not unless you're going to help him."

"I'll help him," I said.

Reggie paused, staring at me.

"To get away?" he asked.

"Yeah," I said. "To get away."

"No," Peaches said. "Don't do this."

"Are you for real?" Reggie asked.

"I'm for real," I said.

"Then I'm coming too," Peaches said.

"No," Reggie said. "She can't come."

"Why not?" Peaches asked.

"Because Curtis don't want you to," Reggie said. "He wants only his brother."

"Baby," I said. "Please go home. I'll talk to you when I get back."

14

Peaches left first. Reggie and I waited a few minutes, and then he helped me to his truck. When we were certain that we were not being watched, we headed north on Highway 17, exiting Brownsville and passing through one small town after another. Confused, I watched the mile markers, trying to figure out where we were going. Twenty miles into the drive, Reggie slowed, then turned right off the main highway, guiding the truck deeper into the countryside, winding between vast tracks of farmland before turning onto a piece of densely wooded property located somewhere near the Arkansas line. A moment later, we were traveling over a narrow dirt road that led to a shed behind an abandoned farmhouse. We got out and cautiously approached the shed. Reggie eased the door open. Inside, Little Man was huddled on the floor underneath a blanket. The sound of the creaking door startled him, and he snapped to his feet. He was holding a gun.

"Don't shoot!" Reggie shouted. "It's me!"

Little Man cringed, and when he did, I looked at him. His face was unshaven, his eyes were red, and I could tell he had not slept in days. I saw him look at Reggie and then at me. Suddenly, his eyes widened and he eased forward, staring with a look of disbelief.

"D'Ray." He whispered my name, then fell into my arms. I held him for a long time. I could tell he was exhausted.

"You alright?" I asked.

"Yeah," he said. "I'm alright." I saw him studying my face. "What happened?"

"Pete got him," Reggie said.

"Pete!" he shouted, alarmed.

"Yeah," he said. "Pete."

He stared at my face for a moment. "Did he do that because of me?"

"No," I said. "At least I don't think so."

"Then why?"

"Because he could," I said.

"He crazy," Reggie said. "You know that."

Suddenly, I thought about the chief, remembering his dire warning. I grabbed Little Man about the shoulders, looking him in the eye.

"I'm scared for you," I said. "They want you. They want you bad."

"I don't care," he said, pulling away. "I'm not going back."

"I'm not asking you to."

"Good," he said. "Because I wouldn't even if you did. I'm not ever going back—at least not alive." He looked at me. "I hear you talked to Mama?"

"I talked to her."

"How is she?"

"Worried."

"I'm sorry to hear that."

"Did you do what they said you did?"

"No, I didn't."

"Are you being straight with me?"

"I didn't do it," he said again. "I swear."

"That don't matter," Reggie said. "They say he did it, so did that jury. They gonna send him to Angola anyway."

"I can't go to Angola," Curtis said. "I can't go there and

do all of that time for something I didn't do. I just can't. I thought I could . . . but I can't."

"They set him up," Reggie said. "That's what happened."

"Why?"

"I don't know. But they did. I would bet my life on it."

"I need your help, D'Ray."

"I know," I said.

"Will you help me?"

"Yeah," Reggie answered for me. "He already said he would."

"Where are you trying to go?" I asked.

"I don't know."

"How will you live?"

"I don't know."

"You haven't thought this out," I said, "have you?"

"No," he said. "I haven't."

"This is tricky," I said. "Real tricky."

"I know."

"Once you leave, you can't come back."

"I understand."

"I mean, you can't ever come back."

"I know."

"You'll be free," I said, "but you'll also be alone."

"I understand, D'Ray. Believe me, I do."

"One more thing," I said, looking at the gun lying on the ground next to him. "That gun won't do you any good. You use it, your life is over."

"I'm not going back," he said, "at least not alive."

"Get rid of that thing," I said.

"No," he said. "I might need it."

"What about Mama?" I said. "What do you think will happen to her if you pull that thing and somebody kills you?"

"I'm not going back," he said.

I looked at Reggie. He had been facing the window, keeping a lookout, but now he turned and looked at me.

"We don't have time for this," he said. "Are you going to help him or not?"

"I already answered that."

"Then what's the plan?" he asked.

"How do I know I can trust you?"

"You can trust him," Little Man said. "I couldn't have gotten this far without him."

"Are you sure?"

"I'm positive."

"Alright," I said, "if you say so."

"I say so."

"What's the plan?" Reggie pressed again.

I didn't look at him. Instead, I looked at Little Man. "You need to lie low for a few more days," I said. "Then I'll get you out of here."

Little Man shook his head. "I don't know," he said. "The cops are looking for me. I feel like I need to be on the move."

"You need to let things settle down first."

"I don't know," he said again. "I've been here for a couple of days. Sooner of later, they're going to find me."

"They won't find you," I said. "Not if we make them think that you're gone."

"And how are we going to do that?"

"Give them evidence."

"What kind of evidence?"

"Evidence that you're someplace else."

"I can't be two places at the same time."

"Why not?" I asked.

He looked at me but did not speak.

"We're going to need some help," I said.

"What kind of help?"

"Somebody with a good car who don't mind driving a few hundred miles."

"I can get a car," Reggie said.

"No," he said. "Not you."

"Why not?"

"They might be watching you."

"What about Miss Lewis?"

"No," I said. "I don't want to get her involved."

"Then who?"

I paused a minute, thinking. "Any of the fellas around?" I asked.

"Just Pepper and Crust," Little Man said.

"Either one of them have a car?"

"Nah."

"Either one of them have access to a car?"

"Pepper is a truck driver."

"Really," I said.

"Yeah, he drives a carpet truck for one of the department stores."

"Locally?"

"All over the place."

"What's his longest run?"

"Georgia."

"Where in Georgia?"

"Dalton."

"How often does he go?"

"Every week, I think."

"When does he leave?"

"Usually leaves on Wednesday and comes back on Thursday."

"Is Dalton close to Atlanta?"

"I think so."

"That's it," I said.

"That's what?" Reggie asked, confused.

"The answer," I said. "What we say here has to stay here. Understand?"

"Of course."

I stared at Reggie for a moment to let him know that I was serious; then I looked at Little Man. "Are you sure you can trust him?" I asked.

"I'm sure," he said.

I walked to the window and looked out. Yes, things were much clearer now. I turned and looked at Little Man again. "Is Mama still dating Sonny?"

"Yeah," he said. "Why?"

"Does she still tell him everything?"

"Just about."

"Okay," I said. "Here's the plan. I want you to write Mama a letter—"

"What!"

"Just listen," I said.

Little Man looked at me, and I could tell he was weighing what I had to say.

"I want you to write her a letter," I said again. "I want you to tell her that you're alright and that you're sorry for all the trouble you've caused. Tell her you appreciate everything she and Sonny tried to do for you. Then I want you to ask her to tell Sonny that you're sorry for betraying his trust. And that's all I want you to say. Do you understand?"

"No," he said. "I don't understand."

"The letter will buy us some time," I said.

"How?"

"By making them think you're in Atlanta."

"I don't get it," Reggie said.

"Me neither."

"I'll give the letter to Pepper to take to Atlanta. I'll ask him to mail it back to Mama. She'll show it to Sonny. And I guarantee you he'll tell the chief. When he does, they'll all think you're in Atlanta. By the time they figure it out, it will be too late."

"Then what?"

"We'll get you to Memphis. From Memphis, you can

catch a plane to Los Angeles. I have a friend out there who can help you."

"Help me how?"

"Give you a new identity. To make this work, you're going to need a Social Security card, a driver's license, and a birth certificate. He can get those for you. In the meantime, I can get you some money and a few clothes. If we can get through the next day or so, I think you can make it."

"I like it," Reggie said.

"Yeah . . . me too," Little Man said. "Thanks."

"Don't thank me yet," I said. "Let's just see how this all works out."

15

We left the shed and made our way through the small copse of trees before heading back to the car. At the car, I paused and looked about. Yes, this was a good spot. Little Man should be safe here for another day or two. I climbed into the car and shut the door, then looked at my watch. It was one-thirty. Suddenly, I thought of something. Would it not be better to try to find Pepper tonight before there were so many cops on the street? Yes, that made sense. We would look for him while the rest of the world was still asleep. I turned and looked at Reggie. I saw him insert the key into the ignition. I heard the engine roar.

"You think Pepper's at home?" I asked him.

"I don't know," he said. "Why?"

"Like to try to get to him tonight," I said, "while there aren't so many people on the streets."

"Pete is still out there."

"I know," I said. "We'll just have to be careful."

As we drove back, I checked my bruises in the rearview mirror. My eye had begun to swell, and there was a nasty gash high up on my cheekbone where Pete had hit me with his nightstick. The sight of the gash angered me. Yes, this was the right thing to do. I would see Pepper and then I would see Crust, and together we would execute the plan that would get Little Man out of this place and beyond the reach of the Brownsville police once and for all.

Suddenly, I thought about something else. What about a gun? Should I purchase one? The question haunted me, and as I pondered it, I felt hot anger rise in me again. For the second time in my short life, I vowed that I would never allow another man to beat me again—even if that man was a cop. I turned toward the window and looked out into the streets. Yes, I would purchase a gun, and I would know how to handle Pete next time. In the meantime, he would not get his hands on Little Man. No . . . not him, not the chief, not Sonny, not any of them.

When we made it back to the old neighborhood, Reggie circled past Pepper's house a couple of times, and when he was sure that we weren't being followed, he pulled to the shoulder at the head of the street. I leaped out and looked around. From where I stood, I could see Pepper's house. The lights were out, and I feared he had either gone to bed or he wasn't home.

"Be careful," Reggie said. "I'll wait for you up here. When you're done, I'll drive back to get you, alright?"

I nodded, then made my way back to Pepper's house. I climbed onto the porch and knocked on the door. A minute or two passed. The porch light flashed on and the door opened. It was Pepper.

"Well I'll just be," he said. Then he grabbed me and hugged me tight. "Outlaw! Is that really you?"

"It's me," I said, speaking in a hushed tone.

He released me. I smiled and looked over my shoulder to make sure we weren't being watched.

"You got a minute?" I asked.

"Of course I do," he said. "Come on in."

He stepped aside and I followed him into the house. I looked around. The television was off and most of the lights were out.

"Did I wake you up?"

"Wake me up! Man, I just got in—been shooting the breeze with some of the fellas over at Kojak's Place. They told me you were back in town."

"News travels fast," I said.

"Hey, this is a small town. You know that." I saw him looking at my face. "Whose fist did you run into?"

"Pete."

"Pete!"

I nodded.

"Guess he gave you the formal introduction."

"Yeah," I said. "Something like that."

"Want some ice?"

I shook my head.

"Might stop the swelling."

"I'm alright," I said.

"What about something to drink?"

I shook my head again.

"You sure?" he said.

"I'm sure," I said.

"Alright," he said, smiling again. "What brings you out this time of night?"

"Need to ask a favor," I said.

"Alright," he said. "I'm listening."

"I hear you drive for Mr. Wilcox."

"That's right."

"And I hear you make a run to Georgia every now and then."

"I do," he said. "As a matter of fact, I'm pulling out in a few hours."

"Good," I said. "I need you to do something for me."

"What's that?" he asked.

"Mail a letter."

"Mail a letter!"

"Yeah."

"That's it?" he said, frowning.

"Yeah," I said. "That's it."

"Man, you came all the way over here in the middle of the night to ask me to mail a doggone letter?"

"Yeah," I said.

"I don't get it."

"It can't be mailed from here," I said. "It has to be mailed from Atlanta. And it has to be mailed today."

"Today," he said.

"That's right."

He frowned again but remained silent.

"Let me explain."

"Don't bother," he said. "You need it done, it's done."

"No," I said. "I want to be straight with you." I paused, then continued. "You heard about Little Man?"

"I heard," he said. Suddenly, his face became solemn. "Word on the street is that he's long gone."

"Really?" I said, intrigued.

"That's what I heard."

"You hear where he went?"

"Nah," Pepper said, shaking his head. "Just heard he's gone."

"From who?"

"Some of the fellas."

"Did the cops talk to you about him?"

"Nah," he said. "Why?"

I hesitated.

"Talk to me, Ray," he said. "What's going on?"

I hesitated again. It had been a long time since I had seen Pepper, and I didn't know if I should tell him about the plan or not. No, I had to be careful. I would only tell him what he needed to know.

"Little Man wrote Mama a letter," I said. "And I need you to mail it to her from Atlanta. And I need you to keep it quiet—you know, just between us."

"How did you get it?"

"He gave it to me."

"So you know where he is?"

"I know."

"He alright?"

"For the moment."

"Cool," he said. "I was worried about him."

"Cops been sweating me," I said. "The chief wants him. He wants him real bad."

"You got the letter on you?"

"Nah," I said. "I wanted to check with you first—didn't want to carry it around with me, just in case they stopped me again."

"I pull out around four-thirty in the morning," he said. "Can you get it to me before then?"

"Yeah," I said.

"D'Ray, he's a good kid, but he ain't you—I mean, he don't have your head for the streets. So when he ran, I was scared that they were going to catch him. But he'll be alright now. You're here."

"I'm trying to help him," I said. "But I can't do it by myself."

"You don't have to."

"If they catch us—"

"I'm not worried about that. Like I said, I pull out at

four-thirty. Meet me at the old train depot. I'll take it from there."

"Thanks."

"No problem," he said. Then I saw him look at his watch. "Well, I better let you get some sleep."

"Cool," he said. "See you in a couple hours."

16

I left Pepper's house thinking that everything would be okay now. Pepper would mail the letter and that would buy us some time. Yes, while they were focusing on Atlanta, I would move Little Man to Los Angeles. Oh, how wrong I had been. Forcing Little Man to turn himself in was foolish. Yes, the beating reminded me of that which I should have never forgotten. We were black and they were white, and no matter how hard we tried to forget, that would always be reality. But the cop who beat me was not white. But what difference did that make? He was acting on their behalf. He was trying to prove to them that he was not like me. No, he was trying to prove that he was not like us.

As promised, Reggie picked me up near Pepper's house. After I had settled on the seat, he looked at me with eager eyes.

"What did he say?"

"He'll do it. I just need to get the letter to him before he pulls out in the next hour or two."

"Cool!"

"We need something to write the letter with," I said. "Do you have a pen and a piece of paper?"

"Not in the truck. Might be some at home."

"No, that's no good. Your daddy might see us. Besides, I don't want to run into Pete again." I hesitated. "He's going to need an envelope too . . . Is Walmart open?"

"I think so."

"Take me over there."

We drove to Walmart. This time, I remained in the truck while Reggie went inside. When he returned, I thought of something else. If the letter was going to be convincing, everything had to be in Little Man's handwriting—including the express mail label. We drove a couple blocks to the post office. I retrieved the express mail form and envelope from the self-service bin and returned to the truck. I climbed inside and slammed the door. I looked at Reggie.

"You know anything about Atlanta?" I asked him.

"Not much," he said. "Why?"

"I just thought of something," I said. "We need to know the name of a street."

"What for?"

"The return address," I told him. "Express mail requires a return address."

"I can't help you," he said.

"Alright," I said. "Take me to Miss Lewis's house. Maybe she'll let us look it up on her computer."

He sped away, not stopping again until we had reached Peaches's house. I got out and looked about. When I was certain that no one was watching, I hurried beneath her carport and rang the doorbell. Instantly, the door opened. She had been waiting for me. I stepped inside and switched off the outside light. I turned around. She was staring at me.

"Did you see him?" she asked me, excited.

"I saw him," I said, looking beyond her, trying to locate her computer.

"Well," she said. "What happened?"

I didn't answer. Where was her computer? I didn't see it. Maybe she didn't have one. But she was a teacher. Of course she had a computer.

"I need to use your computer," I said, still ignoring her question.

"My computer?" she asked, puzzled.

"Yes," I said. "Where is it?"

She hesitated, then frowned. "What's going on?" she asked me. "Why do you need to use my computer?"

"I'll tell you later," I said.

"Why can't you tell me now?"

"I just can't," I said.

"But—"

"Peaches, please!" I said. "Where is it?"

She paused. "In the study."

"Show me."

I followed her down a short hallway and into a small office. I made my way across the room and sat at the computer. I clicked it on and waited.

"Come on," I said impatiently.

"It's a little slow," she called from the doorway.

I didn't answer. Instead, I kept my eyes fixed on the screen. Suddenly, the icons appeared.

"There it is," I said. I hastily retrieved the information and rose to leave.

She stopped me. "Wait a minute," she said.

"I don't have a minute."

She looked at me with worried eyes. "Is everything alright?"

"Yes." I turned toward the door.

She stopped me again. "But where is he?"

"He's still out there," I said.

"Why didn't you bring him in?"

I didn't answer.

"You're not going through with this, are you?"

I started down the hall.

"Answer me," she shouted.

I whirled and looked at her. "I got to go," I said.

"But—"

I didn't answer. Instead, I bolted from the house and met Reggie on the corner. I climbed in next to him, and we drove back out to the shed. When we got there, Little Man was sitting next to the window, waiting. I gave him the pen and paper and told him to write the note just as I said. When he was done, he placed the letter in the express mail envelope and sealed it. I gave him the phony address, and he filled out the form and handed it to me. I looked at my watch. It was almost two-thirty.

"Does anyone else know that you are here?"

"No," he said.

I looked at Reggie. "Have you told anyone else?"

"No," he said, shaking his head.

"If this is going to work," I said, "we are going to have to work together—the three of us, Mama, and Pepper—and we're going to have to keep our mouths shut, alright?"

They nodded.

"Now, after tonight, I won't be coming back."

"But—"

"It's not safe," I said. "I don't want anyone to follow me. Now, I'm going to move back in with Mama so that it will be easier for me to communicate with everyone." I paused. "Does Sonny still go over there for lunch?"

"Yeah."

"Good," I said. "She should get the letter tomorrow by noon by overnight mail. I'll make sure he sees it."

"Then what?"

"We'll move you," I said.

Suddenly, I recalled that he and I were to have no physical contact after I left. If something went wrong, he was on his own. I turned again and looked at him. "Tomorrow I'll visit you for the last time. After that, don't write, don't e-mail, don't communicate with any of us in any way. You understand?"

"I understand," he said.

I looked at him, then let out a deep sigh. "Are you sure you want to do this?"

Little Man, whose eyes had been lowered, raised his head and stared at me with the look of one uncertain about what lay ahead. "I'm sure," he mumbled, then lowered his eyes again.

"Alright," I said.

I stood and we embraced each other.

"Tell Mama I'm alright," he whispered.

"I will," I said, and then I turned to look at Reggie. He seemed more nervous than usual. I saw him peep out of the window, then back at me.

"We better get out of here," he whispered, fidgeting as he spoke.

I nodded. We left the shed and made our way back to his truck. After we arrived, I tried to figure out what to do. Should I go back to Lake Providence? Or should I wait in my truck for a couple of hours? I felt the package beneath my shirt. What if the cops stopped me again? What if they discovered the letter? No, that would not do. Okay, it was settled—I would go back to Lake Providence, wait there until four, then return to Brownsville and give Pepper the letter and some money for the postage. After that, I'd go to my mother's house.

Convinced that was the best thing to do, I had Reggie drive me back to Lake Providence. Later that morning, I met Pepper at the old train depot. Once he had the letter, I headed to Mama's house, relieved that the letter was on its way.

17

At Mama's house, I parked my truck on the front lawn and killed the engine. If the cops were watching the neighborhood, I wanted them to know that I was here. And while they were watching me, I would send Reggie back out to the shed with the things Little Man needed. I rang the doorbell and waited. I looked at my watch. It was not quite five yet.

Oh, she's probably still asleep. Maybe I ought to just sleep in the truck. I turned to leave. Then I heard the door creak open behind me. I whirled. Mama was standing in the doorway. She was still wearing her nightgown.

"I thought I told you not to come back here," she snapped.

"Just let me in," I whispered. I looked over my shoulder to make sure that we were not being watched.

"You're not welcome here."

"I need to talk to you."

"There's nothing to talk about," she said, attempting to push the door closed. I reached out and stopped it with my hand.

"I saw him," I whispered.

She froze. Her eyes narrowed. "Who?"

"Little Man."

"How is he?" she wanted to know.

"Let me in," I said, "and I'll tell you."

She stepped aside and closed the door behind her. "Is he alright?" she asked anxiously.

"He's fine," I said.

"Thank God for that," she mumbled.

"Mama," I said, looking her in the eye. "I've changed my mind. I'm going to help him."

"Get away?" she said, her tone indicating shock.

"Yes, ma'am," I said. "I'm going to help him get away."

She looked at me as though she didn't know whether she should believe me or not.

"You mean it?" she asked me.

I nodded.

She closed her eyes as if to say, *Thank you, Jesus.* Then she opened them again. Suddenly, her expression changed.

"What happened to your face?"

"They beat me," I said.

"Who beat you?"

"The cops," I told her.

"What did you do?" Her tone was accusatory.

"I didn't do anything," I snapped.

"Then why did they beat you?"

"How am I supposed to know?" I retorted.

"How many of them was it?" she asked, ignoring my question.

"Just one," I said.

"Was he black or white?"

"Black," I said.

"My Lord!" she exclaimed. "That must have been Pete."

"It was Pete," I said.

"My God," she said. Then she looked at me with fearful eyes. "Did he know who you were?"

"No," I said. "I don't think so."

And instantly, I knew she was not thinking about me. No, she was thinking about Little Man. She was praying that Pete would not catch him so that what had happened to me would not happen to Little Man. Suddenly, her eyes dimmed and I could see that she was worried.

"You think you can get him away from here?" she asked me.

"Maybe," I said. "But I'm going to need your help."

"Just tell me what to do."

"I need you to make sure that Sonny comes by for lunch tomorrow. Can you do that?"

"He always comes by," she said.

"Did he come by today?" I asked.

"He came," she said. Then she paused and frowned. "What do you want with Sonny?"

"You're going to get a letter," I said, ignoring her question.

"A letter?" she said.

"Yes, ma'am."

"What kind of letter?"

"It's express mail."

"Express mail?" she asked, trying to understand.

"Yes, ma'am," I said. "It's going to come from Atlanta. It should get here around noon. Now, when it comes, I want you to open it in front of Sonny. And I want you to tell him what it says. And I want you to ask him not to tell anyone. Can you do that?"

"Why?" she asked.

"The letter is going to be from Little Man."

"From Little Man!"

"Yes, ma'am."

She paused and screwed up her face. "What are you talking about? Little Man ain't in Atlanta."

"I know," I said. "But that's what I want them to think."

"Who to think?" she asked, still confused.

"The police," I told her.

"The police!"

"Yes, ma'am," I said. "And while they're looking for him in Atlanta, we'll move him someplace else, someplace where they will never find him."

"We," she said. "Who else knows about this?"

"Just Reggie and Pepper."

"Are you sure?"

"Yes, ma'am," I said. "I'm sure." Then I moved closer to her. "And we need to keep it that way—not a word to anyone else, you hear?"

She nodded, then frowned. "Why are you getting Sonny involved?"

"Because he's a mark," I said. "After he sees the letter, he'll tell the chief. I would bet my life on it."

"And what if he doesn't?"

"He will," I said.

Suddenly, a thought occurred to me. Sonny would be suspicious if Mama simply showed him the letter. No, he had to discover it on his own. He had to be convinced that he had seen the letter merely by happenstance, but how? I paused again, thinking. I got it: Mama could leave the letter on the stoop, and when Sonny came to visit, he would discover it and give it to her. And she would open it in front of him because she was perplexed. *Who in the world would be sending her express mail?* That was it. I looked at Mama and smiled.

"Leave it outside," I said.

"What?"

"The letter," I said. "Leave it on the stoop. Let Sonny find it when he comes. Then I want you to open it in front of him. And I want you to act shocked. When he asks you who it's from, don't tell him at first. Make him promise that he won't tell anyone."

"If he promises, he won't tell."

"Mama, the chief is blaming him for everything that has happened—he'll tell or do whatever he has to do to save his hide."

"You're wrong," she said.

I didn't respond. Instead, I looked in the direction of one of the bedrooms. "That still Little Man's room?" I asked her.

"Yes," she said. "At least it was before they locked him up. Why?"

"Need to take him some clothes," I said.

I went into the bedroom and looked around. Not much had changed. The little sleigh bed was still pressed in the far corner. The dresser was situated against the wall nearest the door, and the same pictures hung over his bed. I made my way to the dresser and removed some of his clothes—two shirts, two pairs of pants, some underwear, and some socks; then I hurried into the bathroom and found a razor, a bar of soap, and some deodorant. I found a plastic bag and stuffed everything inside. I turned to leave, then stopped. Suddenly I thought of something else. A towel . . . He would need a towel.

I searched the cabinets until I found one. I stuffed the towel in the bag and hid the bag beneath the sink. Tomorrow, when Reggie came, I would hide the bag among the trash, and while I was pretending to throw out the trash, I would place the bag in Reggie's truck, and he could take it out to Little Man. Satisfied, I turned and faced Mama. She was standing in the door watching me.

"Might be better if I moved back in here until all of this is over," I said. "Is that okay with you?"

"Whatever it takes to get him away from here," she said.

"Then it's settled," I said. "I'll stay here until he's gone." Involuntarily, I yawned. "Where can I sleep?"

She pointed toward my old room. I went inside, crossed the room, and stretched out across the bed. "God, help us," I mumbled. Then I fell asleep.

18

Two hours later, I awoke to the sound of a chiming door-bell. Startled, I sat up in bed and looked at the clock. Yes, it was a few minutes after seven. I cocked my head and listened, hearing Mama pull the front door open. There was a short span of silence, and then the cheerful sound of her voice filled the quiet void as she greeted her morning guest.

"Good morning, Reverend Jacobs," I heard her say.

Reverend Jacobs. Suddenly, I swung out of bed and hurried next to the door. What was he doing here? Had something happened? I cracked the door open so that I could hear them better.

"Just thought I'd stop by and check on you," I heard Reverend Jacobs tell her. "Didn't catch you at a bad time, did I?"

"No," Mama said. "I was just in the kitchen fixing breakfast. Come on in and have a seat."

I heard their feet on the floor. Then I heard Mama's voice again.

"Can I get you a cup of coffee?"

"Coffee would be fine," he said, "if it's not too much trouble."

"It's no trouble," she said.

She left and I heard her moving about the kitchen. A short while later, I heard her return to the living room.

"Here you go, Reverend," she said. "Be careful—it's hot."

He thanked her. Then I heard him take a swallow. After that, he spoke again.

"Heard anything?"

"No," she lied. "Have you?"

"Not yet," he said.

"Well, I guess no news is good news," she said. "At least, that's what I'm counting on."

"It's what we're all counting on," he said.

"Yes, sir," she said. "I guess we are."

Mama paused and I heard Reverend Jacobs sipping the coffee again.

"Your oldest boy came by to see me yesterday."

"He did!" Mama said, pretending to be surprised.

"Yeah . . . he stopped by yesterday evening."

"What did he want?"

"Well, like all of us, he's concerned about Curtis."

"Is that right?" she said.

"I'm afraid so."

"Did he say anything?" Mama asked. "I mean . . . anything that might be helpful?"

"No," Reverend Jacobs said. "He just wanted to know what I thought he ought to do in the event that he was able to find Curtis."

"He asked you that?"

"Yes, ma'am."

"What did you tell him?"

"I told him to tell Curtis to turn himself in."

"I see," Mama said. Then she was quiet.

"I take it you don't agree."

"No," she said. "I don't."

"May I ask why not?"

"He didn't do what they said he did."

"That doesn't matter," Reverend said. "He still needs to come back."

"I don't see it that way," Mama said.

"Well, Sister Reid, I just don't see any other way to see it," Reverend Jacobs said. "It's the right thing to do. It's the only thing to do."

"How is it right to let them send him to prison for something he didn't do?"

"They sent Jesus to the grave," Reverend said. "And he hadn't done what they said he did. Or did you forget?"

Mama didn't answer.

"Nailed him to the cross and sent him to the grave."

Mama still didn't answer.

"No, there's no point in running. Curtis needs to come back. He needs to come back and face this thing like a man."

"He don't want to go to prison."

"Jesus didn't want to go to the grave," Reverend said. "He even tried to get out of it. But he couldn't because you can't run from what must be."

Mama didn't say anything.

"Sister Reid, we all have to go through something in this life—I wish it wasn't so—but it is. This is his cross. He didn't choose it. It chose him. But he still has to bear it."

"And what if he can't?" Mama asked.

"He can," Reverend Jacobs said.

"How do you know?"

"Because I know God," he said. "And God won't put any more on him than he can bear."

He paused. Mama remained quiet.

"Sooner or later, he's going to contact you," Reverend Jacobs began again. "And when he does, I want you to promise me something. I want you to promise me that you'll tell him to turn himself in."

"I can't do that," Mama said.

"You have to."

"I don't have to do anything," she snapped.

"Sister Reid . . . I—"

"No, Reverend," she said. "Now, I'm sorry. But that's how I feel."

"But—"

"Reverend," she interrupted him again. "That's my child, and I won't turn him over to the law. I just won't."

"Listen to me," he said. "If you love your child, please listen to me."

"You know I love my child," Mama said.

"Then try to understand."

"I understand all I need to understand," she said.

"No," he said. "I don't think you do."

"That's my child," she sobbed. "What else is there to understand?"

"I have a lawyer working on his case," Reverend said. "When I talked to him last night, he told me that if Curtis doesn't come back on his own, he won't be able to help him—innocent or not, he won't be able to help him."

"Probably couldn't help him anyway," Mama said.

"Maybe not," Reverend said. "But at least it's a chance."

"Maybe running is a better chance."

"You don't believe that."

"Yes, I do."

"How could you?"

"He could get away," Mama said.

"You can't believe that."

"My uncle got away."

"What uncle?"

"Uncle Jimmy."

"Who?" Reverend Jacobs asked. "I never heard of him."

"They tried to send him to prison—lied and said he did something he didn't do. So, he left here and never came back, and to my knowledge, they never caught him either. That's been thirty years ago."

"Did you ever see him again?" Reverend Jacobs asked her.

"No, sir," she said. "I didn't."

"Is that what you want for Curtis?" he asked, "to never see him again?"

"Don't matter what I want," Mama said.

"And why is that?" Reverend Jacobs wanted to know.

"Because it ain't never mattered what any of us wanted," she said. "They gonna do whatever they want to do."

"Who?"

"White folks."

"Don't go making this about race."

"It is about race."

"No," he said. "This is about right and wrong."

"I used to believe that," she said.

"And you don't anymore?"

"How can I?" she asked. "And my child's been sitting in jail all this time for something he didn't do."

"Well, if the verdict is wrong—and I believe it is—let's prove it and free him the right way. In the meantime—"

"In the meantime, what?" she asked, interrupting him again. "Let him suffer for something he didn't do?"

"Suffering is part of life," Reverend said. "We all suffer."

"Well, as far as I'm concerned, this family has suffered enough."

"That ain't up to you, Sister Reid," he said. "That's up to God."

"Maybe I don't trust God no more," Mama said.

"Sister Reid!"

"Maybe God has turned his back on this family."

"I can assure you he hasn't," Reverend Jacobs said. "But can you assure me that this family hasn't turned its back on Him?"

"My uncle got away," Mama said again. "Little Man can do the same thing."

"He can't live your uncle's life," Reverend Jacobs said. "He can only live his life. That's the only way he'll ever be happy."

"He can't be happy in prison."

"I beg to differ."

"He can't," she said. "Not him."

"If God is with him, he can be happy anywhere."

"No," Mama said, shaking her head. "Not in prison."

"God was with Jonah," Reverend Jacobs said, "and he was happy in the belly of the whale. God was with Daniel, and he was happy in the lion's den. God was with Job, and he was happy even after he lost everything he had. Maybe God wants Curtis to be like Job. In the midst of it all, maybe God wants him to say, 'The Lord giveth and the Lord taketh away.' Maybe he wants him to say, 'Father let your will be done.'"

"This ain't God's will," Mama said.

"Tell him to come back," Reverend Jacobs pleaded. "Please tell him to come back."

"No," she said. "He's innocent."

"Tell him to face this thing."

"No," she said, "not twenty-five to life for something he didn't do. No, Reverend . . . I won't."

The reverend paused, then let out a deep sigh. "Well," he said. "I guess you've made up your mind."

"I have," she said.

"And there's nothing I can say to change it?"

"No," she said. "There's not."

"Well," he said, rising to leave. "If you need me, call me—day or night, it doesn't matter."

"I will," I heard Mama say.

19

After Reverend Jacobs left, I eased from the bedroom and made my way toward the living room. On the wall in the hallway next to the door was a mirror. I stopped and looked, seeing the gash above my left eye, the large lump on the side of my head, my busted lip, and my swollen face. Yes, Mama was right. This family had suffered enough. And what did we have to show for it? Nothing! Well, that was it. No more. And at that moment, I hated them—the chief, Sonny, Pete, and every other goon who wore the blue uniform of the police department. No, they wouldn't get their crummy little hands on my brother. I would die first.

I entered the room. Mama looked up at me.

"I hope you know what you're doing," she said. Her voice was laced with doubt.

"I know," I said.

"If this doesn't work—"

"It's going to work," I said.

"If something happens to him—"

"Nothing is going to happen."

Suddenly, I saw her eyes well up.

"He's all I got," she cried.

My heart sank. But I remained silent.

"God, why is this happening to us?" she asked, staring questioningly at the ceiling. Suddenly, emotions overtook her, and she rushed from the room. A moment later, I heard her bedroom door slam, and I knew she had collapsed on the bed crying. Agitated, I stood there for a moment, then went back to my room and sat at the foot of my bed. I thought about the letter. Anxiety swept me. "Please, God," I whispered. "Let everything go as planned. For once in my life, please let everything go as planned." I closed my eyes and opened them again. It was strange being here, in this house where I had once lived, and it was nerve-racking knowing that Little Man's freedom depended on Sonny being the snitch I had always believed him to be. Suddenly, I heard Mama moving about in the other room. She had said very little to me since last night. But I was not surprised. She loved Sonny and she hated me, and the fact that I was setting Sonny up fueled the resentment she felt for me even more.

At eleven-thirty, the letter arrived. As she planned, Mama signed for the package, examined it, then left it by the door. A few minutes later, I climbed into the loft and hid. From where I sat, I could see the porch through a tiny crack in the wall and I could hear what was being said in the living room below. At noon, I again placed my eye to the crack. Like clockwork, I saw Sonny pull into the yard. Instantly, excitement quickened within me. I willed myself still as I watched him stroll across the yard and climb onto the porch. He hesitated and I knew he had seen the envelope. I watched him pick it up, examine it, then frown. Yes, he was curious. He studied the letter for a moment, then knocked on the door. No one answered. He hesitated before knocking again—still no answer.

"Mira!" he yelled, frustrated. "You home?"

Mama didn't answer.

"Mira!" he yelled a second time. Then I saw him cup his

hands against the door, trying to peep through the small window. Suddenly, I heard Mama's voice.

"Sonny! Is that you?"

"Yeah," he said. "Let me in."

She opened the door.

"Sorry," she said. "I was in the back, lying down."

"You have a letter," he said.

"A letter?"

"Yeah," he said. "Express mail."

"Who in the world would be sending me express mail?"

"It's from Atlanta," he said. "From somebody named Dennis Ray Reid."

"Dennis?" she said. "Let me see that."

He handed it to her, and I saw her stare at the envelope.

"My Lord!" she exclaimed.

"Who is Dennis?" Sonny asked.

"My husband," Mama told him.

"What?"

"That's my husband's name."

"Your husband!" he said.

He waited. But Mama didn't answer him; instead, she ripped the envelope open and removed the contents.

"What's going on, Mira?"

"Nothing," she said.

"It must be something," he said.

She folded the letter and put it back in the envelope.

"Come on," she said. "Let's eat before your food gets cold."

"Is he out?"

"I don't want to talk about it."

"What is he doing in Atlanta?"

"Let's just eat."

"What does he want?"

"Nothing," she said.

"Why are you being so secretive?"

"Can we talk about it later?"

"Why can't we talk about it now?"

"Because I don't want to," she said.

"Is he coming back here?" Sonny asked. "Is that it? Is he asking you to let him come back home?"

She didn't answer.

"Mira," he said. "I'm talking to you."

I saw Mama turn and face him. "I don't want to discuss it."

"You don't want to discuss it."

"No," she said. "I don't."

"Why not?" he asked.

"I just don't."

She turned to walk away. He stopped her.

"I want to see that letter."

"No," she said.

"Wait a minute," he said. "That letter is not from your husband. It's from Curtis, isn't it?"

"What!"

"He sent the letter."

"No," she said. "It's my husband."

"Don't lie to me."

"I'm not lying."

"Let me use your phone."

"For what?" she asked.

"I'm going to call the warden at Angola to see if World has been released."

"No!" she said.

"Why not?" he asked.

She didn't answer.

"He's still locked up, isn't he?"

She didn't answer.

"It's Curtis," he said. "He's in Atlanta." He started toward her. "Let me see that letter."

"Wait," she said. "This is my mail, and you don't have any business going through it."

"I didn't go through your mail," he said. "It was lying on the stoop."

"Who told you to bring it in?"

"I've brought your mail in before."

"Well, this ain't before."

"It is him," he said, "isn't it?"

She didn't answer.

"Let me see the letter."

"No," she said.

He reached for the letter. She snatched it away, hiding it behind her back. He reached again. She backed against the wall.

"Sonny, I'm going to have to ask you to leave."

"Not until I see that letter."

"You have no right."

"I have every right."

"Why are you doing this?"

"They're blaming me," he said. "Everybody's blaming me."

"I don't care," she said. "I just care about my son. And I thought you cared about him too."

"This thing has gotten out of hand," he said. "Can't you understand that?"

"Please," she said.

"No," he said, ignoring her plea. "I need the letter."

"It's not from him."

"Don't lie to me."

"I'm not lying."

"It's his handwriting," he said. "I've seen it a million times, or have you forgotten?"

"No," she said. "I haven't forgotten."

"Then why are you lying?"

"Alright," she said. "I'll let you see. But first you have to promise you won't say anything."

"I can't do that."

"Why not?" she asked. "He said he's sorry."

"That's not good enough," he said, turning and walking toward the telephone. He lifted the receiver from the hook.

She stopped him. "What are you going to do?"

"Alert the chief."

"Please," she begged.

"He has to know," he said. He dialed the number and placed the receiver to his ear.

"No!" Mama screamed. "I'm begging you." She reached over and hung up the phone.

"Mira! It's out of my hands."

"Can't you just pretend you never saw this?"

"No," he said. "I can't do that."

"Why not?" she asked.

"I'm a police officer," he said. "And Curtis is a fugitive. I'm obligated to turn this information over to the chief."

"Obligated."

"Yes."

"What about your obligation to me?"

"I've been good to you," he said.

"If you do this, I—"

"Don't say something you'll regret."

"I mean it," she said. "If you do this, it's over."

He looked at her and frowned. "Give me the letter," he said, extending his hand. She sank to the floor, sobbing. He reached over and took the letter. Then he opened it and read it. He lowered the letter and looked at her. "Is this the first time he's written you?"

She didn't answer.

"Do you know where he's staying?"

She didn't answer.

"Do you know how to contact him?"

She remained silent.

"Very well," he said. "You don't have to answer." He removed his police radio. "Come in, chief."

"Yeah," the chief said. "Go ahead."

"He's in Atlanta."

"Are you sure?"

"I'm sure," Sonny said. "He wrote his mother a letter."

"Well, I'll be," the chief said. "Do you have an address?"

"He used an alias, so I would assume the address is a fake as well. But the postmark is real. He's in Atlanta. At least he was yesterday."

"I want to see you in my office," the chief said. "And bring the letter."

"Yes, sir, Chief."

He paused and looked at Mama. "I'm sorry, Mira," he said. He took the letter and left.

I waited, and when I was sure Sonny would not return, I climbed down from the loft and entered the living room. Mama was standing near the window, staring out into the streets. I did not speak to her. Instead, I pulled the curtain back and looked out. Yes, he was gone. He had taken the bait and run directly back to the chief. I turned and looked at Mama. She was watching me with eyes that told me that I had been right and she had been wrong. But she was still worried that things would not go as planned.

"What now?" she asked me.

"We wait," I told her.

"For what?"

"Nightfall," I said.

"Then what?" she asked, seeking more details than what I had given her.

I blinked and looked away. "We move him."

She was silent again. I could see the tension in her face.

"Where to?" she asked.

"Memphis," I told her. "And from there to LA."

She looked at me and shook her head. "Don't think you ought to take him to Memphis."

"Why not?" I asked her.

"It's too far," she said. "Suppose somebody sees him. Besides, he needs to get on a plane before they figure out he's not in Atlanta."

"Can't take him to Monroe," I said. "It's too close. Beside, the cops are probably watching that airport."

"What about Jackson?"

"Too close," I said.

"Don't feel good about Memphis," she said again.

"Well, I don't know what to tell you."

"Tell me you won't try to take him to Memphis."

"I can't do that," I said. Then suddenly a thought occurred to me. The hideout was only a few miles from the state line. That was it. Arkansas. I would take him to Arkansas.

"What about Little Rock?" I asked, excited.

"Little Rock," she mumbled to herself, then paused. "I like that better than Memphis . . . not quite as far."

"Then it's settled," I said. "I'll take him to Little Rock."

"You really think this will work?"

"I don't see why not," I said.

"You got money for the ticket?"

"Yes, ma'am," I said, turning toward the door again. "As a matter of fact, I'm going to go book his flight right now."

"Going where?" she asked. I could still hear the apprehension in her voice.

"Bastrop," I said.

"Ain't no airport in Bastrop."

"I'm not going to the airport," I said. "Cops might be watching. I'm going to a travel agent."

"Why don't you just call?" she asked. "That might be safer than running up and down the street."

"It's a long-distance call," I said. "It will leave a record. Plus, I would have to use a credit card. The cops could trace that back to me."

"Why don't you—"

"Mama," I said, interrupting her. "I got to go."

20

I checked the window again to make sure that the house wasn't being watched. Then I pulled the door open and bolted from the house. I started toward my truck, then stopped. What if they were watching me? Maybe I shouldn't drive my truck. Maybe I should call Reggie. No, that wouldn't do. For all I knew, they were watching him too. It had to be someone else, someone who they would not suspect. Suddenly, I remembered what Pepper had said. All of the fellas were gone except him and Crust. Yes, that was it—Crust, he would do it. He would give me a ride to Bastrop. I checked the streets again to make sure that no cops were around. Then I thought of something else. Crust lived on the opposite side of the slough. Would it not be better to travel through the woods, avoiding the prying eyes of Mama's nosy neighbors? Yes, that's what I would do. I looked around, and when I was sure that I was not being watched, I cut through Ole Man Harper's cotton field, hopped the fence, walked across Mr. William's hog pasture, and made my way through the small copse of trees leading to Crust's backyard.

When I arrived, I approached his house from the rear on the off chance his house was being watched. I pushed through the small gate and followed the narrow path to his rear door.

I looked over my shoulder and knocked on the door. A minute later, the door swung open and Crust was standing before me, barefoot and shirtless.

"Yeah?" he said, frowning. I could tell he did not recognize me.

"Crust!" I said. "It's me, D'Ray."

He squinted. "Well I'll be a monkey's uncle," he said, gazing at me with disbelieving eyes. "It is you."

"Yeah," I said softly, looking over my shoulder. "Can I come in?"

He eased the door open and stepped aside. I walked inside and quickly shut the door. He stared at me for a minute, then frowned.

"You in trouble?" he asked.

"No," I said, shaking my head. "Just need a favor."

"What kind of favor?"

"Your car working?" I asked him.

"It's working," he said. "Why?"

"I need a ride."

"Where to?" he asked, studying my face. I could tell he was trying to figure out what was going on.

"Bastrop," I said. "I need to go to Bastrop."

"Now?" he asked, still looking me in the eye.

"Yeah," I said. "Right now, if it's no trouble."

"Ain't no trouble," he said. "Let me find a shirt and put on some shoes." He disappeared into his bedroom and emerged a few minutes later wearing a pair of heavy brogan shoes. He was holding his keys in his hand.

"Cops were out behind the house last night searching the slough," he said. "I heard they were looking for Little Man."

"Yeah," I said. "They were."

"Didn't find him, did they?"

"Nah," I said, shaking my head.

"Good," he said. "I hope he long gone by now."

"Yeah, me too."

We made the short trip to Bastrop. I went inside, purchased the ticket, and returned to Brownsville. Crust dropped me off near my truck. I got out, then paused and looked at him.

"If the cops ask you anything, tell them you haven't seen me."

"Well, that's the truth," he said. "I haven't."

"Right," I said.

He pulled off and I drove out to meet Little Man. When I arrived, he was sitting in the shed. He was dressed and his suitcase was packed.

"Everything set?" he asked anxiously.

"Yeah," I said. "Everything's set."

I reached into my back pocket and removed an envelope. "Here's your ticket," I said.

He took the envelope and stuffed it into his suitcase.

"Reggie will pick you up later tonight."

"What time?" he mumbled.

"Seven," I said, "seven on the dot."

"Okay," he said. "I'll be ready." He looked down for a moment and then raised his head again. "Does Mama know what's happening?"

"She knows," I said.

"And she's alright?"

"She's alright," I said. Then I eased to the window and looked out. The little shed was completely surrounded by trees and weeds, and there was not another house in sight for what seemed like miles and miles.

"Must get lonely out here," I said.

"It's alright," he mumbled.

I turned and faced him.

"I'm so sorry you have to go through this."

He looked at me and shook his head. "I just don't know how it happened," he said. "I mean, it all seems like a bad dream. One day I'm sitting at home, minding my own business. The next day, I'm in handcuffs and they're telling me that I assaulted a white woman." He shook his head again. "I just don't know how it happened."

"Do you know the guy who fingered you?"

"Never seen him before in my life."

"Then why would he say you were with him?"

"I don't know."

"Has to be a reason."

"If there is, I don't get it."

"It just doesn't make sense," I said.

"Maybe this family is cursed," he said, offering a possible explanation.

"I don't believe in curses," I said.

"How else can you explain it?"

"I don't know," I said. "Just know I don't believe in curses."

"Don't know what I believe in," he finally admitted. "Just wish we could have been a real family, that's all."

"Me too," I said.

He paused a minute, then continued. "I think about Daddy all the time," he said. "I used to wonder if things would have been different if he hadn't gone to prison." He looked at me. "Do you remember him?"

"Yeah," I said. "I remember him."

"What was he like?"

"He was big and strong," I said. "And he had muscles everywhere."

"For real?"

"Yeah . . . And he liked to laugh too. I mean, he would laugh at anything. And he liked to talk. Boy, could he tell a story."

"Is that right?"

"Yeah, he was a real cutup."

"Wish I could have met him."

"Yeah," I said.

He paused again and looked far off. "Wonder why he never tried to contact me?"

"I don't know."

"I tried to hate him," he said. "But I couldn't." He looked off for a second longer, and then he looked directly at me. His eyes began to water. "It wasn't just Daddy I tried to hate. I tried to hate you too." His voice broke, and he took a deep, calming breath. "I tried to hate you because you left me just like he did."

"I'm sorry," I mumbled, overcome with guilt. "It was never my intent to leave you. You're right. I should have come back. If I had, maybe none of this would have happened."

"No," Little Man said, releasing me as quickly as he had condemned me. "You couldn't have stopped that man from lying on me."

"Maybe not," I said. "But maybe together we could have gotten out of this godforsaken place."

"Maybe getting out wasn't the answer," he said. Then he looked beyond me. His eyes became blank. "Maybe fixing it was."

"Is that what you were trying to do?"

He didn't answer immediately. He stared straight ahead as though deep in thought.

"I guess so," he finally mumbled.

"That's admirable," I said.

"No," he said. "Don't get me wrong. I thought about leaving too. And I would have. It's just that I didn't want to leave Mama by herself. So, I just figured if I had to stay here, I might as well try to make things better." He gazed at me with a tender stare. "D'Ray, there're so many of 'em."

"So many of who?" I asked.

"Boys just like us," he said. "Boys with no daddy, no hope, no future." He paused. "They needed somebody, somebody to show them the way. That's all I was trying to do. Show a few kids the way." Suddenly, he smiled and looked at me.

"Reggie was my favorite. I guess he reminded me of myself. And, oh, he was doing so good before all of this happened. But now I hear he's drinking again. Don't think he's using—at least, I hope he's not."

"I don't know," I said.

"I want you to do something for me," he said.

"What's that?"

"Keep an eye on him."

I hesitated.

"I know it's asking a lot," he said. "But he needs some-body—just like we needed somebody."

"Alright," I said. "I'll keep an eye on him."

"You promise?"

"I promise."

"He could be somebody given half a chance."

"Maybe he will be."

"I hope so," he said. He was quiet a moment. He looked off as if lost in thought again. A moment or two passed; then he resumed speaking. "I don't know what tomorrow holds for me. I just know I can't sit in that cage day in and day out staring at those walls knowing that the only crime I commit-ted was being born black in Brownsville." He lowered his eyes and shook his head. "It's funny," he said. "But the one thing I spent so much time teaching my boys not to do is the thing they accused me of." I could hear the sadness in his voice. "I would rather they had said I killed a man than to say I broke into some woman's house to steal money to feed a drug habit."

"It doesn't matter what they say."

"It matters to me."

"We'll get to the bottom of this one day," I said. "I promise."

"Yeah," he said, his voice trailing off. "One day."

I looked at my watch. "I better go," I said.

I rose; so did he.

"Tell Mama I love her."

"I will."

"Tell her not to worry."

"I'll tell her."

"D'Ray."

"Yeah."

"Try to fix things with her."

"Don't know if I can."

"She loves you," he said. "She just doesn't know how to show it."

"No," I said. "She loves you—she just tolerated me."

"You're wrong."

"I'm not wrong," I said. "I remind her too much of the man who broke her heart. But that's okay—I'm a big boy. I can take it."

"Well, I love you," he said.

Suddenly, I became full.

"Take care of yourself," I said.

"You do the same," he told me.

"I won't be coming tonight," I said. "It's just not safe."

"I understand," he said.

"Reggie will be here at seven. Your plane leaves at ten."

"D'Ray . . ."

"Yeah."

"If I don't see you again—"

"You'll see me again," I said.

"But if I don't—"

"You will."

I turned to leave, but he stopped me. "D'Ray."

"Yeah."

"Pray for me."

21

With bated breath, I walked outside and leaned against the truck. Despair overtook me and I tilted my head back and gazed into the heavens. "Oh, God," I sobbed. "Why is this happening? Why?" I turned and looked back at the shed, feeling hot hate rise in me again. No, I would not turn him over to the police. Not now, not ever.

I climbed into the truck and drove back to Brownsville. For a few hours, I lingered in my old bedroom at my mother's house, listening carefully for any word regarding the police search for Little Man. Then at six-thirty, after I had heard nothing, I drove to Peaches's house. When I reached the open door, I entered without knocking. She was sitting on the sofa attempting to grade papers. I could see her mind wasn't into it.

"Are you alright?" she asked, snapping to her feet. Her voice was excited. Her roving eyes examined me.

"I'm alright," I said, crossing the room and slumping onto the sofa.

"What happened last night?" she asked, sitting next to me.

"I went back to Lake Providence."

"I expected to hear from you," she said. "And when I didn't, I nearly worried myself to death."

"I'm sorry."

"You should have called."

"I know."

"I didn't sleep a wink."

"I'm sorry," I apologized again.

She touched my swollen face with the tips of her fingers. "It looks worse."

"I'm alright."

"I still think you should see a doctor."

"That's not necessary."

"You could have a concussion."

"I'm alright," I said again. I leaned back against the sofa. She sighed.

A silent moment passed, then she spoke again. "Did you see him?"

"Yeah," I said.

"How did it go?"

"I don't want to talk about it."

She sighed again.

"You aren't really going to help him get away, are you?"

I didn't answer. Instead, I rose and walked to the kitchen counter. My head was swirling. No, I did not want to talk, nor did I want to think. I looked at the clock. In a few minutes, this would all be over. He would be on his way to Little Rock.

"You are going to do it," she said. "Aren't you?"

I didn't answer.

"What about yesterday?" she said. "You told me you would bring him in. Was that a lie? Did you lie to me?"

"No, I didn't lie," I said. "I just changed my mind."

"I won't let you do this," she said.

"I'm going to help him," I said. "That beating last night

knocked some sense into me. I'm going to help him and that's final."

"Final."

"Yeah," I said. "Final."

"Just like that."

"Just like that."

She paused and shook her head. "This is not right."

"I can't turn him over to the cops," I said. "Not knowing what I know."

"Please don't do this," she pleaded. She took my hand and looked deep into my eyes, beseeching me to listen to reason. "You haven't thought this through."

"Yes, I have."

"No," she said. "Maybe you've thought about his escape. But you haven't thought about his life." She paused and furrowed her brow. "How is he going to live?"

"That's all been worked out," I said.

"It has?"

"Yes," I said. "It has."

"Have you worked it out with his wife and children?"

"He's not married," I said. "You know that."

"Not now," she said. "But he is going to get married someday, isn't he?"

"What in the name of God does this have to do with anything?"

"When he gets married, what is he going to tell his wife and children? Is he going to tell them who he is, or will he continue to live the lie the two of you created?" She paused. I didn't answer. "And what happens to them when the law finally catches up to him and he goes to prison?"

"Who says they will catch up to him?"

"You know they will."

"Maybe not," I said.

"Stop lying to yourself," she said.

"I'm not lying."

"This isn't right," she said. "And you know it."

"Right or not," I said, "it's done."

"Then undo it."

"I can't."

"You can't or you won't?"

"I won't."

"Then undo us," she said.

"What?" I said.

She slowly shook her head. "I love you and I'm glad you're back in my life. But I won't be a part of this."

"This has nothing to do with us," I said.

"How can you say that to me?" she asked.

"Because it's true," I said.

"It's not true," she said. "This has everything to do with us."

"No," I said. "It doesn't."

"What happens to you when they find out you helped him escape?"

"I don't know," I said.

"You don't know."

"No," I said. "I don't."

"Alright," she said. "Then I'll tell you what's going to happen. You're going to prison for aiding and abetting. And that has everything to do with me. Because when they send you away, that will destroy us, and it will destroy our future."

"What do you want me to do?"

"The right thing," she said.

"I can't turn my back on him," I said. "I just can't."

"I'm not asking you to."

"Then what are you asking?"

"Turn him in," she said. "And if he's innocent, prove it."

"And if I can't prove it?"

"Let him do his time."

"No," I said, raising my hand, and pointing to my face.

"You see what they did to me. I don't trust 'em. I hate 'em. I hate all of 'em."

"Hate who?" she asked.

"The cops!" I shouted.

"The cops didn't do anything to you," she said. *"Pete* did. And if you want to get him, then get him; but do it the right way. Do it through the system."

"Please," I said, dismissing her idea.

"D'Ray, you're not a thug," she said. "So quit trying to act like one."

"I am who I am."

"No," she said. "You are who you choose to be."

"I didn't choose," I said. "They did."

"Baby," she said, kneeling before me and taking my face in her hands. "You're a college-educated man with an incredible mind. Please don't go back to the life you've worked so hard to escape."

"It's too late," I said.

"It's never too late."

"I gave him my word."

"Then break it."

"Do you know what you're asking?" I said. "You're asking me to send him to prison. My God, he's my brother. I thought I could do it, but that was before I saw him—that was before I talked to him. No, I have to help him. I can't turn him over to them, not knowing what I know. I thought I could, but I can't . . . I just can't. Besides, it's all set up—in a little while, he will be thousands of miles away from here, and this will all be behind him."

"For how long?" she said. "One year, maybe two?"

"I don't know."

"We can't live like this," she said.

"Like what?"

"Running from the law."

"What are you talking about?"

"As long as he's on the run, we're on the run."

"Then so be it," I said.

"So be it?"

"Yes," I said. "So be it."

"Who are you?" she asked.

"What?"

"I need to know who I'm dealing with."

I didn't answer.

"Are you Outlaw? Or are you D'Ray?"

She paused but I still didn't answer.

"Are you the boy who killed Stanley? Or are you the man who tried to give back a portion of that which you took? Who are you? Please tell me so that I can know."

"I am who I am," I blurted.

"Choose," she said.

"Choose between what?" I asked, confused.

"Turning him in or letting me go."

"What kind of choice is that?"

"The only one you have," she said.

"I can't choose," I said.

"Well, I can," she said. "I want to be with you, but I won't go along with this."

"I have to help him."

"No," she said. "He has to help himself."

Suddenly, I felt my hand trembling.

"Why are you doing this to me?" I said. "Everything is set. Why are you doing this to me? Why?"

"Choose," she said.

"It's too late," I said. "Can't you understand that?"

"Please!" she said. "I'm begging you!"

"I can't," I said again.

"Alright," she said. "Then leave."

22

I dashed out of her house, slamming the door behind me. Then I hurried to my truck and climbed inside. Once inside, I looked out into the street. What was I supposed to do now? Oh, I needed to go someplace, someplace where I could feel my way through this terrible moment. I shut my eyes and concentrated. Beneath me, I felt my legs trembling. I was tense and confused. Why had I come back here? Would it not have been better for me had I followed my first mind and fled this place? Why had I listened to Miss Big Siss? Why was I listening to Peaches? Oh, if I could only speak to Mr. Henry, he would know what to do.

Behind me, I heard footsteps on the pavement. I turned and looked; Peaches had come out beneath the carport. No, I did not want to talk to her. Not here, not now. I started the engine and pulled out of the drive, feeling the truck swerve, hearing the tires screech. In the rearview mirror, I saw her running toward me. She called to me. But I did not answer. I looked at the clock. It was a few minutes until seven. It was too late now. I pressed the accelerator and headed north. My troubled mind was whirling. I closed my eyes, feeling Mr. Henry's spirit all about me.

"Help me!" I shouted. "I'm lost."

I paused and listened. No one answered. I opened my eyes and looked at the seat next to me. Oh, what I would give at this moment to have him sitting next to me. Inside, I felt my emotions swirl.

"Oh, Mr. Henry, I miss you so much," I mumbled.

Then I gripped the steering wheel, feeling my hands begin to tremble. Suddenly, my eyes began to tear and my legs began to shake.

"Why did you have to leave me?" I shouted.

Then something occurred to me. He didn't leave me. He had returned to Stanley; he had returned to his wife. Yes, they were all together now. And the sorrows of this world were long behind them. Oh, to have that type of peace and to be free of the burdens of this godforsaken place.

Choose. I heard those words again. But only now they had not come from Peaches but from some distant place, a place far beyond the realities of this place. And I frowned, not knowing what it meant.

"Choose," it said again.

Suddenly, I fell back against the seat and wept, for now I knew that which was being communicated to me. The way was clear. I had but to choose the path I desired to travel. Yes, I recalled the story now: the stranger, the fork in the road, the road less traveled. And at the moment, I knew. To truly save his life, Little Man had to lose it. Mr. Henry had chosen me, the boy who had killed his boy, and in so doing, he had given me life, and now it had fallen upon me to do the same. I was in his place now, and Little Man was in mine. No, there was no escaping that which was inevitable. Little Man had to go back and face his life just as I had had to go back and face mine.

I passed through the tiny town of Terry. Instinct made me turn and look. Darkness had fallen. No, he would not get away. They would catch him just as they had caught me.

Under the circumstances, would it not be better for him to end this thing now on his own terms? But what about Mama? How would she feel about this? She would hate me. There was no doubt about it. She would never speak to me again. Well, I would deal with that when I had to deal with it.

I raced through the village of Kilbourne and turned off the highway just short of the Arkansas state line. I glanced at my watch again. It was seven. It was too late. I was sure that they had gone. I stepped on the accelerator, speeding along the bumpy road, then racing across harrowed grown until I slid to a stop a few feet from the shed. I leaped out and burst through the door. The two of them were huddled together in the corner. Little Man was stuffing something into the suitcase, and Reggie was standing over him. I called to them. They whirled, then bound to their feet. I saw Reggie reach for his waist, and I knew he had a gun. I recoiled. Our eyes met, and I saw him relax.

"You scared me," he said, lowering the gun.

Curtis brought his hands to his face and let out a deep sigh. "Is something wrong?"

I shook my head. Reggie frowned and then hurried to the window and peeped out. I watched him for a moment, and then turned back toward Little Man. He was fiddling with the suitcase again.

"We need to talk."

He shook his head. "No time," he said. "I got to get out of here." He lifted the suitcase and started toward the door. I grabbed his arm.

"We need to make time," I said.

He paused.

"Come on!" Reggie insisted. "We got to go."

"Please," I said. "Just hear me out."

He glanced at his watch, then back at me.

"Alright," he said. "But hurry."

I swallowed and looked at him. "I thought I could do this," I said. "But I can't. This is a mistake—a gigantic mistake."

I saw Reggie shake his head. "We don't have time for this," he said. "Let's get out of here before it's too late."

Little Man looked at me. "I'm not going back to that cage," he said adamantly. He lifted the suitcase again. "I'm going to Los Angeles just like we planned." He turned to leave and I grabbed his arm again.

"Listen to me," I said. "Nothing good is going to come of this. Even if you make it to LA. Nothing good will come of this."

"That's for me to decide," he said. "Not you."

"Listen to me."

He pulled away from me. His eyes narrowed. "Why should I?"

"Because we're family."

"Family!" he shouted.

"Yeah," I said. "Family."

"Man! I haven't seen you in years."

"That was a mistake," I said. "I shouldn't have stayed away so long."

"No," he said. "That was your choice and this is mine." He reached in his pocket and removed the ticket. "I'm going to take this ticket and this money, and I'm going to get out of here."

"I can't let you do it," I said.

"It ain't up to you." He turned to leave again.

"Wait," I shouted.

He whirled. "What!"

"Reverend Jacobs talked to the DA—if you come back, they won't file new charges. You'll be right back where you were—no worse for the wear."

"And no better," Reggie said.

"Did you do it?" I asked.

"No!"

"Then I'll help you prove it," I said.

"Let's go," Reggie said.

"D'Ray," he said. "Please . . . Move out of my way."

"It might take some time," I said. "But I won't rest until your name has been cleared, and you're a free man. I promise."

"Don't listen to him," Reggie said. "You can't trust him. He will betray you, just like he's betraying you now."

"He's right," Little Man said. "I can't trust you."

"And you can trust him?"

"Yeah," he said. "I trust Reggie with my life."

"When I was down, Mr. Henry stood by me," I said. "And he helped me do my time. If you go back, I'll stand by you. I'll help you do your time—just like he helped me do mine."

"He's lying," Reggie said.

"It's the only way," I said.

"Let's go," Reggie said. He pulled the door open, and I felt a gush of hot wind sweep across my face. "Let's go before somebody comes."

"Comes a time when you have to stop running," I said, "and stand up. There comes a time when you have to be a man. Mama said you can't do time, but she's wrong. You can do time. You can do time because you're a man—not a little man, but a grown man."

"Come on," Reggie shouted.

I saw him step through the door. He looked back at Little Man; Little Man didn't move.

"Come on," he said again, "before it's too late."

"I'm going to Angola," I said. "And I'm going to speak to Daddy. I'm going to ask him to look out for you while you're there. In the meantime, you just keep yourself busy until I can get you out, and when you get out, we'll make up for all of the time we lost. I shouldn't have stayed away so long. I should have been here for you, but I can't do anything about that now. That's water under the bridge. But I can do something about tomorrow. You just have to hold on until I can get you out of there. You can do that," I said. "Can't you?"

"No!" Reggie said.

I snapped around and looked at him. "I'm not talking to you."

Reggie frowned. "Why should he rot away in Angola when he could be free?"

"He will be free," I said. "As soon as I clear his name."

"Let's get the hell out of here," Reggie said.

"No," I said.

"Don't listen to him," Reggie said.

"I've made up my mind," Little Man said. "I'm not going back."

He lifted the suitcase and started toward the door.

"One of these days, you're going to have a family," I said. "A wife and maybe a son, and in my heart, I know you don't want to do to them what Daddy did to us, do you?"

He didn't answer.

"You don't have to answer," I said. "I know you don't want them to live the same life we lived. I know you don't want your boy to cry at night for a daddy he can't see. I know you don't want your wife to have to fight this world for life because the man who vowed to protect her is not there to fight it for her. And that's what will happen if you live the life of a fugitive. Every day will be a lie. And in the end, those lies will hurt the people you love more than prison will ever hurt you."

He froze again. Reggie became hysterical.

"Don't listen to him," Reggie said.

"One time I told you that I would be the daddy you never had. Do you remember?"

He didn't answer.

"Well, I tried. I did everything I knew to do—I fought for you, I killed for you, and I went to prison for you, but didn't any of that make up for the fact that Daddy was gone.

So, I'm finished trying to be your daddy. I just want to be your brother, and as your brother, I'm asking you to go back with me so that one day we can be what we never had a chance to be—a family."

"It's too late for that," he said.

"No," I said. "All you have to do is go back."

"It's time to go," Reggie said again. "You got a plane to catch."

Little Man looked at Reggie; then he turned to me. "I can't, D'Ray." He turned to leave.

I stopped him. "I'm not going to let you walk out of here," I said.

"You're going to have to."

"No," I said. "I don't."

"Man! What are you trying to prove?" Reggie shouted.

I didn't answer him; instead, I looked at Little Man. I started toward him, and as I did, Little Man reached into his waist and removed the gun, then pointed it at me. I froze.

"Don't make me hurt you, D'Ray," he pleaded in a trembling voice.

"Put that gun away," I scolded him. "Put it away before somebody gets hurt." I started toward him again.

"D'Ray," he said sternly. "Whatever happens to me from this point on ain't got nothing to do with you, you hear? This is my life, and from this moment on, I'm going to live it my own way."

I looked at the gun and then at him.

"Is this what it's come to?"

"I'm afraid so," he said.

"What," I said. "You gonna shoot me?"

"If I have to," he said.

"I don't think so," I challenged him.

"Don't make me hurt you, D'Ray," he pleaded.

"This ain't you," I said.

"You don't know me, D'Ray."

"Maybe I don't," I said. "But Reverend Jacobs tells me you're a spiritual man. He said that you are a true believer, not a killer."

"Let's go," Reggie said.

I looked at Little Man. His eyes were wide and his lips were parted, but he didn't answer; instead, he simply stared at me.

"Give me the gun," I said.

"No," Reggie said. "Don't listen to him."

"You have to go back," I said. "It's the only way."

Little Man shook his head. "I'm not going back, D'Ray," he said. "And I mean that."

I stepped toward him and reached out my hand. "Give me the gun," I said.

"No!" he shouted.

"You're not going to shoot me," I said. "So give me the gun."

"Don't push me, Ray."

"Leave him alone," Reggie yelled.

"D'Ray!" Little Man shouted. "Look out!"

I turned and looked. Reggie was holding a gun of his own. His eyes were wide; his hands were trembling. I dropped to the floor. I heard the loud blast of the gun being fired. I saw Little Man flinch, clutching his chest. I heard him scream. Then I saw him fall back against the table. The tiny lamp fell, and the pale, yellow light faded to darkness.

23

On hands and knees, I crawled next to Little Man's wounded body, seeing bright red blood gushing from a gaping hole in the center of his chest. When I reached him, he moaned. Panic swept me. I yelled his name, then shook him hard, but he did not move. I shook him again. Suddenly his lips parted. I waited for him to speak but no words came. Then, as if in a dream, I lifted his limp body and cradled him in my arms. The room reeled. My heart was racing. Suddenly we were in a haze of dimming light, and all was quiet except the gurgled sound of Little Man's labored breathing. I shook him a third time, and when I did, his bloody body began to convulse. Instantly, my head snapped around, and I looked about frantically, searching for something to stop the bleeding. In the far corner, I spotted a cloth lying next to an empty basin. I looked at Reggie. His mouth was agape, and the recently fired gun was dangling below his waist. He was paralyzed, staring at us with bulging eyes.

"Quick! Get me that cloth!"

I paused. Reggie didn't move.

"Hurry!" I shouted frantically.

He dashed toward the corner and retrieved the cloth. He gave it to me, and I pressed it against Little Man's bloody chest. Little Man flinched, then moaned. I called to him. He didn't answer. He couldn't.

I looked at Reggie again. "Help me get him to the truck." Reggie shook his head. "We shouldn't move him."

"For God's sake, man!" I shouted. "Can't you understand? He's hurt bad. If we don't get him to the hospital, he'll die. Now, come on!" I rose and pushed him hard. He stumbled, then gathered himself.

"Grab his feet!"

He grabbed Little Man's feet and I grabbed his arms. Together, we lifted him and carried him to my truck. And when we were close, I lowered the tailgate and eased him into the back, and then climbed in next to him.

I tossed Reggie the keys. "To the hospital," I said. "Hurry!"

He jumped behind the wheel. I heard the engine roar. The tires spun on the loose, dry dirt; then the truck lurched forward. Little Man moaned again. I lifted his head and placed it on my lap. His eyelids fluttered, then closed.

"Hurry!" I shouted again. "We're losing him!"

I felt the tires leaping over the harrowed ground as we sped toward the highway. I looked at him. His eyes were closed, and I could hear his labored breathing coming and going. I swabbed his wound with the saturated cloth, trying to stop the bleeding. Suddenly, I felt his hands on me.

"D'Ray!" he called to me. His voice was feeble. I lowered my ear next to his mouth, straining to hear. I could feel the wind gushing past the speeding truck.

"Yes," I said. "I'm here."

He swallowed, struggling to speak. "M-my . . . f-fault," he whispered in a raspy voice.

"No," I said, shaking my head. "This shouldn't have happened." I glanced over my shoulder. Through the window, I could see the back of Reggie's head. My emotions seared. If

Little Man died, I would kill him. I would kill him dead. I turned and looked at Little Man again. I felt the truck swerve and then accelerate. He swallowed again.

"T-tell t-them . . . i-it was an . . . a-accident." He moaned. I looked at him. His eyes were wide. His pupils seemed dilated.

"Who?"

"T-the . . . p-police."

I looked around. There was a huge cloud of dust in our wake. Up ahead, I could see the road leading back to town. The truck bounced through a rut and onto the highway. Little Man moaned, then grimaced. He squeezed my hand again.

"I . . . I . . . d-don't . . . w-want . . . R-Reggie . . . i-in . . . t-trouble . . . b-behind . . . t-this." He moaned. "Y-you . . . h-hear?"

I didn't answer.

"T-tell t-them . . . I . . . I . . . w-was c-cleaning m-my g-gun." He paused, struggling to continue. "A-and i-it w-went off. T-that's h-how I . . . I g-got s-shot."

He closed his eyes again. He was losing consciousness. I pounded on the hood of the truck. "Speed up!" I shouted. "For the love of Jesus, man! Speed up!" I looked at Little Man again. His eyes were closed and his lips were trembling. I leaned closer, pressing the saturated cloth over the bloody wound as the truck weaved in and out of traffic.

"Just a little farther," I said. "Hold on."

Reggie slowed, turned off the main highway onto the hospital road, then sped up again. He flew down the narrow road and slammed on the brakes before the emergency room door. He leaped from the truck and raced toward the hospital door. A nurse stopped him.

"What's the matter?"

"Help me!" he shouted.

"Are you injured?"

"Not me!" he shouted, looking over his shoulder toward us. "A man's been shot!"

I crawled from the truck, cradling Little Man in my arms. He was weak. His head hung limp. I saw two men in white coats burst from the hospital and run toward me.

"What happened?"

"He accidentally shot himself," I said. I saw Reggie frown, then lower his eyes. The nurse looked at me.

"Where?"

"In the chest," I said.

She ripped open his shirt, exposing the large gaping hole through which blood poured.

"What's his name?"

"Curtis," I said. "Curtis Reid."

"And who are you?"

"I'm his brother," I said.

"When did this happen?"

"A few minutes ago."

"Okay," she said. "We'll take it from here."

They placed him on a gurney and wheeled him inside.

"Is he going to be alright?" I shouted.

She didn't answer. I looked at Reggie. His wide eyes were fearful.

"Go get Reverend Jacobs," I said. "Tell him that Little Man has been shot and that he's in the hospital. Then go home and stay there. Don't talk to anybody. And I mean anybody."

"What about your mama?"

"Tell the reverend to tell her."

"What about—"

"Go!" I shouted.

He left, running, and I stumbled inside and made my way to the waiting room, where I sank into a chair. My hands were trembling. I looked at them and then at my shirt. I was covered in blood. Fear overcame me. *What if he dies? Oh, God! What if he dies?* I buried my face in my hands and began to sob. Why was this happening? Why? In the hallway, I was aware of the sound of muddled voices. Some folks had gathered next to the door. I could hear them talking, but I could not determine what they were saying. I raised my head and looked. My exhausted mind whirled. "Has something happened?" I rose from my seat and hurried next to the door. Yes, they were discussing him.

"I think it's him," I heard one of them say.

"What should we do?"

"Call the police?"

"Did they find the gun?"

"No?"

"Who do you think shot him?"

"I don't know. Maybe he tried to kill himself."

I went back to my seat. Yes, the police would be here any minute now—the chief, Sonny, the district attorney. Oh, I didn't want to talk to them right now. I paused, thinking. They had him now, but that would not be enough. They would make an example of him, and if not him, somebody. There was a long space of time in which I did not move. I sat with my eyes cast down, staring at the floor. Then the doctor came out. He told me that they had rushed Little Man into surgery and that he had lost a lot of blood, that it did not look good. He left. A moment later, Reverend Jacobs arrived and Mama was with him. I rose and faced them. He was calm but Mama was not.

She stared at me, wide-eyed. "What did you do?"

"Nothing," I said.

"Where is he?" Reverend Jacobs asked.

"In surgery," I said.

"Have you spoken to anyone?" Reverend Jacobs wanted to know.

"Yes, sir," I said. "The doctor just left."

"What did he say?"

"Things don't look good."

Mama let out a piercing scream, and when she did, I buried my face in my trembling hands. Reverend Jacobs tried to console her but could not. And when she refused to settled down, he looked at me.

"Son," he said. "What happened?"

I hesitated, thinking. I didn't know what to tell him.

"What happened?"

"Did you shoot him?" Mama asked.

"Me?!"

"Yes!" she snapped. "You!"

"No!" I shouted back.

"Don't lie to me," she screamed.

"I'm not lying."

"Who shot my child?"

"Reggie!" I shouted. "Reggie shot him."

"That's a lie," Mama said.

"It's the truth. Little Man asked me not to tell. He didn't want to get Reggie in trouble, but it's true—Reggie shot him. It was an accident. But he shot him."

"I don't believe you."

"It's true."

Reverend Jacobs looked at me, stunned. His eyes narrowed. He opened his mouth to speak, but no words came.

"I tried to bring him in."

Suddenly, Mama's head snapped back. "What!" she shouted.

"But he refused to come."

"You had no right," she said.

"Then what happened?" Reverend Jacobs asked.

"When I tried to force him, he pulled a gun."

"On you?"

"Yes, sir," I said.

"That's a lie!" Mama said.

"We struggled. Then Reggie shot him—he was trying to shoot me, but he missed. He shot Little Man instead."

"My God," Reverend Jacobs whispered.

Next to him, Mama fell into the seat, weeping. Reverend Jacobs kneeled and placed his arm around her. He looked at her, then back at me. I was quiet, remembering the scene. "Help me, Jesus!" I heard my mother wail. I wanted to go to her. I commanded my feet to move, but they would not obey. Then a series of images came to me. They were sporadic, disjointed, unrelenting. Mr. Henry lying in a coffin. Papa in a cell. Mama crying. Little Man dying. I closed my eyes as if to make the images stop. When I opened them again, Mama was staring at me.

"Why did you have to interfere?" she wailed.

"I was just trying to help."

"You had no right."

"Sister Reid."

She fell to the floor, clutching her stomach. "Why couldn't it have been you?" she wailed. "My God in heaven, why couldn't it have been you?"

I fell against the wall, stunned.

"Sister Reid!" Reverend Jacobs said.

Mama didn't answer him. Then he looked at me.

"Son, she doesn't mean that."

"I do mean it," she said, weeping. "God knows I do."

"It was an accident," I said.

"Get out of here."

I stared at her. But I did not move.

"You're not welcome here."

"Sister Reid! Please!"

"Get out!"

"Son, please go," Reverend Jacobs said. "There's nothing more you can do here."

I shook my head. "I'm not leaving," I said. "Not until I

know that Little Man is alright. When that's done, I'll leave and I won't ever bother you again. But until then, I'm staying right here."

Mama looked at me. "Why did you have to come back here? I wish you had stayed away."

"So do I," I said.

She buried her head in her hands again, and I went out into the hall. "Lord, I hate this world." I drew my arm back and pounded the wall, hard. I felt someone grab my hand. I turned and looked. It was Peaches.

"I just heard," she said. I looked at her, then fell into her arms, sobbing. "Hush now," she said.

"He shot him," I sobbed.

"I know."

"How?"

"He told me."

"Who told you?"

"Reggie."

"What?" I said.

Behind me, I heard the sound of a man's surly voice. I turned and saw the chief and Sonny walking toward me. Reggie was with them. I stared at Reggie. His shoulders were drooping. His head was down. He was crying.

24

I pulled away from Peaches, and for a moment, I had no idea what to do. Should I start toward them, or should I stand and wait? I paused, watching the three approaching men with curious eyes. Why was Reggie with them? Had he talked? I looked at him but he refused to look at me. Yes, he had talked. I could tell by the way he was behaving. But what had he told them? I glanced at the chief. I saw him smile. Suddenly I furrowed my brow. He was gloating. My brother was in there dying, and the chief of police was walking toward me, gloating. Suddenly, I let out a deep sigh. I felt raging hot hate rising within me. I bit my lip hard and shook my head. If the chief said anything to me, anything at all, I would knock that smile off his face. Yes, I would ball my fist and raise my hand and hit him so hard, he'd think God himself had laid hands on him.

I stood still, watching them. As they drew closer, my tense body tingled with anxiousness.

"Just be calm," Peaches whispered to me. "Just be calm."

When they reached me, the chief spoke first.

"Well, it's over." He smirked.

Suddenly, I felt light-headed and the room began to reel.

Yes, this was it. I slowly doubled my fist, feeling a keen sense of excitement, but before I could do that which I had promised myself I would, I felt Peaches's hand atop mine, and then I saw Reverend Jacobs make his way out into the hall.

"Good evening, Chief."

Instantly, the chief turned and looked at him.

"Evening, Reverend," the chief said, then quickly added, "How's the boy?"

"Not good," Reverend Jacobs said.

The chief paused and wiped his brow. I looked at him and then at Reggie. Reggie's eyes were still diverted. An awkward moment passed, and then the chief spoke again.

"His mama here?"

"She's here," the reverend said.

"Where?" Sonny asked, speaking for the first time.

"In there," Reverend Jacobs said, pointing toward the waiting room. I saw Sonny's head turn as his eyes followed the direction of Reverend Jacobs's outstretched hand. Then I saw him turn and look at the chief again.

"Alright if I check on her, Chief?"

The chief nodded and Sonny left. A moment later, I heard Mama cry out again. The agony in her voice filled the hallway. I frowned and turned toward Reggie. Our eyes met and he quickly looked away. Anger overcame me again, and at that moment, the desire to ram my fist into something returned. I continued to stare at Reggie. Yes, I wanted to hit him so hard, until all the rage that was in me exploded and released me from the burden I was no longer able to carry. That thought caused me to close my eyes, and when I opened them again, I saw the chief turn toward the waiting room. Then I saw him look at Reverend Jacobs again.

"I don't feel sorry for her, Reverend," he said. "And I'm not ashamed to say it. Now, don't get me wrong. I know she's hurting, but that boy has no one to blame for this but him-self. I don't know what possessed him to run off like that. I was good to him—we all were."

"He just panicked," Reverend Jacobs said. "That's all."

"That's no excuse." The chief sneered.

"It's not intended to be," Reverend Jacobs said. "It's just an explanation."

"Well," the chief said dismissively. "It's all water off a duck's back now. He's back in custody, and that's all that mat-ters."

I heard Mama cry out again, and the sound of her voice caused Reverend Jacobs to look toward the waiting room.

"Well, Chief," he said. "I better go see after her."

"Yeah," he said. "I think I'll go with you."

The two of them left. I followed them to the waiting room but hung back, looming near the doorway with Peaches. Inside the room, I could see that Sonny was sitting next to Mama, but as the Chief approached them, I saw Sonny pat Mama on the shoulder, then rise and move next to the chief. Mama dropped her head and began to weep again.

"Go to her," Peaches advised me.

"No," I said, rejecting her advice. "She doesn't want that." And then I saw the chief staring at Mama.

"Mira," he finally said in a loud, forceful voice. "I don't want any trouble out of you, you hear?"

"There's not going to be any trouble," Reverend Jacobs said, looking at Mama with stern eyes. "Isn't that right, Sister Reid?"

Mama nodded.

"Then, it's over," the chief said. "As soon as Curtis can travel, I'm taking him to Angola, just like the law stipulates. You understand?"

"What about our agreement?" the reverend interrupted him.

"What agreement?" the chief asked, whirling and looking at Reverend Jacobs with cold, menacing eyes. The reverend blinked, sensing the need to proceed cautiously.

"Chief, you promised me you wouldn't file additional charges if he turned himself in. Don't you remember?"

"He didn't turn himself in," the chief snapped. "He was captured."

"Captured!" the reverend said.

"Yes," the chief said, "captured." He turned and looked at Reggie. "That boy told me what happened. He tried to bring Curtis in, and Curtis pulled a gun on him. And he shot him in self-defense." The chief paused, then spoke directly to Reggie. "Ain't that right, son?"

Reggie nodded and lowered his eyes again. Hot rage simmered within me. Now I understood. He had gone to the chief to protect himself, knowing that I could not dispute his account without implicating myself. "That dirty bastard," I mumbled to myself.

"Just be calm," Peaches said to me again.

I saw Reverend Jacobs look at Reggie and then back at the chief, and I knew he was trying to figure out what it all meant.

"So, you will be filing additional charges?"

"You bet," the chief said.

"May I ask what they are?"

"Well," the chief said, gazing at the reverend with serious eyes. "He's looking at felony escape, assault with a deadly weapon, and who knows what else. Hell, because of this little stunt, he'll serve twenty more years, easy."

"Please, Chief," Mama sobbed. "Please have mercy on him. He just got scared, that's all."

"That's no excuse," the chief said again.

"Please!" Mama wailed.

"It's out of my hands."

"No!" Mama protested. "You can help him if you want to."

"I can't," the chief said. "The DA has decided to throw the book at him, and I can't say that I blame him."

Mama fell to her knees. "Please," she sobbed. "I'm begging you."

"Mira!" Sonny said, embarrassed that she was behaving this way in front of the chief. "If you want to help Curtis, you need to be strong." He reached over and gently helped her to her feet.

"How can I be strong?" she asked. "They're sending my child to the penitentiary."

"Ask God to help you," Sonny said. "Ask him to give you the strength."

"Why don't you help her?" I said.

"D'Ray!" Peaches whispered.

"If I could, I would," Sonny said.

"Don't lie," I said, challenging him. "You could if you wanted to."

"What!" Sonny said.

"Let's go outside," Peaches said. She grabbed my arm, but I pulled away from her and turned back to Sonny.

"You heard me," I said to him.

"I heard you," he said, "but I don't know what you're talking about."

"Curtis is doing somebody else's time," I said. "You know it and the chief knows it. So instead of sitting here fronting, why don't you go out there and find the real perp?"

"He is the real perp," the chief snapped.

"That's not true," Mama whimpered.

"Mira, it is true," Sonny said.

"It's not," she sobbed. "I'm telling you, it's not."

"It is," Sonny said again, "and you all need to accept it."

"I thought you cared about us," Mama shouted.

"This is not about me," he said. "Nor is it about you. This is about justice."

"Justice!" I shouted.

"Yes," he said. "Justice."

"Please," I mumbled.

"Lord, help us," Mama cried. "Please help us."

"Mira, I love you," Sonny said, angling his face so that he could look into her eyes. "And I don't care who knows it. But Curtis committed this crime, and now he's going to have to do his time. And that's all there is to it."

"You told me you were going to help him," Mama wailed hysterically.

"I tried to help him," Sonny said. "But now there is nothing more I can do. I wish there was but there's not."

"He can't make it in prison," Mama said. "He just can't."

"Yes, he can," Sonny said. "He just has to get his mind right and face this thing like a man." He paused and his voice softened. "Now, after they process him into the facility, I'll do what I can for him. I don't want anything to happen to him. I love that boy like he was my own—"

"Don't say it!" I shouted. "Don't you dare say it."

I took a step toward him. My eyes were wide. My voice had become shrill. I could feel my hands shaking.

"Let's go," Peaches said, grabbing my arm for the second time. I pulled away, and the chief stepped between me and Sonny.

"Calm down," the chief snarled. "Calm down right now."

"It's alright, Chief," Sonny said. Then he looked at me. "Son—"

"Don't call me that," I shouted. "Don't ever call me that, you hear?"

"I'm warning you," the chief said.

"It's alright," Sonny told him again.

"No," the chief said. "It's not alright. Now, this boy can be disrespectful to his mama if he wants to. But by God he's gonna respect the law."

Sonny stepped from behind the chief and looked directly at me. "What have I ever done to you?" he asked.

"You joking," I said. "Right?"

"No," he said. "What?"

"Why are you still running around with my mama?"

"D'Ray!" Mama exclaimed.

"It's alright," Sonny said. "I don't mind telling him. I love her—that's why."

"Please!"

"It's true."

"You have no right," I said.

"Why not?"

"Because she's still married to my daddy."

"D'Ray!" Mama shouted again.

"Well, it's true," I said. "Ain't it?"

"Enough!" the chief shouted. "This is not a barrel house. This is a hospital, and the only business I'm concerned about is that boy in there." He paused and looked around. "Has anyone spoken to the doctor?"

"Not since they took him into surgery," the reverend said.

"Wonder how he's doing?"

"If he's lucky, he'll die on the table," Mama mumbled.

"Sister Reid!" Reverend Jacobs said, shocked.

"Well, I mean it."

"No, you don't," Reverend Jacobs said, shaking his head.

"Yes, I do."

"Sister Reid, why would you say such a thing?"

"Reverend," Mama said, exasperated. "That doctor in there can patch him up. And he might even be able to make him whole again. But what good will it do? The law done sentenced him to die anyway."

"You can't think that way," Reverend Jacobs admonished her.

"How else am I supposed to think?" she asked, raising her head and looking Reverend Jacobs in the eye. "Reverend, he's not going to make it through this. He had one chance, and they took that away from him." She paused and looked at me. "You should have stayed out of it."

She waited for me to respond, but when I remained quiet, she turned and looked at the chief.

"I had hoped he would get away," she said matter-of-factly. "But he didn't. And you got him now. And I'm not going to beg anymore. I'm just going to pray to my God and ask him to take him home to a place where you can't hurt him no more."

"You do that," the chief said. "In the meantime, I'm going to monitor his situation. And if the good Lord doesn't answer your prayers and take him on home, I'm going to do my job and take him on to Angola."

"That ain't your job," I said. "Your job is to find the person who actually committed this crime."

"And that's what I've done."

"That's a lie."

"D'Ray, please," Peaches scolded him.

"That's it," the chief said. He removed his cuffs and started toward me. I looked at him and then at Sonny.

"You gonna arrest him too?" I asked.

The chief froze. Sonny looked at me, puzzled.

"Arrest me for what?"

"Last time I looked, adultery was against the law in the state of Louisiana." I looked at the chief. "Ain't that right, Chief?"

"Lower your voice," the chief said. "This is a public place."

I mockingly stretched my hands toward the chief. "Go ahead, Chief," I said. "Arrest me if you want to. But if you do, I want him arrested too."

I looked as Sonny remained quiet.

Suddenly, Reverend Jacobs stepped forward. "Chief, there is no need to arrest anybody. This young man is just upset. His brother is lying in there with a bullet in his chest."

"Alright," the chief said. "But he better calm down."

"I'll go to jail," I said. "As long as he goes with me."

"Son, please," Reverend Jacobs said. "This is neither the time nor the place for this."

I looked at Reverend Jacobs and shook my head. "Preachers used to stand for what's right," I said. "Now I don't know what they stand for."

"I'm not here to judge this man," Reverend Jacobs said. "I'm here on behalf of Curtis. The other is of no consequence to me, at least not right now."

"That's disappointing," I said.

"So be it," Reverend Jacobs said. Then he turned and looked at the chief. I could tell he was no longer thinking about me. He was thinking about Curtis.

"How much time before you transport him?"

"I don't know," the chief said. "Could be tomorrow, could be the next day. It all depends on the doctor. But we're going to take him as soon as possible."

"Well, what's the big hurry?" Reverend said.

"You're joking," the chief said. "Right?"

"No, Chief," Reverend Jacobs said. "I'm serious. Curtis has been shot. And his mother is grief stricken. I'm just asking for a little compassion. That's all."

"Compassion!"

"Yes, sir, Chief—compassion."

"Well, Reverend, I tried that," the chief said. "And look where it got me. No. From here on out, it's strictly by the book."

"But—"

"No buts, Reverend," the chief said. "As soon as Curtis can travel, he's going to Angola. And that's final." He looked at his watch and then at Sonny. "Come on, Officer, walk with me. I could use a cup of coffee."

25

After the two officers left, Mama and Reverend Jacobs moved to the far corner of the waiting room and sat next to the window. Neither one of them said much. For the most part, Reverend Jacobs kept his head bowed, and I figured he was praying. Mama sat statuelike with her arms folded across her lap, gently rocking back and forth while quietly staring blankly into space. I sat near the doorway, holding Peaches's hand while anxiously awaiting word from the doctor. From where I sat, I could see Reggie. He was sitting in the hallway with his back against the wall.

"Wonder what's taking so long?" I finally asked.

"I don't know," Peaches said. "But I'm sure they'll tell us something as soon as they have something to tell."

I sighed. "What time is it anyway?"

She raised her arm and looked at her watch. "Almost ten," she said.

"Ten!" I exclaimed, shocked. "It's been nearly three hours. My God, something must have gone wrong."

"Not necessarily."

"Why else would it be taking so long?"

"It hasn't been that long," she said. "He's been shot. His wounds are serious."

"Well, I can't just sit here," I said, rising to my feet. "I need to see if I can find out something."

I started toward the door, but before I made it out of the room, the doctor appeared. He was still wearing his scrubs.

"Doctor!" I said. "How is he?"

Suddenly, Reverend Jacobs snapped to his feet. Mama remained seated, her eyes still staring blankly ahead. Out in the hallway, Reggie eased closer to the door. Peaches moved next to me.

"We removed the bullet," he said, "but he's slipped into a coma."

"A coma!" I exclaimed.

"I'm afraid so," the doctor said. "Right now he's on a ventilator."

"My God," I said. I looked at Mama. She was still staring into space.

"Will he recover?" Reverend Jacobs asked.

"I'm hopeful," the doctor said. "But I have to be honest. His condition is critical. The bullet punctured his lungs, and he's extremely weak. The next twenty-four hours are crucial."

"Oh, God!" I wailed. "This can't be. This just can't be."

I felt Peaches slip her arm around my waist.

"It's going to be alright," she said.

"Yes," Reverend Jacobs said, echoing her sentiment. "God is able. Just remember that. God is able."

"When can we see him?" I asked the doctor.

"You can see him now. But I have to warn you, he's unconscious. He won't be able to respond to you."

"I don't care," I said. "Just take us to him."

Reverend Jacobs helped Mama to her feet, then we followed the doctor down the narrow hallway, through the large double doors leading to the ICU. When we arrived, Little Man was lying on his back with a huge tube taped in his mouth. Mama eased next to his bed and gazed at him for a moment, then gently laid her hand on his chest. Reverend Jacobs was standing next to her, holding her steady. I stood back watching. Peaches remained in the doorway.

"Son," Mama called to him softly. She paused. Little Man didn't move. She turned her head and sobbed.

"It's alright," Reverend Jacobs said, trying to console her. "Just remember, God is able."

"Reverend," Mama said, cocking her head and looking beseechingly into Reverend Jacobs's face. "You heard what the doctor said. He said it's bad. He said he could die."

"It doesn't matter what he said," Reverend Jacobs told her. "It only matters what God says."

I entered the room and moved closer to the bed.

Mama whirled and looked at me with hate-filled eyes. "Guess you satisfied now," she said, spewing hot hate.

"What!" I said, staring at her with infuriated eyes. "You think I wanted this to happen?"

"Don't matter what you wanted," she said. "He lying here, ain't he?"

"I didn't shoot him!" I said. "Or did you forget?"

"You didn't pull the trigger," she said, "but you're responsible."

"Please," Reverend Jacobs said. "This isn't helping anything." He turned and gazed at Little Man. "Let's just pray he makes it through this."

"Be better for him if he don't," Mama echoed her earlier sentiment.

"Sister Reid!" Reverend Jacobs said. "Don't talk like that. He may be able to hear you."

"She don't care," I said, feeling my emotions surge. "She don't care about nobody but herself."

"Now is not the time for this," Reverend Jacobs said. "Now is the time to think about Curtis."

"I am thinking about him," I said.

"Had you been thinking about him, you wouldn't have interfered," Mama said. "You would have—"

"I did what I thought was best," I said.

"Everybody calm down," Reverend Jacobs said forcefully. "Everybody calm down right now."

"Why did you have to come back here?" Mama wailed. Then she bent forward in a fit of weeping. "Why didn't you stay where you were? Oh, God, why did he have to get shot? Why couldn't it have been you?" she said for the second time.

"Sister, Reid!" Reverend said, shocked. "You don't mean that."

"Yes, I do," she said. "God knows I do."

Suddenly, a nurse entered the room.

"You all need to keep it down," she said in a strong, forceful voice. "Or else I'm going to have to ask you to leave."

"I'll leave," Mama sobbed. "I can't stand seeing him like this anyway. I just can't."

She turned and walked out. I followed her back to the waiting room.

"What did I ever do to you?"

"Just leave me be," she said.

"Why do you hate me so?"

"She doesn't hate you, son," Reverend Jacobs said, entering the room. "That's just fear talking. That's all."

"When I was locked down, I needed you," I said. "But you wasn't there. I reached out to you, but you turned your back on me. And that hurt me more than you will ever know. But you know what? I survived. A stranger showed me more compassion than my own mother. How do you think that made me feel?"

"I did the best I could."

"No, you didn't," I said. "When they sent Daddy away, you quit trying."

"That's not true."

"It is true. And you know it. You quit trying because every time you looked at me, you saw Daddy—admit it!"

She looked at me but didn't answer.

"Admit it!"

Suddenly, she began to weep again.

"Son, that's enough!" Reverend Jacobs said.

"Admit it!" I said again.

"He hurt me," she wailed.

"What?" I said.

"Your daddy hurt me!"

"That's no excuse."

"I gave up everything for him," she sobbed. "I gave up my family, my friends, my life. But that wasn't enough. He had to take my future, and I hated him for it. He took everything. When he killed that white man, he killed everything this family was supposed to be."

"It was an accident!" I shouted.

"No," she said. "It was stupid."

"He was standing up for himself."

"He should have walked away."

"Maybe he got tired of walking away," I said. "Maybe he thought about you and his children and the world we were living in and decided to take a stand. Maybe he decided that he was a man and that that white man was going to respect him as such. Maybe that was his gift to us. Maybe he was teaching us that nothing is more important than respect. He's in a cage now, doing life without the possibility of parole, because he demanded something worth dying for—respect. And I'm proud of him for that."

"You don't know what you're talking about."

"Before they sent him to Angola, he talked to me."

"What!"

"I went to see him."

"You went to see him?"

"Yes, ma'am, I did."

"How?"

"Aunt Peggy took me."

"Peggy!"

"I know you told me to stay away from him, but I went to that jail, anyway, and I saw my daddy. And he was a man. He wasn't acting scared, or like he was less than human. He just looked at me through those bars and told me that he loved me and that he was sorry things had to be this way and that he wanted me to help take care of you and that baby that was in your stomach. He told me that at that moment, I was a man. I wasn't but five years old, and he told me I was a man. And I wasn't scared anymore, because my daddy told me I was a man."

There was silence.

"That's why I did what I did. Maybe I was wrong—no, I was wrong, but I was trying to take responsibility for a child when I was just a child myself. Little Man was green, and he was naïve, and I hated the way you babied him, knowing where we lived and how we lived. But you didn't care. You just pretended that we weren't living in the projects and that our reality wasn't real at all."

"I did the best I could."

"No, you didn't!" I shouted.

"I did!"

"My brother had a right to know his daddy," I said. "And Daddy had a right to know his child."

"Your daddy had a responsibility," she said. "And he should have lived up to it."

"So you punished us because you were mad at him."

"I didn't punish anybody," she said.

"What if Little Man don't make it?" I said. "What if this is all the time he has left? It ain't right. It ain't right at all."

"I did the best I could," she said for the third time.

"You should have supported him," I said. "You should have tried to get him out. But you never thought about him. And you never thought about us. You just thought about yourself."

"Don't go blaming me for this."

"Who else am I supposed to blame?"

"I lost my husband."

"We lost our daddy," I said. "That boy needed to know his daddy."

"He had Sonny."

"Sonny ain't his daddy," I said. "Just because you love Sonny don't mean that Sonny loves us."

"Sonny was good to him."

"I tried to make excuses for you," I said. "For a long time, I even blamed myself. But in prison, I saw you for what you are. What kind of mother turns her back on her own child?"

"My life has been hard," she said.

"Because you made it that way."

"You just a child," she said. "You don't know what I've been through."

"See?" I said. "There you go again. Always a victim, always casting blame and never accepting responsibility. Has anything ever been your fault?"

"Son," Reverend Jacobs said. "That's your mama."

"Has it?" I shouted, ignoring him.

"Please!" he said. "That's your mother."

"Then why doesn't she act like it?"

"Son," Reverend Jacobs called to me again. "May I speak to you in the hallway?"

I looked at him and then at Mama.

"I'm gone," I said, looking at her with teary eyes. "I'm just wasting my time here. You never cared and you never will."

I walked out of the room and into the hallway. Peaches remained by the doorway. I looked at her. She was crying too.

26

I stumbled out into the hallway, feeling the veins pulsating on either side of my temple. I grabbed my head and slowly slid to the floor. No, it could not end like this, for if it did, nothing about my life would make sense—my birth, Stanley's death, Mr. Henry's words, nothing. Behind me, I heard footsteps in the hallway. I looked up and saw Reverend Jacobs coming toward me. He knelt in front of me and placed his hand on my knee. My knees were trembling.

"Son," he said. "I know you're hurting. But you need to calm down. Both of you do."

Inside of me, a voice told me I was dreaming. I raised my head and looked around. No, I wasn't dreaming. This was real—Peaches, Reverend Jacobs, the hospital, the chief, Little Man, my mother. I shook my head again. No, this could not be. Suddenly, the old, hot sensation came back to me, and I felt a strong desire to rise and flee this place. Why stay here? There was nothing I could do except wait for Little Man's breathing to cease and his heart to stop. No, I would not do that. I would not sit back and watch death take him from me. I rose to my feet. Inside the room, I heard my mother's voice again, looming loud and shrill.

"My God in heaven," she wailed. "Please have mercy on me!"

I turned toward the room, secretly wishing that she would shut up. But she did not. Over and over again she pleaded. No, I could not stay here and be tormented by the sound of her agonizing voice. I closed my eyes, trying to think. She cried out and opened them again. *She's losing it,* I thought. I stepped away from the wall.

"I'm leaving," I said.

I turned to leave. I felt Reverend Jacobs's hand tugging on the sleeve of my shirt. I pulled away. No, I would not stay here. I couldn't.

"Son," he said, grabbing me again. "Listen to me!"

"No," I said, struggling to free myself. "I can't stay here."

"Brother Reid!"

"No," I shouted. "He's going to die. My God, he's going to die."

I pulled against him again. Suddenly, Reverend Jacobs pinned me against the wall.

"Oh, my God!" I heard Peaches say. She was still lingering near the doorway.

"Let me go!" I shouted.

"Brother Reid," he yelled. "Get a hold of yourself."

"Why didn't I let him go?" I moaned.

"This is not your fault," he said.

"He's going to die," I wailed again.

"No," he said. "You can't think like that."

"I should have let him go," I said.

"Son, listen to me. You did the right thing."

"God, please, don't let him die."

"Son, we can still help Curtis, but you have to calm down first."

"It's too late."

"No," he said. "It's not too late."

Inside the room, I heard Mama wail again. I froze, then stared in the direction of her voice.

"She should have listened to me," I said.

"You can't worry about that now."

"But if she had—"

"Son, don't you understand? We can still help Curtis. But we can't do it fighting each other. Now, I'm praying he gets better. But when he does, the chief is determined to ship him off to the pen. Now, we can stop him if we focus. Don't you understand that?"

I nodded.

"Good," he said. "Now, let's concentrate on that and let God take care of Curtis. Okay?"

I nodded again. Yes, the reverend was right. We needed to help Little Man. None of the other stuff mattered now.

I turned and faced him. "Where do we begin?" I asked.

He didn't answer immediately. Instead, he furrowed his brow and looked off again, concentrating.

"There has to be someone who knows the truth," he finally said.

"Yeah," I said, "but who?"

He didn't answer. Suddenly, I thought of something.

"What about the guy they caught?" I blurted.

"Wilson?" Reverend Jacobs said, lowering his eyes and looking directly at me.

"Yes, sir," I said. "He knows the truth."

"But he won't talk," he said. "I've tried."

"What about the girl?" I asked, my mind quickly sorting through other possibilities. "Will she talk?"

"No," he said. "I tried her too. She wouldn't say a word."

"Alright," I said, going back to my original suggestion. "Then Wilson is the key. Let's go see him."

"He won't talk to us," the reverend said again. "Don't you understand that? I've tried."

"Let's try again."

"That's a waste of time, and we don't have time to waste."

Behind me, I heard Mama cry out again. I looked toward the door and then back at Reverend Jacobs. Then I thought of something else. What if Wilson's mother was like my mother? What if she was fed up with him? Yes, that was it. Maybe she would help us.

"Wilson's mother," I said. "Let's talk to his mother."

"His mother?" Reverend said, shocked.

"Yes," I said. "Maybe she can convince him to talk to us."

"Why would she do that?"

"Because she's a mother," I said. "And deep down, every mother wants to know the truth about her child."

"I don't know."

"What do we have to lose?"

He paused. I could tell he didn't like the idea.

"Nothing," he said after a moment of reflection.

"Then let's go talk to her," I said. Then I turned and looked toward the waiting room. I could hear Mama crying. As I listened to her, my mind drifted to Little Man. *If God lets him live, I'm going to make sure he talks to Daddy.* I paused and looked at Reverend Jacobs.

"Little Man needs to know why Daddy never reached out to him," I said. "He needs to be whole."

"He did . . ." Reverend Jacobs said, his voice trailing off.

"Excuse me?" I said. My voice was slightly elevated.

"His daddy wrote him," Reverend Jacobs said. "He wrote both of you."

Suddenly my mouth fell open. I stared at him, shocked.

"Who told you that?" I asked, dumbfounded.

"Your mother."

"No!" I said.

"It's true," he mumbled.

Overcome by hot rage, I shouted, "Why didn't she tell us?"

"She thought it was best not to."

"She had no right."

"You were minors," Reverend Jacobs said. "And he was a convict. She was trying to protect you. But over the years, she's been looking for the right time to tell you. She just hasn't been able to. She feels bad about what she's done, and under the circumstances, I don't think she would mind me telling you."

"Are you defending her?"

"No," he said. "But I am saying she had her reasons."

"Where are the letters?"

"I don't know."

"Did she destroy them?"

"No," he said. "She kept them."

"She told you that?"

"Yes," he said. "She told me."

Anger overtook me. "I'm going in there," I said, whirling to leave.

"No," he said, grabbing my arm. "Now is not the time."

Inside the room, I heard Mama wail again.

"How could she?" I asked.

"She had her reasons," Reverend Jacobs said again.

"I would love to hear them," I said.

"In due time, I'm sure you will," he said. "But right now, we need to go see Mrs. Wilson, and after all of this is over, maybe the three of you can sit down and talk."

I said good-bye to Peaches, and I waited while Reverend Jacobs told Mama we were leaving. Then I followed him down the hall and out of the building. Soon, we were sitting in his car, heading out of the parking lot.

27

For a long time, after we had left, I said nothing. Mentally, I was in a strange place. I did not know what to think, nor was I certain of what to do, and that uncertainty filled me with uneasiness. I closed my eyes and leaned back against the seat, seeing before me an image of Little Man's unconscious body lying prone on the narrow white hospital bed. Why did Reggie have to shoot? If he hadn't, none of this would have happened.

I opened my eyes and looked at the tiny clock mounted in the dashboard. It was fifteen minutes after ten. Next to me, I could hear Reverend Jacobs breathing in and out as he guided the car through the narrow streets of Brownsville. We crossed the tracks into the black neighborhood. Yes, we had made it to the south side of town. In a few minutes, we would know if Mrs. Wilson would help us. He stopped the car on the shoulder before an old run-down trailer. The trailer loomed just off the highway—isolated and silent. I paused, looking. The lights were on, and through the thin curtains, I could see the silhouette of someone sitting in a chair next to what appeared to be the living room window. I got out of the car and followed Reverend Jacobs to the front steps. He raised his hand and knocked on the door. A moment later, the door creaked open and a middle-aged woman appeared. In the dim glare of the full moon, I saw her squint and stare. She seemed to be peering hard, trying to make out our faces.

"Good evening, Mrs. Wilson," Reverend Jacobs spoke first.

"Evening, Reverend," she said, then looked at me.

"This is Mr. Reid," Reverend Jacobs introduced me. I nodded and the reverend continued. "We would like to speak to you if you have a minute."

"About what?" she asked.

"Your son," he told her.

"My son!" she exclaimed.

"Yes, ma'am," he said.

Suddenly, her eyes narrowed. "Did something happen? Is he alright?"

"No," Reverend Jacobs said. "Nothing happened."

"Then what's this all about?"

"He testified against my brother," I said, inserting myself into the conversation. Suddenly, she snapped her head around.

"Your brother!"

"Yes, ma'am," I said. "My brother."

She paused, looking me over again.

"What's your name again?"

"D'Ray," I said. "D'Ray Reid."

"Reid," she said. Suddenly, her expression changed. "I don't have anything to say to you."

"Ma'am, this is important," Reverend Jacobs said.

"Important to who?"

"To us," I said.

"I ain't got nothing to say," she said again.

"Mrs. Wilson," Reverend Jacobs said softly. "I know this may be asking a lot, but I would like for you to ask your son to see us."

"And why would I do that?"

"Because we need to know the truth."

"He told the truth."

"No, ma'am," Reverend Jacobs said. "I believed he lied."

"No offense, Reverend, but I don't really care what you believe."

"You should," I said. "An innocent man is in jail."

"Says who?"

"Says me."

"My boy said your brother was with him and I believe him."

"Were they friends?" I asked her.

"Who?"

"Your son and my brother."

"I don't know," she said.

"Well, had you ever seen them together before?"

"No, I hadn't."

"Had you ever seen Curtis before?"

"No."

"Then that doesn't make sense to me," I said.

"What are you talking about?" she asked, irritated.

"If they were close enough to pull a job together, don't you think you would know him? I mean, you're his mother. It stands to reason that you would know who your child is hanging out with."

"I work two full-time jobs," she said. "Besides, Donald Wayne is a grown man. He came and went as he pleased."

"He's twenty," I said.

"Like I said, he's a grown man."

"Where's his father?"

"What's it to you?"

"Just curious," I said.

"He's in San Quentin," Reverend Jacobs answered for her.

"Sorry to hear that," I said.

"Don't be," she said. "It's where he belongs."

"Lots of people belong there," I said, "but not my brother. He's innocent."

"I don't know what to tell you," she said.

"You don't have to tell me anything," I said. "Just tell your son to talk to us."

"He has his own mind," she said. "And he talks to who he wants to. Besides, what's done is done."

"It doesn't have to be."

She looked at me, then at Reverend Jacobs.

"Reverend, I'm busy," she said. "Now, if there's nothing else, please excuse me." She stepped back to close the door, but I stopped her.

"Curtis was shot last night," I said. "Did you know that?"

"No," she said, "I didn't."

"The doctor said he might not make it."

"That's too bad," she said matter-of-factly.

"I'd like to clear his name before he dies."

"Good luck." She was blunt.

"You could help me," I said.

"It's none of my business."

"Ask your son to speak to us."

"I can't do that."

"Please," I said. "I'm begging you."

"My son is getting out in a few months," she said. "Why should he ruin his life?"

"I don't want to ruin his life," I said. "I just want to talk to him."

"Can't help you."

"Would you just—"

"Reverend," she said, interrupting me. "I'm busy."

"Okay," he said. "Thank you for your time."

"But, ma'am," I said.

She looked at me, then closed the door. I glanced at Reverend Jacobs, but he wasn't looking at me. He was already peering at the road. I paused, feeling the anxiousness return. I tilted my head back and gazed at the beautiful, starlit sky. "Oh, God," I mumbled. "Please help us." Then I followed Reverend Jacobs back to his car.

28

As we headed back to the hospital, I sat stone-still, listening to the soft, steady hum of Reverend Jacobs's Cadillac, wondering, *What now?* Then, as we approached Kojak's Place, an image flashed before my eyes, one in which I did not at first understand. Then it came to me, suddenly, forcefully. The answer to this dilemma was not to be found among those who lived up on the hill. No, it was to be found in the streets among those who lived beyond the law. I stared at the tiny little juke joint. It was Friday night, and hoards of cars were parked along the street. I leaned forward, smiling. Yes, this was it.

"Let me out," I said.

Reverend Jacobs looked at me and frowned. "Here?"

"Yes, sir."

"Why?" he asked, confused.

"I need to do something."

He hesitated. Then he looked at the rickety building before looking back at me. I could tell that he did not like the idea of stopping in front of this place.

"Are you sure?"

"I'm sure," I said.

He guided the car off the road and pulled to a stop on the

shoulder in front of Kojak's Place. I got out, leaned against the door, and peered at him through the window.

"If it's not too late, I'll meet you at the hospital when I'm done."

"Okay," he said, and pulled off.

I watched him for a moment. When he was out of sight, I hurried across the parking lot and made my way up the wooden steps. I pushed the door open and stood in the doorway. I looked around the room. My eyes fell on the old black man standing behind the bar. I approached the bar. His back was to me.

"Mr. Walter," I said.

"What's left of him," he said. He turned and looked at me. Suddenly, he recognized me. "Outlaw! Is that you?"

"Yes, sir," I said. "It's me."

Walter smiled, then hurried from behind the bar. When he was close, he grabbed me with both arms.

"Boy, look at you," he said, laughing as he talked. "Ain't you a sight for sore eyes?" He paused and looked at me. "You back or just visiting?"

"I'm back," I said.

"Well, welcome home."

"Thanks."

"Come on," he said, turning toward an empty table. "Take a load off."

I pulled out a chair and flopped down on it. In the distance, I heard a tune blaring over the jukebox. A man and a woman had been sitting. They rose and made their way to the dance floor. I was watching them dance when I heard Walter's voice again. He removed a towel from his back pocket and began wiping the top of the table.

"Seen any of the fellas yet?"

"Couple of 'em," I said.

"Know they were glad to see you."

"They were," I said.

"Yeah," he said. "Ain't nothing like seeing old friends." He stuffed the towel back in one pocket and removed a tiny pad from the other. Then he retrieved a pencil from behind his ear. "Can I get you anything?"

"Nah," I said. "Just some information."

"What kind of information?"

"Do you know a cat named Donald Wayne Wilson?"

"Donald Wayne!" He paused and looked at me. "Yeah," he said. "I know him."

"What can you tell me about him?"

"Ain't much to tell," he said. "Nigger used to come in here every Tuesday night. He always sat at that far table there. He always ate the same meal, he always ordered the same drink, and he always asked for the same girl."

"Is that right?"

"Yeah," he said, smiling. "He had this thing for a little yellow number from Eudora named Phoebe."

"Phoebe."

"Yeah."

"Is she here?"

"Nah," he said, then looked at the clock. "But she will be in the next fifteen or twenty minutes."

"When she comes in, tell her I would like to talk to her."

"Will do," he said.

"Thanks."

A quiet moment passed; then he looked toward the bar again. "Sure I can't get you anything?"

"I'm sure," I said.

"Alright," he said, "if you change your mind, holler." He turned as if to leave, but then curiosity seemed to get the best of him. "Why you interested in Donald Wayne anyway?" he asked, quickly adding, "If you don't mind me asking."

"He testified against my brother."

"That's right," Walter said, snapping his fingers. "He sho' did."

"I've been looking into the situation for the last day or two. It looks like he lied. I just need to know why."

"You should talk to your boy," Walter advised.

"Who?" I asked.

"Beggar Man."

"Beggar Man!" I said.

"Yeah, he knows Donald Wayne better than I do. They used to drive tractors together for Ole Man Watson."

"Is that right?"

"Yeah," Walter said, nodding as he spoke. "But that was a long time ago."

"Where is he now?"

"Beggar Man?"

"Yeah."

"He's locked up."

"What?"

"Yeah, he's in Hunts."

"I didn't know that."

"Oh, he's been locked up for a couple of years now."

"What happened?"

"He got in a fight. I mean a terrible fight. As a matter of fact, it happened right about where you're sitting. He cut somebody. Cut 'em real bad. Nigger he cut almost died. They locked Beggar Man up that night. He ain't been home since."

"That's too bad," I said.

"Well, that's life in Brownsville," he said. "But I don't have to tell you. You grew up around here."

"When is he getting out?"

"In a couple of months," Walter said. Suddenly, he smiled again. "Nigger called here last week, said he's counting down the days."

"I know the feeling," I said.

"Go talk to him," Walter said. "Maybe he can tell you something."

"I will," I said.

Then I looked at the clock. Walter saw me and chuckled.

"She'll be here in a minute. In the meantime, let me get you a beer. It's on the house."

"Alright," I said. "I sure appreciate it."

He left, and the two gentlemen at the adjacent table turned and looked at me.

"Excuse me," one of them said. "But I couldn't help over-hearing your conversation." He paused and squinted. "Are you Curtis Reid's brother?"

"I am," I said.

"How is he?"

"He's hanging on."

"Well, I'm glad to hear that," he said. "He's a good boy, and he sho' didn't deserve what happened to him."

"You know him?" I asked.

"I know him," the man said. "And I admire what I know." He smiled and extended his hand. "The name's Jenkins," he said. "Bobby Jenkins."

"I'm D'Ray," I said.

"Pleased to meet you, D'Ray."

"Likewise," I said.

We shook hands. Then I saw Mr. Jenkins staring at me.

"I came along with your granddaddy," he said. "He and I used to work in the field together."

"Is that right?"

"Yeah," he said, smiling. "He was a good man."

"That's what I hear," I said. "But I didn't really know Granddaddy. He died when I was young."

"Well, take my word for it," Jenkins said. "He was a class act, a real community man. And that brother of yours is a lot like him. Looks like he inherited your granddaddy's love for the community."

"He inherited it," the man sitting next to him said. "But in my opinion, he would have been better off if he hadn't."

"Well, now, I don't agree with that," Jenkins said. "When

I was young, our trouble was white folks. Now it's black folks
who don't give a flying flip about nothing. Curtis was different. He was in the community working. He was always trying
to help somebody. I'm telling you that boy was making a difference."

"And look where it got him," the second man said. "He
spent all of that time trying to help the community, and all it
did was get him sent to the pen."

"Well, that don't take away from what he was trying to
do," Jenkins said.

"Might not take away from it," he said, "but I bet you a
beer it got something to do with his troubles."

"How you figure?" Jenkins asked.

"He in jail, ain't he? At least he was before he escaped."

"One thing ain't got nothing to do with the other."

"So you say."

"Believe me when I tell you, this thing is upside down."

"What are you talking about?"

"Just hear what I'm telling you."

"You ain't telling me nothing."

"Just remember it anyway."

"Remember what?"

He didn't answer. Instead, he turned his head and looked
at me. "Brother Reid, you keep looking into this thing."

"I plan to," I said.

"Good," he said. "Because I don't know exactly what
happened, but I do know there's more to it than what they
telling. Now, that Donald Wayne, he's a lowlife, and crime is
right up his alley. But your brother ain't the kind of fellow to
go around breaking into folks' houses. You look low and you
look high. Sooner or later, you'll get to the bottom of this."

Walter returned with my drink and placed it on the table.
"That's Phoebe over there," he said, motioning toward the
door. "Now, if I were you, I would catch her before she gets
busy."

"Yeah," I said, excusing myself. "I think I'll do that."

I pushed from the table and made my way across the room. Phoebe was standing next to the jukebox. Her back was to me.

"Phoebe," I called to her.

"Yeah," she said, turning and looking at me.

"Can I talk to you for a minute?" I asked her.

"Talk?" she said.

"Yeah," I said. "Talk."

"Mister, I'm not really in the talking business."

"I understand," I said. "But I just need a few minutes of your time."

"My time ain't cheap," she said.

"I understand," I said. "Now, can we go someplace private?"

"Follow me," she said.

She led me out of the room, through a door, and down a short hall. She stopped before a room on the left side of the hallway. She pushed the door open, and I followed her inside.

"Now, what do you want to talk about?" she asked, sitting on the bed and crossing her legs.

"Donald Wayne Wilson," I said.

Suddenly her body became tense. "Are you a cop?"

"No," I said.

"Then why are you interested in Donald Wayne?"

"Not interested in him," I said. "I'm interested in something he said."

"And what's that?"

"That my brother was with him when he broke into that woman's house."

"Don't know anything about it," she said.

"He never talked to you about that night?"

"He didn't come to me for talk. Like I said, I'm not in the talking business."

"Who did he hang out with?"

"Don't know," she said. "That's none of my business."

"Does he have any friends?"

"You have to ask him."

"What about a girlfriend?"

"None of my business."

"He never mentioned anyone?"

"Why would he?"

"Did he do drugs?"

"Not around me, he didn't."

"So he wasn't stealing to support a drug habit."

"Don't know nothing about his habits," she said. "He came to me for sex. I never saw him do drugs, and I never did drugs with him."

"I don't get it."

"I don't know what to tell you," she said, "except that I'm on the clock. And time is money."

"You're going to get your money," I said.

"It's a shame to spend good money on talk," she said seductively. "You sure I can't do anything else for you?"

"Did he live alone?" I ignored her question.

She sighed. I could tell she was getting agitated.

"He lived with his mother."

"Do you know any other person he hung out with besides her?"

"No, I don't," she said. "As far as I could tell, he was a loner."

"Then why would he lie?"

"Mister," she said, agitated. "It's just who he is."

"Has to be more to it than that," I said.

"I don't know what to tell you."

"Are you sure he never said anything about this?"

"Look!" she said, cutting me off. "I need to go to work. I got rent to pay."

"Alright," I said. I rose, reached in my pocket, removed a twenty-dollar bill, and handed it to her.

"Thanks," she said.

"You're welcome," I said. Then I turned to leave.

"Hey," she said, stopping me.

"What?" I asked.

"Donald Wayne never said anything to me about that night, but one of my other johns did."

"You remember what he said?"

"Yeah."

"What?"

" 'Payback is a real mother for you.' "

"Payback!"

"That's what he said."

"What does that mean?"

"Mister, I don't know."

"Alright," I said. I walked out. When I made it back to the bar, Walter was waiting for me. He had a big smile on his face.

"Guess who just called?"

"Who?"

"Beggar Man."

"You lying!"

"Nah," he said, laughing. "He was just on the phone. I told him he was gonna live a long time, because we were just talking about him."

"Man," I said, "sure wish I could have talked to him."

"Hey, I'm sorry," Walter said. "But when I told him you were with Phoebe, he said don't bother you."

"Did you tell him about Little Man?"

"Yeah, I told him."

"What did he say?"

"He said he has something to tell you. But what he got to tell you he can't say over the phone. He said tomorrow is visiting day, and if you can come down, what he got to say is worth the drive."

"He said that?"

"Yeah, he said it's about Donald Wayne."

"Really!"

"That's what he said."

"If he calls back, tell him I'll be there."

"Will do," he said.

I looked at the clock. It was almost eleven.

"I'm out of here," I said.

"Alright," Walter said. "It's good to have you back."

I nodded, then made my way outside. Now that I was alone, I felt the awful strain of having Little Man's fate in my hands. Suddenly, an image of him flashed before my eyes, and I fought against the emotions it stirred within me. Yes, he had given up and he had done so because, like my mother, he believed that I had taken from him his last opportunity to be free. I had betrayed him. Me—the brother whom he trusted with his life had betrayed him. Suddenly, my heart ached. What if I was wrong? What if he died because of my decision? No, I could not let that happen. I wouldn't. Spurred on by a new sense of purpose, I descended the steps, staring determinedly ahead. No, he would not die. He would live and he would be free. I would see to that.

29

At 6:00 the next morning, I headed to Baton Rouge, driving well over the speed limit, clutching the wheel and staring mindlessly ahead as the truck gobbled up mile after mile of desolate highway. Exactly four hours after my departure, I arrived at Hunts Penitentiary. I passed through the ominous-looking gates complete with concerting wire and armed guards, and entered the facility. Once inside the building, I was searched and escorted to a small visitation room just beyond the entrance. A few minutes later, the door opened and Beggar Man walked in, flanked by two prison guards. He approached me and we embraced.

"It's been a long time," he said. His voice was low and his body was rigid.

"Too long," I told him.

He pulled out a chair and sat on one side of the table; I sat on the other. I glanced at him, and then looked beyond him. There was a second officer in the room with us. He was standing against the far wall. I stared at him for a moment, then straightened in my seat and looked at Beggar Man again. He was sitting with his hands folded on the table in front of him.

"Glad you could come," he said.

"Walter said it was important."

"It is," he said. He paused and looked at the guard, and when he was certain the guard wasn't listening, he continued. "Walter said you're looking into Little Man's case."

"I am," I said.

"Maybe I can help you out."

"How?"

"I have some information," he said.

I leaned forward. "What kind of information?" I asked, looking at him with intense eyes.

"Information that proves Curtis is innocent."

"What!" I said, louder than intended. The officer standing next to the door looked at me, and I quickly averted my eyes. I hesitated, then settled back in my seat. "How do you know he's innocent?"

"Donald Wayne told me."

"You lying!"

"No," he said. "Nigger just up and confessed to me. I couldn't believe it. But he did."

"I don't understand."

"I knew the nigger back in Brownsville. We used to work together."

"Yeah," I said, nodding. "Walter told me."

"Well, after his conviction, they sent him down here to do his time."

"Okay," I said, then waited.

"As fate would have it, they put him in the cell with me. Well, when they locked that door and left, the nigger just started talking."

"What did he say?" I asked anxiously.

"At first, he wasn't talking about nothing. You know, he was just rambling about the white man. But then he started talking about Brownsville, and before I knew it, the fool started talking about his case."

"You joking!"

"No! He told me it didn't go down like they said. He told me he said what he said to the police because he had to do what he had to do."

"What does that mean?"

"I don't know. The nigger was just talking crazy. So I told him I didn't know what he was talking about. And he just burst out and said he felt bad for Little Man."

"You lying."

"No," Beggar Man said. "I'm telling it to you just the way he told it to me. He said he didn't even know Little Man and that he had never even seen him before they arrested him."

"Then why did he lie?"

"He said his lawyer told him to."

"His lawyer!"

"Yeah, he had a white lawyer from the public defender's office. And he said he told his lawyer that he was going to confess to the whole thing. But his lawyer told him not to. His lawyer told him that the cops had arrested his accomplice, and they were building a case against him. The prosecutor was willing to cut him a deal if he would agree to turn state's evidence. But when his attorney told him that the cops had arrested Little Man as his accomplice, he told his lawyer that the police had the wrong guy. But his lawyer told him that the police were certain that Little Man was the right guy and that they were willing to be very lenient with him if he would say the same. So, he did it, but he was lying. His cousin was with him that night, not Little Man. His cousin hit that woman."

"He said that."

"Yeah."

"Did he tell you his cousin's name?"

"Yeah, his name's Oscar."

"I don't get," I said. "Why would he confess after he had already gotten away with it?"

"I don't know. At first, I figured the nigger was trying to

con me. Then I found out he had never been to the pen before. He had been to jail but not the pen. So, all I can figure is
that he was trying to get on my good side—you know, hoping I would look out for him, seeing how we were the only
two cats in here from Brownsville."

I peered over my shoulder, then back at Beggar Man. "It's
over," I said. "It's really over."

"No," he said. "Unfortunately it's not."

"But he confessed."

"It's not that simple."

"Why not?"

"He changed his story."

"What!"

"A couple of days after he confessed to me, I went to the
warden, and I told him what Donald Wayne had told me. The
warden told me that he would look into it. A day or two
passed, and then the warden told me that Donald Wayne
changed his story. He said that Donald Wayne told him that I
had threatened him."

"Threatened him?"

"Yeah, but get this. The warden also told me that Donald
Wayne told him that Little Man was a friend of mine and that
I had said I was going to kill Donald Wayne for ratting Little
Man out unless he changed his original story. So, Donald
Wayne changed it, saying that his cousin was with him that
night, not Little Man. But he told the warden he only said
that because I forced him to."

"And they believed him?"

"They believed him."

"Then what happened?"

"Well, the warden called me into his office and told me
that if I didn't drop the matter, he would be forced to file additional charges against me for threatening to kill another in-
mate. I agreed and a day or two later, they moved Donald

Wayne to another prison near Alexandria. They tell me the
nigger is doing easy time."

"Why do you think he changed his story?"

"I don't know."

"You think somebody got to him?"

"Maybe."

"Who?"

"I don't know."

I leaned back and let out a deep sigh. "Why would anyone want to frame Little Man?"

"I don't know that either," Beggar Man said. "But if you
find the answer to that question, I have a funny feeling that
this whole thing will make sense."

"I need to go see him," I said.

"Who?"

"Donald Wayne."

"That's a waste of time."

"Why?"

"He ain't gonna talk."

"I got to do something," I said.

"Go talk to my sister," Beggar Man said.

"Marilyn?"

"Yeah."

"Why?"

"Because this is a small world," he said. "And she can help
you get to where you need to be."

"I don't get it," I said.

"She's dating that bastard," he said angrily.

"Donald Wayne?" I asked, guessing.

"No," he said. "His cousin."

"You got to be joking."

"I wish I was."

"Have you talked to her?"

He shook his head.

"Does she know that Little Man is doing her boyfriend's time?"

"No," he said, "at least not that I know of."

"Is she still in Brownsville?"

"Yeah," he said. "She's staying in Mama's house."

I pushed away from the table to leave, but before I could, he stopped me. "D'Ray," he called to me.

"Yeah," I said.

"That nigger knows something," he said. "Don't let him jive you."

"I won't," I said. I rose to leave, then stopped. "You need anything?"

"Nah," he said. "I'm cool."

"Alright," I said. "See you in a couple of months."

"Right," he said.

Then I left.

30

It was a little after three when I made it to Marilyn's house. Emotionally, I was drained. Yet, for the first time in five days, I was actually hopeful. When I pulled into her yard, she was sitting on the porch. A man was sitting next to her. I got out and started toward them. When I reached the porch, Marilyn looked at me and smiled.

"D'Ray!"

"Yeah," I said. "It's me." I mounted the steps and greeted her with a hug. The man instantly rose and approached me. He seemed nervous.

"This is Oscar," she said.

"Oscar," I said.

He nodded and we shook hands; then I turned to Marilyn again.

"Did Beggar Man call you?"

"Yeah," she said. "He called this morning."

"Did he tell you we talked?"

"Yeah," she said again.

"Did he tell you what we talked about?"

"He told me," she said. "And I told Oscar. That's why he's here."

"Donald Wayne's lying," Oscar said, with no prompting

from me. "I didn't break in that house with him that night. I swear."

"Why would he lie on you?"

"Because he blames me for what happened, that's why."

"What are you talking about?"

"He said if I would have helped him that night, he wouldn't have gotten caught."

"He told you that?"

"No, he didn't tell me. He told one of our homeboys, and our homeboy told me."

"Did he ever say who was really with him?"

"He didn't have to. I already knew."

"What?" I said, shocked.

"I saw him."

"You saw him?" I said, stunned.

"Yeah," he said, nodding. "He walked up just as Donald Wayne was trying to talk me into pulling that job with him."

"Who is he?"

"I don't know his name," he said.

"Nigger, you're trying to hustle me," I said. "Aren't you?"

"No," he said. "I swear. I saw him. He was a kid, some strung-out kid trying to buy some reefer."

"What do you mean by kid?"

"Just what I said—he was a kid. He could have been thir-teen or fourteen, but no older."

"That doesn't make any sense," I said. "Little Man was nineteen at the time of the crime. How could a witness mis-take him for a thirteen-year-old?"

"I don't know," he said. "But this kid was thirteen or four-teen."

"How old are you?" I asked.

"I'm twenty," Oscar said.

"The same age as Little Man," I said.

He didn't answer.

"Had you ever seen this kid before?"

"No," he said. "I hadn't."

"Well, do you at least remember what he looks like?"

"Yeah, he was kind of thin—I would say he was about five foot six. He had short wavy black hair, light brown skin, and he was wearing a pair of faded blue jeans and a red T-shirt."

"Are you sure about this?"

"I'm positive," he said. "I was there. I saw him."

He paused but I didn't answer. Instead, I stood staring at him with eyes indicating disbelief.

"I'm not lying," he said. "Now, I didn't know the dude, but Donald Wayne did. I could tell by the way the two of them talked."

"They talked?"

"Actually, they argued."

"About what?"

"I told you," he said, becoming excited. "The kid wanted drugs. But Donald Wayne wouldn't give him any."

"So Donald Wayne was dealing drugs."

"No, he wasn't dealing. But he did have access."

"I don't understand."

"He worked for Kojak," Oscar said, trying to make me understand. "He was Kojak's pickup man."

"Pickup man?"

"Yeah," he said.

I looked at him and frowned.

"You know," he said, looking at me with serious eyes. "When the drugs came in, he picked them up and delivered them to Kojak."

"Oh, I see."

"Actually, that was his main hustle. Breaking into houses was his side hustle. That was just something he did every now and then."

"How do you know that?" I asked.

"I used to run with him."

"You did?"

"Not here," he said, clarifying himself. "Back home in Ferriday."

"So, you're telling me that you and he used to pull jobs together."

"Yeah," he said. "When we were younger, when he was staying with my auntie in Ferriday."

"Then maybe it was you," I said.

"No," he said, shaking his head violently. "It wasn't me. I swear. I was here that night. If you don't believe me, you can ask my girl."

"That's right," Marilyn said, coming to his defense. "He was with me."

"With you?" I said.

"Yes," she said. "I can vouch for that."

"Can you vouch for where he was before he was with you?" I asked her. I waited. She didn't answer.

"It wasn't me," he said. "I swear, it was a kid—a kid trying to score drugs."

"Did you tell the police?"

"No."

"Why not?"

"They wouldn't have believed me," he said. "Besides, Donald Wayne's my cousin. I wasn't going to rat him out."

"Then why are you ratting him out now?"

"I'm not ratting him out," he said. "I'm just defending myself. He's telling folks I broke into that house with him that night and that's a lie."

"Have you seen the kid since that night?" I asked, changing the subject again.

"No," he said. "I haven't."

"How convenient," I said.

"Look," he said. "I haven't seen him because I don't live in Brownsville. I live in Ferriday. I just come over here to see my lady."

"Do you know my brother?"

"No," he said. "I don't know him. But I saw his picture in the paper."

"And you're sure it wasn't him?"

"I'm positive," he said. "I'm telling you the guy who was with Donald Wayne was younger, a lot younger."

"Are you lying to me?"

"No," he said. "I'm telling the truth."

"Okay," I said. "Then I need to find that guy."

"No," Oscar said. "*We* need to find him. This is causing problems between me and my girl. She called me saying that you're a friend of the family and that if I was involved in this, I better come clear or else we're done. I need to find this guy. I need to clear my name."

"So you'll help me?"

"Yeah," he said. "I'll help you."

"If he was as young as you say," Marilyn interjected, "he was probably still in school."

"That's right," I said.

"And if he was in school," she continued, "his picture should be in the yearbook."

"Right!" I said again. Then I turned and looked at Oscar. "If you saw his picture, could you pick him out?"

"No doubt about it," he said.

"Marilyn," I said, excited. "Do you have a yearbook?"

"No . . . ," she said, her voice trailing off. "We never purchased one. We couldn't afford it."

I paused. Then I thought of something. Peaches was a teacher—she might have a yearbook. Yes, that was it.

"Oscar," I said, turning my attention to him again. "How long are you going to be in Brownsville?"

"Until tomorrow," he said.

"But we're leaving for Monroe in a few minutes," Marilyn said. "And we won't be back until late tonight."

"What time?"

"I don't know," she said. "Maybe eleven or twelve."

"Alright," I said. "I think I know where I can get a year-book. I'll see y'all when you get back." I turned to leave.

Marilyn stopped me. "Is it true?" she asked me. "Was Curtis really shot last night?"

"It's true," I said.

"How is he?" she asked.

"Not good," I said. "Not good at all."

"But he is going to make it," she said. "Isn't he?"

"I hope so," I said.

"When you see him, tell him I'm praying for him."

"Might be nice if you told him yourself," I said. "I'm sure he would appreciate it."

"Can he have visitors?"

"Yeah," I said. "He can."

"Maybe I'll stop by to see him tomorrow."

"I wish you would," I said.

"Then count on it," she said. "I'll stop by in the morning on our way to church."

I looked at Oscar. "Are you coming too?"

"Yeah," he said.

"Good," I said. "Then I'll bring the yearbook to the hospital. You can take a look at it then."

"Okay," he said.

"Good," I said again. "I'll see you in the morning." Then I turned and hurried from the porch. My excited mind was whirling.

"D'Ray," Marilyn called to me again.

"Yes," I said.

"I never thanked you," she said.

"For what?"

"What you did that day."

"What day?"

"The day you found me eating the raw potato," she said. "Don't you remember?"

"No," I said. "I don't."

"You were looking for Beggar Man, and I was home alone. When you came by, I was eating a raw white potato because it was all the food we had left in the house. And you went to the store and bought me a bag of groceries. Don't you remember?"

"Yeah," I said. "Now I remember."

"I want to thank you again."

"It was nothing," I said.

"It was something to me," she said, and her eyes began to water. "We didn't have any money, and I was so hungry."

"I'm glad I could help."

"Now it's my time to help you," she said, wiping back tears. "We're going to find the guy who was with Donald Wayne that night. I promise."

31

I sped from Marilyn's driveway, hurrying through the streets until I finally reached the street on which Peaches lived. When I arrived at Peaches's house, she was backing out of her driveway. I braked to a stop, sprang from my truck, and raced to her car. Her head was turned and she did not see me. I banged on the window. She stepped on the brake, then snapped her head around. Her eyes were wide with fright.

"My God, D'Ray!" she said, lowering the window. "What's wrong with you? You nearly scared me to death."

I didn't answer her. My mind was on the yearbook picture.

"I need a 1996 yearbook," I said, still excited.

"A yearbook?"

"Yes," I said. "Do you have one?"

"Are you crazy?" she asked, eyeing me. "You almost gave me a heart attack."

"I'm sorry," I said. "But it's important."

"What's important?"

"I talked to a man who was there that night. He saw the person who was with Donald Wayne. He said it definitely wasn't Curtis. He said it was a younger boy."

"He told you that?"

"Yes."

"And he said he actually saw him?"

"Yes," I said. Then I grabbed the handle of her car door and flung it open. She got out and I grabbed her with both hands.

"My God, Peaches," I said. "Do you realize what this means? This could all be over tomorrow."

She gasped. I looked toward her house and then back at her.

"The yearbook," I said. "Do you have one?"

"Yeah," she said. "Follow me."

I followed her into the house, waiting in the hallway near the living room door while she disappeared into the study. When she returned, she was clutching the book. I looked at it and then at her. Suddenly, my hands began to shake.

"Is that it?"

"Yes," she said, handing me the book.

I took it from her, pulling it close to my bosom, clutching it tightly. Then I thought of something. Marilyn and Oscar said they were going out of town for the night. Maybe I could catch them before they left. I turned toward the door, then stopped. No, surely they were gone by now. Suddenly, my head felt light. I stumbled and fell back against the windowsill. Peaches raced to my side. I leaned against her.

"You're exhausted," she said.

"I'm alright," I told her.

"No, you're not," she said, slipping her arm around my waist. "Come on and sit down. You need to rest."

"I can't," I said, pulling away. "I have to check on Little Man." I started toward the door.

She grabbed my hand again. "I just left him," she said. "There's no change."

"I would still like to sit with him."

"Take a nap first," she said. "Your mother is with him. So is Reverend Jacobs. So is Reggie." She looked at me again. "Now, please, lie down and rest."

"Alright," I said.

I sat on the sofa and began removing my shoes.

"I cooked some red beans and rice," she said. "You want some?"

I did not answer. I tried to recall the last time I had eaten. Yesterday . . . yes, that was it. I had not eaten since yesterday. Suddenly, the thought of food caused my stomach to rumble. The sound betrayed me and she looked at me with stern eyes.

"Lie down," she said. "I'll be back with your food."

She left the room, but I did not lie down. Instead, I sat on the sofa, facing the window, wondering if there was a picture in this book that would solve this mystery and free my brother once and for all. A thousand tons of weight had been balanced on my shoulders. But now there was hope.

Peaches returned and placed the plate on a small wooden tray, which she positioned before me. I looked at her and then at the food. My mind began to wander again.

"Eat your food," she chided, "before it gets cold."

I raised the fork of food to my mouth and took a bite. As I chewed, she didn't say anything. Instead, she stared into space like a person does when they are thinking about something.

"What is it?" I asked her.

"Something happened today," she said.

"What?"

"Curtis mumbled something."

I dropped the fork and looked at her.

"He spoke?" I said, louder than intended.

"Yes."

"What did he say?"

"Daddy," she said, barely above a whisper. "He said, 'daddy.' "

I was quiet a moment, then I rose and walked to the window. I looked out, but I wasn't seeing the barren streets of Brownsville. I was seeing Little Man. He was lying in a hospital bed dying, and yet he was not thinking about death; he was thinking about Daddy. I lifted my head and looked far up the dark, desolate road.

"Daddy wrote him," I said, and then my voice broke. "He's been writing him for years. He's been writing both of us."

"How do you know that?"

"Reverend Jacobs told me."

"My God!" she said, covering her mouth with her hand. "And how does he know?"

"Mama told him."

"What happened to the letters?"

"Mama kept them," I said. "She just put them away and never said a word to either one of us."

"That's not right," Peaches said. "That's not right at all."

"No," I said. "But that's Mama."

"Get them from her."

"I can't."

"Why not?"

"She doesn't know that I know."

"Then tell her."

"I can't," I said. "She told Reverend Jacobs in confidence. I don't want to betray him."

"Under the circumstances, I don't think he would mind," she said. "I've known the reverend for a long time. He wouldn't have told you if he didn't want it out."

"I can't," I said.

"This is not right," she said again. "What if he dies thinking his daddy didn't care about him? Would you be able to live with that?"

"I guess I would have to."

"He has a right to know."

"It's not that simple."

"Why not?"

"Even if the reverend doesn't mind, Little Man loves Mama, and he trusts her. If I tell him that she has betrayed him, it will kill him."

"So, what are you going to do?"

"Nothing I can do," I said.

She eased next to me and gave me a hug. "Why don't you rest now?"

"Alright," I said. "I think I will."

She took the tray and headed back toward the kitchen. When she left, I made my way to the sofa, lay down, closed my eyes, and fell asleep.

32

Outside, on the street, a truck rumbled past. The loud noise roused me. Startled, I snapped upright on the sofa and looked around. In the dim and silent room, my weary eyes settled on the clock. It was nearly eleven. "My God," I mumbled, swinging my legs to the floor. "I overslept." Suddenly, panic overcame me. The hospital. I needed to go to the hospital. I rose to leave, then stopped. What was I thinking? It was too late to go to the hospital. Well, I could not stay here. It would not look right. In the other room, I heard the soft steady sound of Peaches's breathing. Well, there was no point in waking her now. I would stop by tomorrow.

That decided, I eased outside and climbed into my truck, then drove back to Mama's house. When I arrived, the lights were out but the front door was unlocked. I went inside and looked around, checking the living room and the kitchen before finally knocking on Mama's bedroom door. When I was satisfied that she was not home, I went to bed, certain that she had decided to spend the night at the hospital. And though I was still exhausted, I could not sleep. I tossed and turned most of the night, rising every hour or so to check the time. When morning finally came, I was lying flat on my back, staring at the ceiling. Out of the blue, a thought occurred to me. What if Oscar did not come? What if he changed his mind? What if he was long gone by now? I threw the covers back and sat straight up in bed. Oh, what had I been thinking? I should have attempted to find him last night. I stumbled from bed and hastily dressed.

Instinct told me to hurry. I tossed the yearbook on the seat of my truck, jumped in, and tore off toward Marilyn's house. I swung onto Jackson Avenue, and when I arrived at her house, I braked to a halt in front of her driveway. I glanced around. The lights were out inside her house, and her car was gone. Panic gripped me. If they had fled, I would never forgive myself. Oh, God, how could I have been so careless? My mind began to whirl. The hospital—perhaps they were at the hospital.

I roared through streets only dimly lit by the rising sun. I turned onto Hospital Road and sailed into the parking lot, braking to a halt near the main entrance. I leaped from the car and rushed into the building. I saw a policeman lingering near the reception area. I paused and looked at him. Why was he here? Had Little Man awakened? I turned right and rushed toward the intensive care unit. I pushed through the double doors and entered the waiting room. I paused and looked about. The place was empty. I crossed the waiting room and made my way to Little Man's unit. I stopped in the doorway and looked. Reggie was sitting next to the bed holding Little Man's hand. Mama was sitting in a chair clutching a Bible, and Reverend Jacobs was staring out the window.

"Any change?" I asked.

"No change," Reverend Jacobs said, and when he did, I saw Mama bite down on her lips as if she was going to start crying again. I looked at Reggie; he still refused to look at me. I watched him for a second or two and then turned my attention back to Reverend Jacobs. He crossed the room and stopped directly before me.

"Can I talk to you?" he whispered.

I didn't respond. My mind was not on the reverend. I was concerned about Oscar. My roving eyes scanned the room. Where was he and Marilyn? They should have been here by now. Nervous energy made me fidget. Well, if they did not show up in the next minute or two, I would go look for them. I looked toward the door again. Maybe they were waiting for me outside. Perhaps it would be better if I waited for them out there. Instinctively, I turned to leave. The sound of Reverend Jacobs's voice stopped me.

"Can I?" he said.

"Sure," I mumbled, still looking around. I followed him out into the hallway.

He walked a short distance from the door and then stopped. "Did you find out anything?"

I stared at him, remembering the events of a day ago. An image of Oscar glared before me. The image excited me. I looked up the hall again and then back at the reverend.

"Yes," I said, my voice rising. "I talked to a man who was there that night. He said it wasn't Curtis who was with Donald Wayne that night. He said it was a young boy, a boy who couldn't have been any more than thirteen or fourteen years old."

"He told you that?"

"Yes, sir."

"Is he sure?"

"He said he's positive."

Reverend Jacobs hesitated again. "Where is this man?"

"I don't know. He's supposed to meet me here this morning."

"What time?"

"He just said morning."

"Well, I hope he gets here soon."

"Me too," I said.

I turned and looked far up the hall again.

"Curtis spoke yesterday," Reverend Jacobs said. "Did you know that?"

"I know," I said. "Miss Lewis told me."

"Did she also tell you that the chief came by?"

"No," I said. "She didn't."

"Well, he did," Reverend Jacobs said.

"What did he want?"

"To see if Curtis had truly spoken."

"So he knows."

"Yeah," the reverend said. "He knows. And, son, when he found out that it was true, he said something else."

"What?"

"He said that as soon as Curtis regains consciousness, he was going to have him transported to the prison hospital."

"He said that?"

"Yes."

Now I understood. The cop around the corner was waiting for Little Man to awaken. He was the chief's lookout. Fear made me look toward the door again.

"I hope your friend gets here soon," Reverend said.

Behind me, I heard footsteps in the hall. I turned and looked. It was Sonny, and he was wearing his uniform. I watched him approach us, and as I did, I felt my anger rise. He stopped before Reverend Jacobs and nodded.

"What are you doing here?" I snapped.

"The chief sent me."

"Why?"

"He wants him cuffed."

"Cuffed!"

"That's right."

"But he's in a coma."

"The chief thinks he will come out of it any day. And he's afraid that when he wakes up, he might run again."

"He won't run," Reverend Jacobs said. "I'll see to that."

"The chief wants him restrained."

"But—"

"Reverend, it's out of my hands."

I looked at him to let him know what I thought of him. But he did not look at me; instead, he started toward the room with the reverend in tow. I hesitated. Should I follow them, or should I go look for Oscar? I swallowed. No, I ought to be there. I followed them through the waiting area and back into the ICU. I watched Sonny enter the room and remove the cuffs from his belt. Mama snapped to her feet and faced him. She looked at him and then at the cuffs.

"What are you doing?" she shouted hysterically.

"My job," he said.

"You're not going to put those on him."

"Mira, I have to."

"No," she said. "I won't let you."

He started toward the bed, but she blocked him.

"Mira," he said. "Please!"

"No," she said.

Reggie stood and faced him.

"Officer," he said. "Is this necessary?"

"I'm afraid so."

"No!" Mama insisted. "I'm not going to let you put those things on him—I'm not."

"It's alright," Reverend Jacobs said, placing his arm around Mama's waist. "It's alright."

"No!" Mama babbled. "It's not alright."

"Mira, I don't like this any more than you do," Sonny said, moving next to Little Man's bed. "But I have to do what I have to do."

He raised Curtis's left arm and placed the cuff around his wrist, then snapped the other cuff to the frame of the bed. Incensed, Mama pulled from Reverend Jacobs's grasp.

"Leave him alone!"

She dashed across the room and shoved Sonny hard. He fell against the bed, sending it crashing into the wall. Instantly,

Little Man grimaced, then groaned. Stunned, Mama spun about. Little Man had opened his eyes and was staring at her.

"My Jesus!" Mama exclaimed. "He's awake—call the nurse—he's awake."

"Nurse," Reverend Jacobs shouted. "Nurse! We need a nurse."

A moment later, a nurse raced into the room. "What's going on in here?" she asked.

"He's awake!" Mama shouted again. "He's awake."

The nurse moved next to the bed. "Mr. Reid," she called to Little Man softly. "Can you hear me?"

For an answer, Little Man groaned. Instantly the nurse pressed the buzzer. Someone at the nurse's station answered.

"Yes," the voice on the other end said.

"Page Dr. Ryan," she said excitedly. "Tell him Reid has come out of his coma."

33

I moved closer to the bed. My breath became short and my eyes bulged. Little Man was awake, lying flat on his back, looking around the dimly lit room with wide, confused eyes. Reggie rushed next to me, as did Mama. Little Man opened his mouth to speak, but no sound came.

"Don't try to talk," I told him. "The doctor is coming."

Little Man hesitated for a moment, and then I saw him look at the handcuffs binding him to the bed. Panic quickened within him; he lifted his arm and yanked against the cuffs.

"Calm down," Sonny said. "Calm down before you hurt yourself."

"Where is that doctor?" I shouted, and no sooner had I spoken than I heard the sound of a deep, surly voice behind me.

"I'm here," he said.

I turned and looked. The doctor entered the room and made his way to the bed. Then he bent over Little Man.

"Son," he whispered. "Can you hear me?"

Little Man nodded. And when he did, the doctor placed the stethoscope on Little Man's chest and listened to his heartbeat. Then he removed a tiny flashlight from his front pocket and shined it in Little Man's eyes. He lowered the flashlight and looked at Little Man.

"Can you tell me your name?"

Little Man hesitated. His lips trembled. He lifted his head, and I saw him struggling to speak. *My God!* I thought. *He can't talk.* He closed his eyes and concentrated.

The doctor waited, and when Little Man said nothing, the doctor spoke again. "Son," he said. "Can you tell me your name?"

A moment passed. Little Man swallowed, then his lips parted. "C-Curtis," he mumbled. "C-Curtis R-Reid."

"Thank you, Master," I heard Reverend Jacobs praising God.

Relief swept over me. I turned my back and closed my eyes. My emotions broke. I felt my hands trembling. Then I felt Reverend Jacobs's arm around my shoulder. "God is good!" he said. "God is good!"

I opened my eyes. They were wet with tears. Across the room, I saw a dim figure emerge from the shadows and stop in the doorway. It was Marilyn and next to her was Oscar. I stumbled across the room, and when I reached them, Marilyn spoke first.

"What's wrong?"

"He's awake," I sobbed.

She raised her hands to her mouth. "Then he's okay?"

I nodded and she eased into the room, but Oscar did not follow. Instead, he lingered near the door. I stared at him. Again, panic swept over me. Now that Little Man was awake, the chief was sure to transport him. I walked over to Oscar. Suddenly, I realized something.

"The yearbook," I said. "I left it in the truck. I'll go get it."

I turned to leave, but Oscar stopped me.

"Don't bother," he said.

"Why not?" I asked.

"I don't need to see it."

"What do you mean you don't need to see it?"

"You see that guy?" he said.

"What guy?" I asked, turning and looking.

"Him," he said, pointing at Reggie.

"Yeah," I said. "What about him?"

"That's him," he said. "That's the guy who was with Donald Wayne."

"No," I said. "You're mistaken."

"Ain't no mistake about it," he said. "It's him."

I shook my head. "No," I said. "It can't be."

"It's him, I tell you. That's the guy who broke into that lady's house." Suddenly, I felt the room reeling. How could this be? I looked at Oscar and then at Reggie. I didn't know what to believe.

"What is he doing here?" Oscar asked me.

"They're friends," I said. "Best friends."

Across the room, I saw Reverend Jacobs looking at me, and I knew he was wondering if this was the person I had been waiting on. I nodded at Reverend Jacobs, asking him to come over. He quietly made his way to me.

"Tell him," I said to Oscar.

"Tell me what?"

"It was Reggie," I answered for him.

"Excuse me?"

"It was Reggie," I said again.

"Reggie!"

"Yes, sir."

"No," Reverend Jacobs said. "Couldn't be."

"I saw him," Oscar said emphatically.

"No." Reverend Jacobs shook his head. "That doesn't make sense. It doesn't make sense at all."

Suddenly, I crossed the room and grabbed Reggie by the shoulders. He whirled and faced me, with a dazed look in his eyes.

"It was you!" I shouted.

"What are you talking about?" he asked, pulling away.

"You broke into that house," I said. "Not Little Man."

"That's a lie!" Reggie yelled, recoiling and falling back against the wall.

"I saw you," Oscar hollered.

"He's lying," Reggie shouted, looking around the room with wild, roving eyes.

"Why would I lie?" Oscar asked.

"I don't know," Reggie said. "You tell me."

"I saw you," he said again. "You were wearing a red shirt and a pair of dingy blue jeans."

"I don't know what you're talking about."

"You were talking to Donald Wayne."

"You got me confused with somebody else."

"You were buying drugs."

"I've been clean for years."

"Why are you lying?"

"I'm not," he said. "You are."

"Son, just tell the truth," Reverend Jacobs advised.

"I am telling the truth."

"Everybody calm down," Sonny said.

Reggie walked over to Oscar. "What are you trying to pull?" he asked, pointing an angry finger.

"Nothing!" Oscar said.

"Then why are you saying these things?"

"Because they're true," he said.

"Stop it!" Little Man shouted.

I turned and looked. He had risen to his elbows. Reggie rushed to him and knelt down beside the bed.

"It wasn't me," he wailed. "I swear!"

"Don't lie, son," Reverend Jacobs said. "If you were involved, just tell the truth."

"I am telling the truth."

"He wouldn't lie to me," Curtis mumbled. "If he said he didn't do it, I believe him."

"I saw him with my own eyes," Oscar said.

"I don't know you," Curtis mumbled. "But I do know him. And I'm telling you he wouldn't lie to me. I would stake my life on that."

"But—"

"No buts," Little Man said.

"But what if he's right?" I said.

"He's not." Little Man dismissed me.

I paused and looked at him. "Do you know what you're saying?"

"I know," he said.

"But Oscar said he saw him."

"Two people said they saw me," Little Man said. "And I know I wasn't there."

"But—"

"No," he said. "He wouldn't lie to me, just like I wouldn't lie to you."

"Okay," Sonny said, pulling Reggie away from the bed. "Everybody calm down and let the doctor do his job."

I looked at the doctor. He had backed against the far wall. I could tell that the entire ordeal had alarmed him.

He stepped forward. "Everybody out," the doctor said. "I need to examine the patient."

Everyone left the room and made their way to the waiting room.

34

I lingered a moment. Then I tried to say something else to Little Man, but the doctor would not let me. I stifled a sob and decided to join the others in the waiting room. When I got there, Reverend Jacobs was standing next to the large bay window. His back was to me. I did not see Oscar or Marilyn, but I did see Mama and Reggie. They were huddled together in the far corner. I watched them for a moment; then I walked over to Reverend Jacobs.

"Where's Oscar?" I asked him, looking around.

"He left."

"Did you talk to him?"

"Yeah," Reverend Jacobs replied. "I talked to him."

"What did he say?"

"He just kept saying it was Reggie."

"Then Reggie's lying."

"I don't know," Reverend Jacobs said. I could hear the doubt in his voice. "Somebody's lying. I just don't know who."

From the window overlooking the parking lot, I saw the chief approaching, taking long, quick strides. He was holding his radio close to his mouth, talking to someone. I watched him enter the building. A few minutes later, I heard his footsteps in the hallway. The door swung open, and the chief appeared. He stood for a moment, taking in the room. He opened his mouth to speak, but before he had a chance to say anything, the officer I had seen lingering near the reception area burst into the room. From the redness of his face and the sound of his breathing, I could tell that he had come running.

"You called, Chief?" he said.

"Reid has regained consciousness," the chief said. "Were you aware of that?"

"No, sir," he said. "I was not."

"Well, he has," the chief told him. "And from this moment on, I want you in the room with him at all times, you hear?"

"Yes, sir, Chief."

"And I want him cuffed every second of every day," the chief said. Then he paused, looking around. "He got away once. By God he won't do it twice."

The officer turned to leave, then stopped.

"What about visitors, Chief?"

The chief paused. I saw him look at me and Reverend Jacobs, and then at Mama and Reggie. "Just the folks in here now," he said emphatically. "No one else."

"Yes, sir, Chief."

The chief paused again. "And I want them searched," he said. "Before they're allowed to pass through those doors, I want them searched. You understand?"

"Yes, sir, Chief."

The officer disappeared through the double doors, and when he did, the chief turned and faced us.

"Now, let's get one thing straight," he said, looking at Mama with raging eyes. "One more stunt like the one you pulled a few minutes ago and I'll end this thing. No one is to ever put their hands on one of my officers. Is that clear?"

The reverend nodded, as did Mama and Reggie. I remained still.

"Good!" he said.

He left and I turned to Reverend Jacobs.

"What now?" I asked him.

He paused. "What do you know about Oscar?" he asked me.

"Not much," I said. "Why?"

"I was just thinking," Reverend Jacobs said. "Maybe he's pointing the finger at Reggie so that no one will point the finger at him."

"No," I said. "I don't think so."

"But that is a possibility?" Reverend Jacobs said. "Isn't it?"

"Oscar didn't know that Reggie was going to be here," I said. "He came to look at a picture, not to finger a live suspect."

"But, son—"

"Reverend," I said, cutting him off. "I believe him—it was Reggie. I can feel it in my bones."

"But that doesn't make sense," Reverend Jacobs said. "Why would Reggie do this?"

"I don't know," I said. "Something must have happened."

"Something like what?"

"I don't know," I said again. "But whatever it was, it was bad enough to make him turn on his best friend."

Reverend Jacobs paused and let out a deep sigh.

"I can't see it," he said. And then he looked far beyond the window again.

"Stranger things have happened," I said.

Reverend Jacobs sighed again. "Maybe I better talk to him," he said.

"I think that's a good idea," I said. I watched him turn and walk toward Reggie.

When he reached Reggie, he stood over him for a moment, and as he did, Reggie continued to look down at the floor.

"I need to talk to you, son," Reverend Jacobs said. "I need

to talk to you man to man. Is that alright with you? Can the two of us talk?"

Reggie looked up but did not answer. Instead, he looked around the room with jittery eyes.

"Forget about what's going on in that room over there," Reverend Jacobs said. "Forget about what everybody is saying, and forget about what's going to happen tomorrow morning. Forget about all of that, and let's me and you talk. Can we do that? Can you and I talk like two grown men?"

He nodded.

"Good," he said. "Then I'm going to ask you a question. And I want you to think long and hard before you answer it. Can you do that for me?"

He nodded again.

"Son, were you involved in this?"

Reggie shook his head.

"I know you're scared," he said. "But I want you to stop and think. Think long and hard before you answer. Are you sure? Are you sure you weren't involved?"

"I'm sure."

"Why would that man lie?"

"I don't know."

"I will stand by you," Reverend Jacobs said. "I know that may be difficult for you to believe. But I will stand by you. No matter what, I just want you to tell me the truth."

"I am telling the truth, Reverend."

"Curtis has been good to you," he said. "Hasn't he?"

"Yes, sir."

"He's stood by you when no one else would. Is that right?"

"Yes, sir."

"He has been your friend."

"Yes, sir."

"He's been your good friend."

"Yes, sir."

"Well, son, it's your turn to return the favor. It's time for you to be a friend. No, it's time for you to be a man. You owe him that much. After all he has sacrificed for you, you owe him that much. You owe him that and much, much more."

There was silence.

"You know what happened that night," he said. "Don't you?"

"No, sir," he said. "I don't."

"You can end this," Reverend Jacobs said. "You can end this right now. All you have to do is tell the truth. It's that simple, son."

"I am telling the truth," he said, sobbing. "I would never hurt Curtis. I would die first."

"Are you happy, son?"

"Sir?"

"Are you happy?"

There was silence.

"No," Reverend Jacobs said, answering for him. "You're not happy. And you're not going to be happy—not until you tell the truth. Your conscience won't let you—it won't let you keep this terrible secret that's destroying the happiness of the only man who's ever stood by you."

"It wasn't me," he cried.

"You believe in God, don't you, son?"

"Yes, sir." He nodded.

"Then you believe in God's word."

"Yes, sir."

"God said the truth will set you free. Do you believe that?"

He didn't answer.

"Don't you want to be free, son?"

"Yes, sir, I do."

"Then tell the truth," he said. "Tell the truth and give Curtis his life back."

"I am telling the truth," he said. "I swear, Reverend. I swear on a stack of Bibles. I am telling the truth."

"Well, son, I pray that you are. I pray that you are, for your sake and for the sake of that young man lying on that bed in there facing twenty-five years in the state penitentiary for a crime he did not commit. And I pray that you are, for the sake of that woman sitting over there in that corner crying because the child she carried inside her for nine months and raised for twenty years is about to be taken from her. And I pray that you are, for the sake of that young man over there who has been away from his brother for much of his life only to return home to find him trapped in a living hell much worse than any he could have imagined. And I pray that you are, because it would be a shame to think that one human being could be so callous as to allow another human being to suffer such a fate because he himself is not man enough to stand up and take responsibility for that which he has done. I'll pray for you, son. And when I'm done, hopefully you will pray for yourself."

"I am telling the truth," Reggie said.

"I believe you," Mama said. I saw her ease closer to Reggie and put her arm around him. "I believe you."

He laid his head on her shoulder and began to cry.

"This ain't your fault," she said. "None of this is your fault."

35

I called Peaches and told her what was going on. Then I went back into the waiting room with the others and waited. At noon they moved Little Man out of the ICU and onto the medical floor. And as instructed, the officer searched us before allowing us to enter his room. Mama and Reverend Jacobs entered first. The two of them made their way to one side of the bed while Reggie went to the other. From where I stood, near the center of the room, I could see Little Man's eyes. They were solemn and distant, and I could not help but wonder if he was thinking about prison or about how much time he was facing or about how long it would be before he would see any of us again. A chill swept over me. Then I saw Mama gently lift Little Man's limp hand. Little Man didn't move.

"Son," she whispered to him. "How you feeling?"

He lifted his head slightly and looked at her as if he was going to answer. Then he paused, closed his eyes again, and swallowed. His throat was bothering him. I could tell by the way he grimaced when he swallowed. Mama must have noticed it, too, for as soon as he grimaced, she frowned, then retrieved a pitcher of ice water from his night tray, filled a cup, and held it to his lips. He drank in slow, steady gulps until the cup was drained.

"More?" she asked.

He shook his head, then lay back on the pillow.

Reverend Jacobs eased forward. "Son," he said somberly. "You gave us quite a scare."

Little Man looked at him but did not try to answer.

"We're going to stay on our knees," Reverend Jacobs said. "We're going to stay on our knees until God delivers you from this burden, you hear?"

Little Man nodded and then his eyes fluttered and began to close again.

"He's tired," Reverend Jacobs said. "Maybe we should let him rest."

"Maybe so," Mama said.

She adjusted his covers and gently kissed him on the forehead. Instantly, his eyes opened. He slowly turned his head and stared blankly at the ceiling.

"Is something the matter?" Mama asked him.

A quiet moment passed.

"I almost died," he finally murmured. "Didn't I?"

He waited. But she didn't answer.

"I thought I was ready to die," he said. "But I'm not ready. I don't want to die."

"Son," Reverend Jacobs whispered. "No one wants to die."

"I did," he said, still staring at the ceiling.

"But you don't now?"

"No, sir," he mumbled.

"Well, I'm glad to hear that."

"When all of this happened, I thought going to the grave would be better than going to prison. But I was wrong."

"You were scared," Reverend Jacobs said. "That's all."

"When I was riding in the back of that truck, and that

bullet was trying to take my life, I realized that my time here was up and I hadn't even lived yet, and that scared me more than prison."

"My Lord," Reverend Jacobs said.

"Mama, do you know what it's like to stare death square in the eyes?" he asked her. "And realize that you have never lived? Not even for one day—not even for one second?"

She shook her head.

"It's a terrible feeling," he said.

He paused and looked at her. But she wasn't looking at him. She was looking through the open door, staring out into the hallway.

"Mama," he said. "Look at me."

He waited and she slowly turned her head, and when she was facing him, he gazed deep into her eyes.

"Mama, there's something else I want you to know."

"Yes," she said, still looking at him.

"I made a deal with God," he said.

"A deal?"

"Yes, ma'am," he said. "I told Him if He let me live, I would go to that prison and do my time and I wouldn't complain anymore."

"God don't want you to go to prison," I said, speaking for the first time. "Don't you understand that?"

"It must be His will," he said. "Otherwise He wouldn't have allowed it to happen. Would He?"

"It's not God's will," I said. "It's the state's will."

"It doesn't matter," he said.

"It does matter."

"No," he said. "It doesn't." He turned and looked at Mama again. "Mama, a few minutes ago, I heard the doctor tell Sonny and the chief that I could travel. And then I heard the chief say that they were going to let me rest here tonight. But by this time tomorrow, I will be in Angola."

"My God!" Mama wailed. "My God in heaven."

"Sister Reid, this is just a storm," Reverend Jacobs said. "It won't last forever. It's just a storm."

"Don't worry about me, Mama," Little Man said. "I'm alright—really, I'm alright."

"But, son—"

"I'm alright," he said again.

Mama looked at him. I could tell she was fighting back tears.

"Before you go, there's something else I want to tell you. Something that's really important."

"Something like what?" she asked.

"Mama . . . I saw Daddy."

"What!" she said. And when she did, she leaned back on her heels, staring at him as if she could not believe what she had heard.

"While I was talking to God, Daddy came to me."

"That's not possible," Mama said.

"He said he was sorry."

"No," she said. "You were dreaming. Your daddy is in the pen."

"He said he shouldn't have ever abandoned me the way he did. He said he should have reached out to me. He should have called me. He should have written me."

"No," Mama said.

"And he said that he would understand if I hated him—and I wanted to hate him, but I couldn't. So I told him I forgave him. Then he hugged me and told me that everything was going to be alright."

"He told you right." Reverend Jacobs played along.

"When I get to Angola, I'm not going to make any trouble for him. I don't even plan to see him. I'll just let things stay the way they have always been."

"No," I said. "You need to talk to him."

"Why?"

"He can help you."

"I'll be alright," he said. "I'm alive—that's all that matters."

"No," I said. "You need to talk to Daddy."

"I'll be alright," he said again. Then he looked at Mama. "I don't want you to worry. I'll be alright. I don't want to go to prison, but I'm not scared anymore. I'm alive, and that's all that matters."

I looked at Mama. I could tell she didn't know what to say.

"Tell him," I said, angrily. "Tell him about the letters."

Little Man frowned and looked at me.

"What letters?" he asked.

I didn't answer. Instead, I continued to stare at Mama.

"I mean it," I said. "Either you tell him about the letters or I will."

"Maybe he's right," Reverend Jacobs said. "Maybe it's time."

"Time for what?" Little Man asked.

Mama didn't answer.

"Alright," I said. "I'll tell him."

I opened my mouth to speak again, but footsteps on the hallway made me turn and look. Sonny entered the room. He was wearing his uniform.

"What do you want?" I asked him.

He didn't answer. Instead, he made his way to the bed, and as he stood there, looking at Little Man, everyone became deathly quiet.

"How are you?" he asked Little Man.

"I'm alright," Little Man said.

And then Sonny looked at him and then at the cuffs binding him to the bed. "I wish it didn't have to be like this," he said, still looking at the cuffs. "But in the eyes of the law, you're a convicted felon."

"What about in your eyes?" Little Man asked.

"My eyes don't matter," Sonny said.

"They matter to me."

"I believe in you," Sonny said. "I always have and I always will."

"That's good to know," Little Man told him.

"Son, I'm going to do everything I can to help you get through this, alright?"

Little Man nodded.

"Is it true?" Mama asked, interrupting them. "Are you all moving him tomorrow?"

"It's true," Sonny said.

"But he's not well."

"The doctor said he can travel."

"But—"

"Mira," Sonny cut her off. "If I could change this, I would."

"Will we be able to see him before he goes?" Reverend Jacobs asked.

"I don't know," Sonny said. "I'll have to ask the chief."

"I hate you for this," Mama said.

"I'm sorry you feel that way," Sonny said. "But I'm not the enemy. I'm just doing my job."

"We understand that," Reverend Jacobs said.

"Yeah," Little Man said. "We do."

"Hang in there," Sonny told him.

"I will," Little Man said.

Sonny turned and looked at Mama. "Mira," he said. "If you need me, call me."

He waited for a response but when Mama didn't answer, he turned and left. After he was gone, I looked at her.

"Now tell him," I said.

She dropped her eyes and stared at the floor.

"Alright," I said. "I'll tell him." I turned and faced Little Man. "Daddy wrote you," I said.

He cocked his head and looked at me with narrow, confused eyes. "What?"

"Daddy wrote you," I said again.

He frowned, then sat upright. "When?"

"He's been writing you for years," I said.

"What are you talking about?"

"Mama kept the letters from you."

"No," he said. "That's not true."

He looked at Mama, but she remained silent.

"Mama, he's lying . . . right?"

She didn't answer.

"It is true," I said.

"No," Little Man said again. "It can't be."

He looked at Mama again. Her head was still bowed.

"Mama," he said, gazing at her.

She did not answer.

"Mama," he called to her again.

She still didn't answer.

"Why would you do that to me?" he asked. "Why?"

"I'm sorry," Mama sobbed.

Little Man's mouth fell open. He looked at her. His eyes narrowed. Then, without warning, he yanked violently against the cuffs. Mama recoiled.

Reverend Jacobs stepped forward. "Son," he said. "Calm down."

"You knew I was hurting," he yelled, looking past Reverend Jacobs. "You knew I needed him. Why? Why?" He raised his hand and pounded the bed. "Why?"

"I'm gonna make it right," Mama said. "I promise."

She reached over to touch him, but he pulled away.

"Son," she said. "Please don't act like this."

"Get out," he said.

"No," she said. "Please, son, no."

"I mean it," he shouted. "GET OUT!"

"Son," Reverend Jacobs cautioned him. "She's your mother."

"I'm sorry," she said. "I'm so sorry."

"All these years," he wailed. "All these years, I thought he didn't care. But he did care. He reached out to me but you wouldn't let him touch me."

"I'm sorry," she said again.

"Sorry!" he yelled, yanking at the cuff again. "How could you? How could you?"

"Son!" Reverend Jacobs said. "Calm down. Please calm down."

"What if I had gone to see him?" Little Man said. "Maybe my life would have been different."

"I'm sorry."

"Maybe I wouldn't be lying here cuffed to this bed facing twenty-five to life for something I didn't do."

"I'm gonna make it up to you," Mama said. "I promise."

"What did I ever do to you?"

"I'm sorry."

"I thought you loved me."

"I do."

"I thought you cared about me."

"I do."

"No," he said. "You don't. If you did, you wouldn't have taken my father from me."

"I'm sorry."

"D'Ray," he sobbed. "How could she do this to me?"

I didn't answer. I couldn't.

"Little Man—" Mama said.

"Get out!" he shouted, cutting her off.

"Son—"

"I mean it," he shouted. "Get out and leave me alone."

"Alright," Mama sobbed. "I'll leave."

She hurried from the room, and Reverend Jacobs raced after her. When they were gone, Little Man sat staring at the door through which they had exited. Anger seemed to grip him. He pulled hard against the bed with his cuffed arm. The bed rocked. He screamed, then removed the pitcher of water from his tray and flung it across the room.

"Little Man!" I shouted

He looked at me. He was crying.

36

After they had gone, Little Man clasped his hands over his mouth and looked toward the ceiling.

"You were right," he said.

"About what?" I asked him.

"Not trusting anybody." He paused and sighed heavily. "My God, man," he wailed. "If you can't trust your own mother, who can you trust?" Suddenly his eyes fell on Reggie.

"Come here."

Reggie inched closer. His head was down. His eyes were averted.

"It was you," he said. "Wasn't it?"

"No," Reggie said, shaking his head.

"Don't lie to me," Little Man snapped. "Not now, not in my condition—not after all I've been through."

"I'm not lying," Reggie whimpered. "It wasn't me. I swear."

"He said you were wearing a red shirt. We had a meeting that day, remember? I saw you. You were wearing a red shirt. You always wore that red shirt."

"I'm telling the truth."

"No," he said. "You're lying. And I would rather you had

killed me than have you stand here and lie to me like this."
He paused and his voice broke. Then, without warning, he
grabbed Reggie by the collar with his free hand and yanked
him hard. Reggie fell to his knees. Little Man stared at him
with cold, angry eyes. He pushed Reggie hard. Reggie fell
back and slid against the wall. His eyes were wide. His hands
were trembling.

"I loved you," Little Man said. "When nobody else
would, I loved you. Didn't I?"

Reggie didn't answer.

"GET OUT," Little Man said. "JUST GET OUT."

Reggie stumbled to his feet and staggered out into the
hallway. I followed him. He took a few steps, then fell to the
floor, clutching his stomach and wailing loudly. Reverend Jacobs, who had escorted Mama into the waiting room, came
back out into hall. When he saw us, he made his way to Reggie.

"Son, what's wrong?" he asked, kneeling.

"It was me," he said. "I was with Donald Wayne."

"What!"

"I knew it," I said. "I knew it all along."

Reverend Jacobs raised his hand, signaling me to keep
silent; then he turned back toward Reggie.

"It's alright," he said. "Just tell us what happened."

"I was in a bad way," Reggie said.

"A bad way," Reverend Jacobs said. "I don't understand.
What do you mean, you were in a bad way?"

"I had just come down off my high."

"High!"

"Yes, sir. I had started smoking again, and I was hurting
for a fix. I needed something bad, but I was broke. Then I saw
Donald Wayne. He had spotted me a few dollars before, and I
thought he might do it again. So I walked up to him, and I
tried to talk to him, but he didn't say nothing—he just kept
talking to the man who was with him."

"What man?"

"The man who was here earlier."

"Oscar."

"Yes, sir."

"Then what happened?"

"The man—Oscar—he started laughing at me, but I didn't care. I was hurting bad. So I kept talking. No, I done lied enough. . . . I kept begging. I got down on my knees and begged him. I begged him to have mercy on me. I told him I would do anything if he would let me hold a couple of dollars."

"What did he say?"

"He told me that he was about to pull a job and that if I helped him, he would hook me up. I just wanted the drugs—that's all I was thinking about. I didn't want to hurt nobody. I just wanted to get high. So I told him yeah, and he broke into that woman's house."

"And you went with him?"

"No, sir. I stayed outside like he told me to. I was his lookout. But he was taking too long, and I had the shakes, and then my mind started talking to me. It said maybe something went wrong—maybe he needed some help. And all I could think about was the drugs, so I went in. He had told me to stay outside, but I went in, anyway, and he was in the lady's den, stealing her computer. When he saw me, he whirled around, and I backed up, and I bumped into something, and the lady came running into the room. When she saw us, she told us to leave before she called the police, and she started toward the phone, and I panicked."

"What did you do?"

"I started toward her, and Donald Wayne tried to stop me. He hollered, 'No! Let's go!' But I hit her anyway."

"Then what happened?"

"Donald Wayne grabbed her purse and computer and we

ran. He went one way and I went the other way. The cops caught him. But I got away."

"Why did you hit her?"

"I don't know. I just panicked."

"Did you try to rape her?"

"No!"

"She said you did."

"I didn't—I swear."

"Are you telling me the truth?"

"Yes, sir."

"Why did you lie on Curtis?"

"I didn't," he said. "Donald Wayne did."

"But you didn't correct him."

"No, sir, I didn't."

"Why not?"

"I didn't think they would convict Curtis. I swear I didn't."

"But they did."

"Yes, sir," he said. "They did."

"How could you?" I shouted. "How could you sit back and let him take the rap for you?"

"I'm sorry."

"You're sorry!"

"Yeah," he said. "I'm sorry."

"Well, being sorry ain't good enough."

"I know," he wailed. "I know."

"Make it right," I shouted. "Make it right, you hear?"

"I can't."

"What do you mean, you can't?"

"It's bigger than me," he said. "It's bigger than this whole town."

"What are you talking about?"

"Please!" he sobbed. "Don't make me say something that could get me killed."

"Killed!" Reverend Jacobs said, frowning. "What are you talking about?"

"Please!" he said. "Don't ask me any more questions. I ain't nobody," he cried. "Neither is Donald Wayne. But they are."

"Who?"

"I need to talk to somebody," he said, "somebody who can protect me."

"What about the chief?"

"No," he said. "Not the chief."

"Why not?"

"The chief is rotten," he said. "He's rotten to the bone." He paused and looked up. "He made me shoot Curtis."

"What!"

"Oh, God, help me," he said. "If I would have listened to Curtis, none of this would have happened. If I would have just listened . . . Why didn't I listen?"

"Son, are you telling me that the chief of police told you to shoot Curtis?"

"Yes, sir, he did."

Suddenly, my mind began to whirl, and I was standing in my mother's house, listening to the chief's ominous warning: *Tell him to run,* he'd said. *Tell him to run hard. Because when I catch him, I'm gonna blow a hole in him big as Texas.*

"It's true," I said.

"Oh, God, help me," Reggie pleaded.

"Why?" Reverend asked. "Why would the chief want to harm Curtis?"

"Please," he said. "Please, don't make me say something that's gonna get me killed."

"Son, what's this all about?"

"We're in this thing deep."

"Who?"

"Donald Wayne and me."

"What are you talking about?"

"I didn't want to lie," he said. "But I was scared."

"Scared of what?"

He turned and looked toward the door.

"I can't say anything else," he said. "Not until I talk to somebody who can protect me."

"The police will protect you."

"No," he said. "I don't trust them. They work for the chief."

"What about the sheriff?"

"I don't know the sheriff."

"He's a good man," Reverend Jacobs said. "I've known him all of my life."

"I don't know," he said. "I just don't know."

"Son, whatever is going on, he will help you."

"I don't know," he said again. "I just don't know."

Reverend Jacobs grabbed him by the shoulder and looked deep into his eyes. "You trust me," he said. "Don't you, son?"

"Yes, sir, Reverend," he said. "You and Curtis are the only two people I do trust."

"Then trust me on this."

"I don't want any harm to come to Curtis," he said. "I don't."

"Well, it will," Reverend Jacobs said, "if you don't talk to the sheriff."

"Alright," he said, wiping his nose with the back of his hand. "I'll talk to him. If that's what you want, I'll talk to him."

"Good," Reverend Jacobs said, rising to his feet. "Let's go."

37

I followed the two of them out of the building. The swirling tides of my frayed emotions spiraled, then spiked again. I looked into the heavens. In less than twenty-four hours, Little Man would be on his way to prison. The thought made me tense. Hot hate rose within me. A sharp pain stabbed at the front of my eyes. I squinted, then climbed into the car next to Reverend Jacobs. I glanced in the rearview mirror. Reggie was sitting in the backseat, staring aimlessly out the window. Oh, what right did I have to be angry at him? Had I not also lived outside the law? And had I not lied to hold on to a freedom I knew someday I was bound to forfeit? Maybe this was payback. Maybe this was my chickens coming home to roost.

I lowered my eyes and watched Reverend Jacobs slowly guide the car out of the parking lot and onto the road. As he navigated the narrow streets, I quietly prayed that the end of this nightmare was but a short ride before us. Outside, a police car whizzed past us. I watched the car for a moment, then turned away. Yes, the law that had brutalized me was the same law to which I now had to turn to plead for my brother's life. Oh, how I hated this world. Oh, how I hated my life.

At the courthouse, Reverend Jacobs parked out front and

we followed him into the building, then to the sheriff's office. When we arrived, the sheriff was sitting behind his desk,
drinking a cup of coffee. He was wearing his uniform, and a
large, tan cowboy hat was sitting on the corner of his desk.
He asked us to come in and have a seat. I entered first, but I
did not sit. I stopped and lingered near the doorway. Reggie
sat in a chair across from the sheriff, and Reverend Jacobs sat
next to Reggie. His shoulders were slumped, and his head
was down. I could tell he was scared.

"What can I do for you?" the sheriff asked.

I looked at Reggie. He remained quiet.

"Go ahead, son," Reverend Jacobs said. "Tell the sheriff
what you told me."

"Is he going to protect me?" Reggie asked, still looking at
the floor.

"Protect you from what?" the sheriff asked.

"What he has to say is quite sensitive," Reverend Jacobs
said.

"Sensitive?"

"Yes, sir," Reverend said. "Sensitive."

The sheriff leaned back in his chair and rubbed his chin.
He looked at Reggie and then back at Reverend Jacobs.

"Well, I can't promise him anything until he tells me what
this is all about." He paused and looked at Reggie again.
"Now, son, what is it?"

Reggie didn't answer.

"It's alright, son." Reverend Jacobs nudged him. "Tell the
sheriff what you told me."

Reggie raised his eyes and looked around nervously. "I . . .
I . . . c-committed . . . a crime," he stammered.

"What kind of crime?" the sheriff asked.

Reggie did not answer.

"It's alright, son," Reverend Jacobs said again. "Just tell the
sheriff what happened."

"I . . . I . . . b-broke . . . into s-somebody's . . . h-h-ouse," he stammered. "A . . . w-white . . . l-lady's house."

"When?" the sheriff snapped.

Reggie recoiled and averted his eyes again.

"It's alright," Reverend Jacobs said. "Just tell the truth."

"About a year ago."

"A year ago."

"Yes, sir," Reggie said.

"I don't recall any burglaries around here that weren't solved," he said. "Was anybody charged?"

"Yes, sir," Reggie said. "Two men were tried and convicted—Donald Wayne Wilson and Curtis Reid."

The sheriff screwed up his face and leaned forward. "Let me get this straight," he said. "You're confessing to a crime that has already been solved?"

"Yes, sir."

"Why?"

"They convicted the wrong person," Reggie said. "Curtis didn't do it. I did."

"If that's the case," the sheriff said, "why didn't you come forward before?"

"I was scared."

"But you aren't scared now?"

"Yes, sir," Reggie mumbled. "I am. That's why I need protection."

"Protection from who?" the sheriff asked.

"The chief," Reverend Jacobs said. "The boy's scared of the chief."

"The chief!" the sheriff said, eyeing Reggie in outrage. "Son, what are you trying to pull here?"

"Nothing," Reggie mumbled, still looking down.

"I know the chief," the sheriff said. "He's a good man. Why would you be afraid of him?"

"He threatened to kill me."

"Do you really expect me to believe that?" the sheriff asked.

"He did," Reggie said.

"Why would he do that?"

"Because I know what they did."

"And what did they do?"

"They framed Curtis Reid."

"Who told you that?" the sheriff asked gruffly.

"Nobody."

"Then how do you know?" the sheriff pressed him.

"I was there," Reggie said.

"You were where?"

"I was in the room when they decided to do it."

"You're lying."

"No, sir," Reggie said, shaking his head. "I'm not."

"You expect me to believe that the chief of police framed an innocent man?"

"Yes, sir," he mumbled. "I do."

"Well, I don't."

"It's true. Curtis was in the way, so they framed him."

"In the way of what?" the sheriff asked.

Reggie didn't answer.

"It's alright, son," Reverend Jacobs said. "Just tell the truth."

"Business," he said.

"What kind of business?" the sheriff asked.

"The kind of business that goes on in the quarters," Reggie said.

"And what kind of business is that?"

"Drugs, gambling, prostitution—you know, business."

"That's not business," the sheriff said. "That's criminal activity."

"Well, that's what they were doing."

"Son, are you sitting here telling me that the chief of police is involved in criminal activity?"

"He was getting kickbacks," Reggie said.

"From who?"

"The people who needed him to turn his head while they did their dirt."

"And how do you know that?"

"I was friends with one of them."

"Which one?"

"Donald Wayne," he said.

"Donald Wayne!"

"Yes, sir. He picked the product up for Kojak. And sometimes I helped him."

"You mean the drugs."

"Yes, sir."

"From where?"

"Different places," he said. "But it was usually a cotton field just west of town."

"How did they get there?"

"They dropped them from a plane."

"A plane?"

"Yes, sir—a crop duster."

"Are you lying to me?"

"No, sir," he said. "I'm telling the truth. The pilot would spray the crops for insects, and while he was doing that, he would drop a package in the fields. That evening, after he was gone, Donald Wayne would go pick it up. Now, if he couldn't make it, he would send me."

"How often would you do that?"

"As often as they told me to."

"And you gave the drugs to Kojak?"

"No, sir. I gave them to Donald Wayne, and he gave them to Kojak."

"And what did Kojak do with them?"

"He gave them to the dealers and the dealers sold them on the street."

"And the chief knew about this?"

"Yes, sir. Kojak paid him a weekly fee to turn his head and allow him to do business."

"You're lying," the sheriff said.

"No, sir."

"Kojak was paying the chief."

"Yes, sir. And he was paying a couple of cops too—they provided protection on the street."

"What cops?"

"There were two of them."

"Who?"

"Sonny and Pete."

I saw the sheriff's eyes widen.

"Pete!"

"Yes, sir."

"The head of the chief's drug task force?"

"Yes, sir."

"You're telling me he's on Kojak's payroll?"

"Yes, sir."

"I don't believe you."

"I'm telling the truth. Officer Pete is the muscle behind the whole thing. From my understanding, he was handpicked by the chief. They say he came from a long line of dirty cops."

"I don't believe you," the sheriff said.

"But it's the truth," Reggie said again.

"I think you're lying to me," the sheriff said.

"No, sir. I'm telling the truth. You got to believe me. Curtis didn't have anything to do with this, I swear. The chief framed him."

"Why would the chief risk his career and his freedom to frame a nobody? Son, what you're saying just doesn't make sense."

"Curtis was running a substance abuse program."

"And?"

"And that program was getting a lot of boys off the street."

"What does that have to do with the chief?"

"A lot of those boys were in the business."

"In the business how?"

"Some were customers and some were dealers."

"I don't get it," the sheriff said.

"Sir, Curtis was hurting some powerful folk and didn't know it. And they wanted him out of the way. So sending him to prison is how they decided to do it."

"Who decided?"

"I don't want to die," he said. "Please don't make me say something that could get me killed."

"You're not going to die," the sheriff said. "But I need to know who came up with the idea to frame Curtis." He paused and looked at Reggie. "Was it the chief?"

"No, sir," Reggie said, shaking his head.

"Then who?"

"Go ahead," Reverend Jacobs said. "Tell him."

"Sonny," he said. "It was Sonny's idea."

"Sonny!" I said. Suddenly, I felt a lump of hate rise and lodge itself in my throat. "Sonny set him up?"

"Yeah."

"Son, are you telling me the truth?" the sheriff asked. "Because if you're not . . ."

"I am," Reggie said. "I swear."

"Sheriff, I believe him," Reverend Jacobs said.

The sheriff looked at Reverend Jacobs and then at Reggie again. "Can you prove any of this?" he asked.

"I can prove I was with Donald Wayne that night."

"How?" the sheriff wanted to know.

"I took something from the girl's house."

"What?"

"A broach," he said. "I was going to pawn it. But after

they picked up Donald Wayne, I got scared. So I hid it under my house, behind the porch steps."

The sheriff paused and leaned back in his chair.

"Are you willing to testify against them?"

"Yes, sir," he said. "I am."

"Then that's it," Reverend Jacobs said. "Isn't it?"

"No," the sheriff said. "Just because he can prove that he was in the house, doesn't prove that Reid wasn't. Now, I'm going to be honest with you. Donald Wayne testified against Reid. He swore under oath that Reid was with him. This boy coming in here confessing after the fact is not likely to change that."

"But I'm telling the truth."

"Donald Wayne said *he's* telling the truth."

"No, he's lying."

"Why would he lie?"

"This was his third strike. He was looking at life without the possibility of parole. They gave him a deal to lie."

"That makes sense," Reverend Jacobs said.

"It was me," Reggie said. "Curtis had nothing to do with it."

"It's your word against theirs."

"But I'm telling the truth."

"You're not credible," he said. "You're an admitted drug addict. No one will believe you."

"I believe him," Reverend Jacobs said. "He confessed to a crime that could send him to the penitentiary. I believe him."

"Maybe someone promised him something," he said. "Or maybe someone threatened him." He paused and looked at me.

"No one threatened me," Reggie said.

"That's right," Reverend Jacobs said. "I was there when the boy confessed. In fact, he confessed to me."

"Maybe we should go to the Feds," I said.

"No," the sheriff said. "I don't want you to say anything to anybody about this. I'll take care of it. In the meantime, son, you need to get yourself a lawyer."

"What about my brother?" I said. "They're planning on sending him to Angola first thing in the morning."

"I will check out this story and see what I can do," the sheriff said. "But I'm going to be honest with you. I don't believe anything will come of this. We need evidence, some kind of proof that would warrant reopening a case that has already been closed."

"This is not right," I said. "Reggie confessed."

"Listen. Your brother had his day in court, and a jury of his peers found him guilty. Now, there's not a judge in his right mind who would throw out his conviction based on what I just heard. But as a favor to Reverend Jacobs, I'll petition the court for a temporary stay."

"Will it work?" the reverend asked.

"I don't know," he said. "Judges are reluctant to intervene in cases that have already been adjudicated."

"Speak to Judge Roberts," Reverend Jacobs said. "He owes me a favor."

"I'll speak to him," the sheriff said. "But don't get your hopes up."

He rose to his feet to signal that this conversation was over. Reverend Jacobs stood and extended his hand.

"Thank you for your time, Sheriff."

They shook hands, and Reggie and I followed Reverend Jacobs down a long corridor and out of the building. We stopped on the stoop in front of the courthouse. I felt anxious, not knowing whether I could trust the sheriff. I looked at Reverend Jacobs. He was quiet, and I could tell he was lost in thought.

"What do you think?" I asked him.

"I think we've done all we can do," he said.

"But do you think the sheriff will go against his friends?"

"He's an honest man," Reverend Jacobs said. "He'll do his job."

"He didn't believe Reggie," I said. "Otherwise he would have taken him into custody."

"We've done all that we can do," Reverend Jacobs said again. "The truth is out. Now all we can do is wait."

"Wish there was some way to verify your story," I told Reggie.

"All I have is the broach," he said.

"There has to be something else."

"That's all there is," he said.

"Then it's your word against theirs."

He didn't answer.

"For all it's worth, I believe you," Reverend Jacobs said.

"Well, the sheriff doesn't," I said. "And if he won't act, I still say we should go to the Feds."

"He's a good man," Reverend Jacobs said. "Let's just give him a chance."

We descended the steps and made our way back to Reverend Jacobs's car. Once inside, I lowered my window and gazed into the heavens. The sun had moved from the center of the sky. Soon, afternoon would give way to evening, and evening would give way to night. Yes, we were running out of time.

38

Back at the hospital, I sat slumped in the waiting room, feeling the tenseness of the moment. What if the sheriff was right? What if Little Man's fate was sealed? What if there was nothing any of us could do to change what had already happened? Well, if that was the case, would it not be better for me to honor my word and leave? Would it not be better for me to pack my truck and go somewhere, just me and Peaches, and begin life anew in a place where I would not have to think about Little Man or about what I had done?

I looked at Mama. She was clutching her Bible and mumbling to herself. Reverend Jacobs was standing near the window again, and Reggie was sitting in the far corner with his head hanging down. High up on the wall, the hands of the clock continued to move until it was time again. Then, as before, we were searched and allowed back into the room. When we arrived, Little Man was lying on his back staring vacantly at the ceiling. Mama eased next to the bed. She reached for his hand, but he pulled it away. And when he did, I saw her take a deep breath, and I knew she wanted to cry again. He furrowed his brow and continued to stare.

"Honey," she called to him softly. "This is the last time the chief is going to let us see you before they take you away, and I don't want it to be like this."

She paused. He remained quiet.

"Ain't you gonna look at me?" she asked him.

His eyes remained fixed on the ceiling.

"I know you're mad," she said. "God knows you got a right to be. But they're going to take you away from me in a little while, and I don't want it to be like this."

He remained quiet.

"I'm old," she said. "And I've seen a lot of misery in this world. But somehow I made it. But I can't make it through this. Not without knowing that things between us can be right again. Please, son, tell me that everything is gonna be alright."

"Just leave me alone," he mumbled.

"How can I leave you alone?" she asked him. "You're my child. How can I leave you alone?"

He didn't answer. Suddenly, Mama's eyes welled and I could tell that she was going to cry again. She looked at Reverend Jacobs. He moved forward, fumbling with his hands.

"Son, don't do this," he said. "This is your mama. Don't push her away. Please don't push her away."

"Just leave me alone," he said again.

"My mama's gone," Reverend Jacobs said. "She gone on to glory, and no matter how bad I want to, I can't talk to her. But, son, you can talk to your mama. You still got time. Fix this thing. Fix it before it gets to a point where it can't be fixed."

Little Man remained quiet.

"Son, talk to me?" Mama pleaded. "Please talk to me."

Little Man didn't answer.

"So, that's it," Reverend Jacobs said. "You're just going to lie there and pout."

Little Man didn't answer.

"Well, that's just what that old devil wants you to do," Reverend Jacobs admonished. "That's just what he wants you to do."

Little Man didn't answer.

"I'm sorry for what I did," Mama said. "Please believe me."

"Believe?" Little Man mumbled. His soft voice seemed far away. His eyes remained fixed on the ceiling.

"Yes," Mama said. "Believe."

"I tried to believe," he mumbled. "I tried to believe in all of you, but where has it gotten me?" He turned his head and looked directly at Mama. "Tell me, where has it gotten me?"

"I made some mistakes," Mama said. "But—"

"Where has it gotten me?" he interrupted her.

"I—"

"Where has it gotten me?"

He paused. Mama became quiet. He turned his head and stared at Reggie.

"Should I believe in you?" he asked him.

Reggie didn't answer.

"That's alright," Little Man said. "You don't have to answer. I already know. You're just like all the rest of them. I already know."

"Don't blame him," Reverend Jacobs said. "It's not his fault. They had him over a barrel."

"It doesn't matter," Little Man said.

"What are you talking about?" Mama asked.

"It was him," Little Man said, still staring at the ceiling. "He was with Donald Wayne that night." He turned and looked at Reggie. "Ain't that right?"

"It's not his fault," Reverend Jacobs said again.

"Oh, my God," Mama cried.

"Believe," Little Man mumbled again. Then he turned his head and stared at the ceiling.

Mama grabbed Reggie by the shoulders and shook him hard. "Tell me it's not true," she cried. "Please tell me it's not true."

"I didn't want to," he sobbed. "But they made me do it."

"No," Mama wailed.

"They made me do it."

"How could you?" she yelled.

"It was Sonny!" he said. "Sonny and the chief."

"No," Mama said. "MY GOD, NO!"

"Sister Reid, it's true," Reverend Jacobs said.

"Believe," Little Man said again, still looking at the ceiling.

"My Lord, my Lord, oh, my Lord," Mama wailed.

"I tried to make it right," Reggie said. "I told the sheriff everything. I tried to make it right. But he wouldn't listen."

"It's true," Reverend Jacobs said. "I was there."

"My God," Mama wept. "My God in heaven."

"You got to believe me," Reggie said. "I tried to make it right."

Little Man refused to look at him.

Talk to him, a voice called from within me. *He doesn't have much time. Talk to him.*

I hesitated, then looked at the clock again. Outside the door, I heard feet approaching. Then I heard the voice telling me to talk to him again. I approached the bed and leaned over the rail.

"Forget about all of this," I said. "Forget about it and just concentrate on what you have to do."

"He don't know what to do," Mama wailed.

I hesitated again. Yes, she was right. He had never been to prison before. How would he know what to do? Well, this was his life now. They had him, and it was time he faced the facts. It was time we all faced the facts.

"Find something to occupy your time," I advised him.

"He don't know what to do," Mama said again. "My God, he don't know what to do."

"Go it alone," I said. "Go it alone until you hook up with Daddy."

"Help him, Jesus," Mama said. "Please help him."

"And don't agitate the guards," I said. "Mind your business and do what you're told."

"Listen to him, son," Reverend Jacobs said. "He's telling you right."

"Now, they probably won't let anybody see you for a while," I said. "But I'll be there as soon as they allow it. And I'm going to keep coming until we get you out." I looked at the clock again. "Do you hear me?"

He didn't answer.

Suddenly, my voice broke. No, I could not leave him. I would not leave him, not until he was free.

"Anything you need before we have to leave?" I sobbed.

He didn't answer.

"Anything at all?"

He still didn't answer.

"Please, son," Mama pleaded. "Talk to us."

He stared at the ceiling.

"Are you going to look for Daddy?" I asked.

He didn't answer.

"Please look for him," I said. "He can help you."

"I'll write him," Mama said. "I'll explain everything to him, and I'll ask him to look out for you. You hear me, son?"

She paused. There was silence.

"Take God with you," Reverend Jacobs said. "Ask him to watch over you. Ask him to protect you."

Suddenly, the door swung open and the officer walked in.

"Times up," he said.

I looked at Little Man. He continued to stare at the ceiling.

"I'll be here in the morning," I said. "They may not let me see you, but I'll be here."

"Me too," Mama said.

"So will I," Reverend Jacobs said.

Reggie remained quiet.

"God bless you, son," Reverend Jacobs said.

"Hang in there," I said.

"I love you, son," Mama said.

"I'm sorry," Reggie said.

And then the officer asked us to leave.

39

I followed the three of them out into the hallway. We had failed. The thought came to me from some faraway place. In spite of everything we had done, it had happened. Like my father, and like my father's father before him, Little Man was going to prison. I looked back toward Little Man's room, then far up the hallway. I could not stay in here. I needed to go outside, in the night air, where I could breathe and where I could put distance between myself and this place and these people and this situation.

Distraught by all that had occurred, I fled from the hospital, leaving the three of them anchored in the tiny waiting room, resolved not to move until morning dawned. And when morning did dawn, they would be on their knees praying to God with the belief—no, the conviction—that He would intervene and the nightmare would be blotted out, and they would be able to live again. Oh, but He would not intervene, and Little Man would not be freed, because this thing was bigger than Little Man, and it was bigger than Brownsville.

Outside, I climbed behind the wheel of my truck and sped away. My head began to ache. My eyes began to blur. I drove on, knowing there was no place I could go or anything

I could do to change what was coming. I looked into the heavens at the twinkling stars. How vast were the heavens. How plentiful were the stars. How peaceful it all seemed lingering high above the dim and dark drudgery of this godforsaken world. Why did it always end like this? What was the point of it all? I was educated now. And yet, the degree hanging high up on my wall could no more save Little Man than the gun I had used to kill Stanley.

But what about the sheriff? Maybe he could help. Maybe he would help. No, that was no good. The sheriff had been too nonchalant. Why would he risk all on the word of a confessed criminal? No, he had made up his mind. Besides, what did I expect? He was white, and Little Man was black, and the law is what it has always been. Oh, I did not want to think that way. But what choice did I have? It has always been that way. Black and white, right and wrong, living and dying.

I turned onto the street leading to Peaches's house. I needed to see her. I needed to be with the only thing that made sense in my life. I made my way to the door and knocked. A moment later, she stood before me, dressed only in her bathrobe. It was nearly ten o'clock. She had taken her bath and was preparing for bed. I entered her house and slumped onto her sofa. She eased next to me. I leaned my head on her bosom and closed my eyes. I did not want to think anymore. I simply wanted to lie in her arms and sleep.

"Did you find out anything?" she asked.

I hesitated, pondering her question. Then I remembered I had not spoken to her about Oscar, and the yearbook, and the missing piece of the puzzle we had so desperately sought. I raised my head and looked at her.

"It was Reggie," I said.

"Reggie!" she gasped.

"Yeah," I mumbled, "Reggie."

"My God!" she said.

I remained quiet.

"Are you sure?" she asked.

"Yes," I said. "He confessed."

Again I heard her gasp. And I knew what she was thinking. *That's it. Case closed. It's over. The system has worked.* But the system had not worked and it would not work. Who were we kidding? Little Man's fate was sealed. I knew it; he knew it— we all knew it. Suddenly, I laid my head on her bosom again. I wanted to cry but tears would not come. I stared blankly into the room, feeling again the helplessness of the situation. She waited for me to say more, but I remained silent. In some ways, this was my fault. Would it not have been better for him to have died than to rot away in prison for a crime he did not commit? Oh, I wanted to believe. I tried to believe. But I had been wrong.

"Where is he now?"

I heard her voice coming to me as if she were some stranger asking a question I had not fully understood.

"Reggie?" I asked, seeking clarification.

"Yes," she said. "Reggie."

"At the hospital," I told her.

Suddenly, I felt her body become tense.

"They didn't arrest him?" she exclaimed.

"No," I said. "They didn't."

"I don't understand."

"They don't believe him," I said.

"But he confessed."

I rose and walked to the window, realizing nothing had changed. This time tomorrow, Little Man would be at Angola. I looked deep into the darkness, recalling the look I had seen in his eyes. Yes, he was scared, and he was broken, and he had every reason to be. Oh, but what could I do that we had not already done?

"I hope he'll be alright," she said.

I didn't answer. Instead, I looked out into the darkness again. Suddenly, my lips began to quiver. Instinctively, I let out a deep sigh; then I looked over the horizon in the general direction of the hospital.

"Wonder what he's thinking?" I asked her.

"I don't know," she said. "What does a person think at a time like this? I would imagine he's scared. I know I would be."

Ten minutes later, she and I lay together in the center of her large floral-covered bed. The lights were dim and the television was off, and the light of the moon seeped through the thin fabric of the loosely drawn curtains. My arms were around her waist, and her body was curled against my own, and her head was on my chest, and I could feel her hands gently caressing the nape of my neck. Yes, in the morning, I would say good-bye to Little Man. And then, one day, when we were beyond all of this, I would say good-bye to this place.

40

After a long, restless night, the alarm clock rang. I threw back the covers and sat upright in bed. I turned off the alarm, then held still for a moment. Through weary eyes, I looked toward the window. Thin bands of daylight seeped through the thin curtains. In the distance, I heard the five o'clock train rumbling past. Yes, the world was awake now, and life was going on as usual. In spite of everything, life was going on as usual.

I swung my legs out of bed and stepped to the floor. I looked at the phone. Instinctively, I knew things had not gone well. If they had, somebody would have called. Suddenly, anxiety swept over me. Inside my head, I felt a throbbing pain. I closed my eyes for a brief moment and then opened them again. Oh, God, in a moment or two, they would bind his hands, shackle his feet, and lead him to the vehicle that would transport him to Angola.

I hesitated a moment, contemplating that image. Then, the seriousness of the moment made me hurry. I dressed, then dashed from the house. Once outside, I climbed into the truck and tore out of the drive. At the intersection, I turned onto Railroad Avenue, following the street through the neighborhood and across the tracks, and then I headed down

Hospital Road before screeching to a halt in the hospital parking lot. From the parking lot, I spied a police car. It was parked next to the emergency room. I stared at the car for a minute. The engine was running but no one was inside. Yes, it was happening. The police had gone inside to get him. I staggered from the truck on wobbly legs, then stumbled into the building, hustling down the long corridor. Near the end of the hallway, I saw Reverend Jacobs; he was talking to Sonny and the chief. When I reached them, they stopped talking and looked at me.

"Where is he?" I asked Reverend Jacobs.

"In there," Reverend Jacobs said, pointing to the last room in the corner of the hallway.

I looked at Sonny. "I want to see him."

"Go on," he said. "You got one minute."

I eased closer to the doorway and peered inside. Little Man was sitting in a wheelchair. His hands were cuffed in front of him. Mama was standing next to him. I hesitated a moment, then entered the room. Little Man looked up. Our eyes met. I eased closer and kneeled on the floor before him. I grabbed his hand; he was trembling.

"Are you alright?" I asked.

He opened his mouth to say something, but anxiety rendered him silent. I squeezed his hand hard. He took a deep breath and composed himself. I looked at him; my voice broke.

"Just find Daddy," I said. "When you get there, just find him. You hear?"

He closed his eyes and nodded. Behind me, I heard feet on the floor. I turned and looked over my shoulder. I saw Reverend Jacobs creeping forward.

"I spoke to the warden," he said. "He won't let me visit you today. But I'll be down there next weekend."

"Me too," I said.

Mama began to sob again.

"I'm going to be alright," he said to her.

"I never meant to hurt you."

He didn't answer.

"Whatever mistakes I made, I made them out of love."

"We don't have time for this," I said.

"I just wanted you to have a chance," Mama said. "I didn't want you to end up like your daddy."

"You had no right," he said angrily.

I heard Mama swallow hard, then turn her back. Reverend Jacobs put his arms around her. I saw her mouth open. I saw her lips quiver.

"I'm so sorry," she said. "God knows I am." Then she lifted her eyes and looked at Little Man. "Can you forgive me, son?"

He still didn't answer. Suddenly, the chief and Sonny entered the room. The chief looked at Mama.

"It's time," he said.

Mama clasped her hands over her mouth and sobbed louder. The chief nodded to the officer. The officer stepped forward and grabbed the handle and pushed. The wheelchair rolled forward. The officer wheeled him out of the room and into the hallway. The chief and Sonny followed them.

Suddenly, I heard Mama scream. Then I saw her lurch forward, her hands outstretched, her mouth agape. Reverend Jacobs grabbed her and held her tight. I turned my back and prayed, asking God to be with him. When I looked again, Little Man had turned in his chair and was looking back at us.

"I'm alright," he mouthed again.

I started down the hall.

The chief whirled. "Stay back!" he shouted. "I mean it. Stay back."

I slowed, following at a distance. Behind me, I heard Reverend Jacobs leading Mama up the hallway. We passed the nurse's station and rounded the corner. The exit door came into view. I heard a commotion behind me. I turned and looked. Mama had shaken free of Reverend Jacobs and was racing toward Little Man. Sonny grabbed her.

"Mira!" he said. "Get a hold of yourself!" He shook her hard. "Do you hear me? Get a hold of yourself."

"This ain't right," she said. "This just ain't right."

"Get him in the car," the chief ordered.

The officer pushed through the door, then stopped. In the distance, I heard the lone voice of an angry man.

"Hold it right there!" he yelled.

I eased closer. It was the sheriff. Beyond him I saw more police cars with lights flashing. I leaned forward, looking. Several deputies stepped forward, wielding guns. I saw one of them remove the gun from the holster of the officer pushing Little Man's chair. Then I saw the chief push forward with a confused look on his face.

"What is this?" he asked, looking around.

"Up against the car," the sheriff shouted.

The chief looked at the sheriff but did not move. Suddenly, raised guns were aimed at his head.

"I mean it, Harland," the sheriff said. "You, too, Sonny— against the car and drop your weapons."

I saw the chief whirl. "What is this?" he asked again.

"Step away from the prisoner."

The chief frowned but did not move.

"I mean it," the sheriff shouted. "Step away from the prisoner and do it right now."

The chief complied. So did Sonny. A deputy stepped forward and removed their weapons. The chief looked at him.

"What's this all about?"

"You're under arrest," the sheriff told him.

"You got to be joking."

"You have the right to remain silent."

"Bobby!"

"Harland!" the sheriff yelled. "It's over."

"What are you talking about?"

"Cuff him," the sheriff said, "and read him his rights."

Two deputies stepped forward. One cuffed the chief and the other cuffed Sonny.

"Wait a minute," the chief said.

"Put them in the car," the sheriff said.

The deputy hesitated.

"Right now!" the sheriff demanded.

The officer complied. I saw Little Man look at his wrist and then at the sheriff, confused.

"Son," the sheriff said, looking at Little Man, "you're free."

"Free?" Little Man whispered. His hands were trembling. His eyes were wide.

The sheriff turned and looked at Reverend Jacobs. "Reverend, the boy's story checked out."

"My God!" Reverend Jacobs said.

"Turns out the Feds have been watching those three for a couple of months," the sheriff said. Then he turned and looked at the chief. "Harland, I'm disappointed in you. I'm real disappointed."

"This is a big mistake," the chief said. "I don't know what that boy told you, but he's lying."

"He's telling the truth," the sheriff said.

"No," the chief said. "He's lying."

"Harland, the Feds picked up Pete last night. When he found out what they had on him, he sang like a bird."

"It's really over," Mama said.

"It's over," the sheriff told her.

She narrowed her eyes and looked at Sonny. "How could you?" she asked him.

He didn't answer.

"That's alright," I said. "He don't have to say anything. He gonna get what's coming to him."

Suddenly, Reverend Jacobs frowned. "Where's Reggie?" he asked.

"In custody," the sheriff told him.

"How is he?"

"Relieved," the sheriff said. "We offered him a deal. But he didn't want it. He said he'll accept whatever sentence the judge hands down."

"What kind of sentence will he get?" Reverend Jacobs asked.

"I don't know," the sheriff said.

"I'll speak for him," Reverend Jacobs said.

"So will I," Little Man seconded.

"Tell him we said that."

"I will," the sheriff said. Then he turned and spoke to his deputy. "Take them away."

The deputy placed Sonny and the chief in the squad car. Our eyes followed the car until it was fully out of view. Then I saw Little Man bury his face in his hands and cry.

"It's alright," Reverend Jacobs said. "Let it all out, son. It's alright."

"I can't believe it's over," Little Man sobbed.

"Well, it is," I told him.

He looked up. Our eyes met.

"Thank you," he said. "Thank you for everything."

"Don't mention it," I said. Then I looked at him and smiled. "You ready to get out of here?"

"Yeah," he sobbed.

"Where to?" I asked him.

"I want to go see my daddy," he said, his voice trembling. "Is that possible? Can I go see my daddy?"

"You can go anywhere you want to," I told him. "You're a free man."

"Praise God," Reverend Jacobs said.

"Son," Mama said, sobbing, "I'm gonna make this up to you. And I'm gonna make it up to World. And I'm gonna do right by you boys from here on out, you hear?"

He didn't answer.

"You believe me," she said. "Don't you?"

She looked at Little Man and then at me.

"Time will tell," I said. "Time will tell."

In the distance, I could see the dim rays of the rising sun illuminating the sky. I looked at the sun for a moment, and then I looked west toward the old neighborhood. Peaches's house was over there somewhere, and I could not wait to go to her. The thought of going to her made me smile. I looked toward the horizon again. Yes, this was going to be a beautiful day.

FAMILY TIES

Ernest Hill

ABOUT THIS GUIDE

The suggested questions are intended
to enhance your group's
reading of this book.

DISCUSSION QUESTIONS

1. Family is a central theme in this story. How would you assess the Reid family? In what ways is this family representative of the typical family?

2. Mira made a decision to confiscate letters that were written to the children by their father. Was she justified in her actions, or was this a blatant example of contemptuous behavior toward her husband? In addition to withholding the letters, she also made sure that her children had no contact with their father. Did she have a right to keep the children separated from their father given the fact that he was incarcerated? Or do you consider her actions to be child abuse? Are there other examples, either stated or implied, where she may have mentally, physically, or verbally abused her children?

3. Little Man never knew his father. In what ways might his life have been different had his mother allowed him and his father to maintain contact? How prevalent is this practice of parental nullification on the part of black women who have children by men who are incarcerated?

4. In his youth, D'Ray killed a boy, and up until the time of his incarceration for that crime, he was considered to be a juvenile delinquent. By the conclusion of this novel, do you believe that D'Ray's life has been redeemed, or do you feel that his past acts were so egregious that redemption is unattainable?

5. Are there other characters in this story who have been redeemed?

6. D'Ray's initial act of defiance toward his mother's request regarding Little Man's escape is later transformed into an act of heroism. How do you think D'Ray's act of heroism will impact his relationship with his mother? Will it make it better, will it make it worse, or will it have no impact?

7. On several occasions, D'Ray questioned whether his mother truly loved him. Do you believe she loved him? Do you believe he deserved her love? Cite examples to support your answer.

8. How would you assess Mira as a mother? Was her treatment of both of her sons the same? If not, discuss the different treatment, the reasons for it, and the impact it had on her relationship with each child.

9. What is your perception of Peaches? What impact does her presence have on D'Ray?

10. Given the tragic episodes in D'Ray's and Peaches's lives, do you think that a romantic relationship between the two of them can be sustained? Or is there just too much for them to overcome?

11. Themes such as friendship, betrayal, and manhood are illustrated throughout this story. Examine each as it relates to D'Ray, Reggie, Little Man, Mira, and Sonny.

12. At various points in the story, D'Ray is confronted with moral dilemmas. Identify the dilemmas he faces

and the ways in which he handles them. What statement does his handling of each dilemma make about him as a person?

13. What role does religion play in sustaining D'Ray, Little Man, Peaches, and Reggie? Do you think Mira was a religious person?

14. In a conversation with D'Ray, Miss Big Siss made the following statement: "Family is everything, but family ain't much good when the circle has been broken." What does she mean by this? Do you agree with her assessment? Does this statement have any implication for understanding the crisis currently plaguing the modern-day black family?

15. Reggie, D'Ray, and Peaches are pivotal characters. In many ways, each of them is tragically flawed. Identify those flaws and identify the similarities in their individual family histories that may have contributed to the manner in which they view the world, as well as the way in which they choose to live their lives. In your discussion, consider their familial relationships, their socioeconomic status, and their level of education.

16. At the conclusion of the story, Mira asks her sons to forgive her. Do you think they will forgive her? Do you think they should?

17. The ending of the book is quite emotional. What feelings does it evoke and what message is revealed?

Don't miss

A Person of Interest

by Ernest Hill

Available now wherever books are sold

Turn the page for an excerpt from *A Person of Interest.* . . .

1

The deafening sounds of the sirens fell silent, and through the partially opened blinds of my bedroom window, I could see the twirling beams of light casting long shadows on the house across the street. And though I was only partially conscious, there was in me an overbearing urge to rise, for I could not imagine, try as I may, what ungodly occurrence could have caused such upheaval in our quaint community at such an unseemly hour of the morning. And as I hastily draped a robe over my scantily clad body and a scarf over my freshly curled hair, I could hear rising from the streets the panicked sound of people scurrying about, and I could hear the muddled sound of a man's authoritative voice barking out a series of unintelligible orders, and could hear the screeching wail of a pained woman screaming at the top of her lungs.

And those sounds incited me again, and I pulled the sash tighter about my waist and slipped my bare feet into my old house slippers and made my way out of the house and into the darkness. And the sight of the yellow police tape strung around Luther's house confused me. As did the ambulance that was backed against his front porch, and the fire truck and three squad cars parked on the shoulder just beyond his front yard. And I was staring at the scene, trying to make some sense of things, when I heard her pained voice again.

And I saw that it was his wife's mother, and she was hanging onto a paramedic, and her limp legs were like spaghetti, and there was an awful smell in the air and I saw Luther standing before the porch with his hands clasped over his mouth and a police officer was standing next to him, and in the officer's hands was a pad. And as my eyes moved beyond his face and I inched closer to the yellow tape, I noticed that the front door of his house was open, and there was a trail of white smoke floating out of the house and billowing high into the early morning air. And until this moment, I had thought that this was simply a fire that had burned out of control, but now I sensed something more.

And I was struggling with those feelings and trying to make some sense of the chaos when I approached the yellow tape and noticed two policemen passing back and forth before the front door. The porch light was on, as were the lights inside the house, and I could see several other officers congregating at a spot just inside the door, and I opened my mouth to question the officer standing on the opposite side of the tape, but before I could summon the words, he spoke first.

"Move back," he said. "You can't go in there." And he looked at me with eyes made stern by the seriousness of the moment.

"What happened?" I asked.

"Move back," he said again. "Please move back."

I stepped back into the street, and though it was a warm, humid morning, I felt a chill sweep over me and I tugged at my robe and as I did, I saw another officer rush from the house and out toward the street. And when he was near the officer guarding the perimeter, he paused and spoke.

"There's gasoline all over the goddamn place," he said.

Then I saw him look toward the cars parked along the street. "They here yet?"

"Over there," the other officer said.

I saw him squint and look. A third officer was struggling to remove a large dog from the rear of his car.

"Get that goddamn dog over here," he yelled.

I watched him for a moment, then I turned and looked at Luther, and I could see that he had collapsed to the ground, crying. And I could see his body trembling, and I could see his large, powerful hands pounding the ground, and I wanted to go to him, but I knew that I could not, and the fact that I could not pained me. And I was staring at Luther when I saw the officer gingerly lift him to his feet and escort him away from the house and out toward one of the squad cars parked just beyond the yard. And as they disappeared into the shadows I was aware of the foul odor again, and the people milling about the streets, and next to me, I heard Brother Jenkins say that Luther had just made it home, and that he had found his wife and son's smoldering bodies huddled together just inside the door, and they had been doused with gasoline, and they were burned beyond recognition, and that it was a goddamn shame for one person to do that to another person, and that when they caught the son of a bitch that did this, they ought to hang him upside down by his baby maker and beat him to death with horse wire.

And in the distance, I saw the car with Luther in it pull out into the street, and I heard the officer say that they were headed downtown to take his statement. And as they passed, I saw Luther slumped over in the front seat with his forearms folded against the dashboard and his head lying against his arms. And as I watched the car disappear into the curb, I felt my eyes moisten, and I wondered how Luther was going to go on without his family, and I wondered how Mrs. Miller was going to go on without her child. And on the horizon, I saw the light of the rising sun breaking through the darkness, illuminating the ugliness of this godforsaken day. And suddenly, I could not help but notice the stillness of the morning, or the way the huge branches of the old oak tree in the yard before Luther's house hung perfectly still in the warm, breezeless air. Or the spot beneath that tree where, from across the street in the window of my parents' house, I had recently watched him and her lying on a blanket laden with food, laughing and frolicking and making merry like it was Christmas. And I was looking at that spot, remembering them, when I heard the distant sound of my mother's feeble voice calling to me from the depths of her front porch.

2

The door to my house was open, and from where I stood, I could see the tiny trail of smoke rising from their badly charred bodies. And I could smell the strong scent of their burning flesh. And the officer they called A.J. was standing next to me. And he was asking me questions and writing on his pad. And I could hear the commotion all about me. And my trembling hands were covering my mouth, and I could not move. And I could not breathe. And I could not stop the tears from streaming down my face. And through the chaos, I heard Chief Harlan Ladue's voice rising above the mayhem.

"A.J., get him out of here!" he screamed. "He don't need to see them like this!"

And I saw A.J. click his ink pen shut and place it in his shirt pocket. And when he did, I heard the chief call to him again.

"And tell Billy Ray to keep everybody behind that god-damn tape. I don't want to see anybody trampling over this crime scene. You hear?"

"Yes, sir, Chief," A.J. called back to him.

And then he eased next to me, and I felt him take my life-less arm and place it about his neck. And his weight was sup-porting my weight. And I felt myself leaning hard against his body, and I felt my weak, wobbly legs keeping time with his as we proceeded to his car, which was parked on the road just beyond the house. And as we walked, I noticed the neighbors standing on their stoops, many of them still wearing their nightclothes, and I saw others standing in the road that ran past my house, and they were all looking at me, and I knew that like me, they were trying to figure out what in the hell had happened.

When we reached the car, A.J. pulled the door open on the passenger's side and I slid onto the seat, and a second officer approached him, and I heard him tell the officer that he was taking me downtown, and that he would get my statement, and that this was one of the most brutal crimes that he had seen in Brownsville in his twenty-three years on the force. Then I heard him tell the officer to keep the crowd behind the tape because the chief didn't want anybody trampling over the crime scene. Then he climbed behind the wheel—the window on the passenger's side of the car was down and the other officer spoke to me. I could see his lips moving and I could hear him talking, but I could not focus.

So I turned my face away from the window, and I closed my eyes, and laid my head upon the dash. And I could feel the car moving out into the street, I could hear the people outside the car talking, and I could smell the scent of burning flesh, and I could feel the tears stinging my eyes. And I could feel the intense pain of my aching heart. I was in a nightmare, and darkness was all about. And the world was spinning, and all I wanted was to die.

I felt the car navigating the curb, and then I felt it accelerate, and I knew we were on the long stretch of highway leading downtown. And inside my tormented mind, I wished that this were a normal day. And I wished I was at work, and I wished Juanita was sitting at the kitchen table having her morning coffee, and I wished Darnell was still in bed, sleeping. And I wished that I had come home sooner, and I wished that none of this had happened.

We passed the old train depot, and my head was still bowed, and my mind was whirling, but in spite of it all, I could hear the townsfolk milling out near the street. And I was certain they had heard the sirens, that by now someone had given them the news, and like everybody else in town, they were speculating on what had happened, and on who in God's name would do such a thing. And I had asked myself that question a thousand times and a thousand times I had drawn a blank. And I had prayed over and over again for this nightmare to end. But pray as I might, I knew that when I again raised my head and opened my eyes, the horror of this day would still be before me. And I wished that I could keep my head bowed and my eyes closed and that I could somehow stave off that terrible moment which, at present, I neither had the courage nor the desire to face.

At the station, A.J. pulled into the large parking lot behind the courthouse just off the square, and I followed him through the side door of the police station. Outside, the sun was just beginning to rise, and there were a few people milling about the square and one of the trustees was outside, washing a car, and I saw him looking at me, and I knew he was wondering if my presence had anything to do with the sirens. I saw him, and yet I did not see him. I was outside of myself, mindlessly following the officer while struggling to stand and struggling to put one foot in front of the other.

I followed him into the building, and he led me down a narrow hall to a small room which sported only a table and two chairs. When I entered the room, he motioned for me to sit down, which I did. Then he pulled the chair out as if he, too, was going to sit, but before he did, he hesitated and looked at me.

"Can I get you a cup of coffee?" he asked.

I looked at him, but I didn't answer. I couldn't. I saw him look at the officer standing just beyond the door.

"Get him a cup of coffee," he said.

I saw him remove an empty cup, fill it with coffee, then hand it to me. I raised the cup to my mouth but my hands were shaking so badly, I only managed to take a sip before I had to set the cup down. I was dead inside—my nerves were shot, and I could not stop trembling. I saw A.J. sit down directly across from me. He took the pad and pencil from his pocket, and after he had flipped through the pad a moment, he looked up at me.

"Mr. Jackson," he said in a low, sympathetic voice.

"Yes, sir," I said, and I could feel my voice breaking.

He paused again, and I saw him study the pad. "I'm sorry to have to put you through this again," he said, "but I'm afraid we need to go over this one more time. Can you do that?"

"I'll try," I said.

I saw him look at the pad again, then click on the tape recorder.

"Let's see," he said. "I believe you said you discovered the bodies at approximately five A.M. Is that correct?"

"Yes, sir," I said.

And through the dazed state which was now my reality, I heard myself sobbing. And I closed my eyes and buried my face in my hands. And I could see the image of their smoldering bodies lying before the door. And I could smell the stench of their burning flesh. And I only wished that I could die.